A MIDNIGHT LOUIE MYSTERY

Tor Books by Carole Nelson Douglas

HISTORICAL

Amberleigh

MYSTERY

IRENE ADLER ADVENTURES:
Good Night, Mr. Holmes
Good Morning, Irene
Irene at Large

MIDNIGHT LOUIE MYSTERIES:
Catnap
Pussyfoot

SCIENCE FICTION

Probe*
*Counterprobe**

FANTASY

TALISWOMAN:
Cup of Clay
Seed Upon the Wind

SWORD AND CIRCLET:
Keepers of Edanvant
Heir of Rengarth
Seven of Swords

*also mystery

CAROLE NELSON DOUGLAS

CATNAP

A MIDNIGHT LOUIE MYSTERY

A TOM DOHERTY ASSOCIATES BOOK
NEW YORK

CATNAP

Cover art by Joe DeVito
Interior art by Elissa Martin

A Tor Book
Published by Tom Doherty Associates, Inc.
175 Fifth Avenue
New York, N.Y. 10010

ISBN: 0-812-51682-6
Library of Congress Catalog Card Number: 91-33293

First edition: March 1992
First mass market printing: March 1993

Printed in the United States of America

0 9 8 7 6 5 4 3 2 1

The adventures of Baker and Taylor—the cats—as depicted in Midnight Louie's memoirs are purely fictional.

For the real and original Midnight Louie:
nine lives weren't enough

Contents

CATNAP
A
MIDNIGHT LOUIE
MYSTERY

Midnight Louie, P.I.

I have a nose for news and pause at nothing. That is why I always find the body.

This time it is one dead dude tucked at the back of one among three thousand booths cramming the half-million-square-foot East Exhibition Hall of the Las Vegas Convention Center.

As usual, my presence on the scene—not to mention my proximity to the corpse—puts me in a delicate position. For one thing, my unappetizing discovery is made in the wee hours of morning. Security with a capital *s* is blissfully unaware of my presence among the aisles of merchandise on display, which is the way I like it.

Now Las Vegas is a twenty-four-hour town and I am a twenty-four-hour kind of guy. That is why they call me Midnight Louie.

It is in my veins, Vegas. I know every back alley and

every gawdy-awful overelectrified Strip sign. Vegas is people on the take, people on the make, people just out to have a good time—to win a little, maybe lose a lot. There are times I might be wiser to skip town (I am no angel), but I stay and even try to go straight.

But it does not pay to know too much in this town, not that the tourists ever suspect half the stuff that goes on. Naw, to them Las Vegas is just a three-day round-trip junket of blackjack, singing slot machines and free drinks with more paper umbrellas than booze in 'em.

Some say that Las Vegas is no longer the hotsy-totsy town that it was back when Bugsy Siegel hung out the first resort hotel-casino sign in the forties. Some even say that a certain Family has loosed its hairy-knuckled grasp on the profits from gambling, girls, and anything that gives the folks any illicit fun, including substances of a pharmaceutical nature. (Drugs are not my vice of choice, let me make clear, though I do take a wee nip now and then.)

Still, it does not behoove a retiring soul like myself to admit to knowing too much. My habits are quiet, my profile low and, while I have a certain rep in this town, it is among a choice acquaintanceship, most of whom are like-minded about discretion always being the better part of discovering dead bodies.

Death broadcasts an unmistakable whiff. No lurid pools of blood need apply to advertise the fact. All five senses recoil from lifelessness, whether in the remains of a mouse or a man. I never met a corpse I liked, but the feeling would be mutual, I suspect. In a philosophical moment, I muse on how the late, possibly lamented (nothing is a sure thing in this town), would view being discovered by the likes of myself, for the fact is that among some circles I am known as something of a rambler, if not a gambler.

So I stand over the *corpus delicti* in *flagrante delicto* and consider the fragile nature of life and death in Las Vegas and my propensity for scenting the scene of the crime. It is dark except for the fluorescent glow of distant security lights, but I see well enough to observe no visible signs of violence on the body—no guarantee of natural causes, not even in this town, which can cause fatal shocks to the pocketbook, if not the system.

I picture explaining my presence to the local constabulary, a ludicrous scene for the simple reason that I always keep my lips buttoned tighter than a flasher's London Fog when he finds himself in custody. Midnight Louie does not talk—ever. I have my ways of getting the word out, however, and I review options. I am not one to pussyfoot around a problem.

First and most important, the Las Vegas Convention Center is far from my normal purview. How I got here is like this: I am undercover house detective at the Crystal Phoenix, the classiest little hotel and casino to flash its name in neon on the Strip. This is a tasteful, if not tasty, sign with a mythical beast of an avian nature exploding its pinfeathers in blue-and-magenta neon with a dash of emerald green; in other words, a first cousin to the NBC peacock, another mythical beast of more recent manufacture.

Some around town find it unusual that a dude with my, shall we say, pinstriped, if not actually checkered, past would snag a responsible job like unofficial house detective. I owe it to the Crystal Phoenix's founder, Nicky Fontana, a sweetheart of a guy and the only one in his large Family to go as straight as the Las Vegas Strip itself.

Nicky inherited eight million in legitimate dough from his grandma's pasta factory in Venice (California, that is). So he throws this considerable yeast into remodeling an abandoned hotel into a showpiece of what Vegas could be if the whole town had the taste to employ a marzipan little doll like Van von Rhine to manage the joint.

This pint-size doll also managed to marry Nicky, and therein lies the source of my present disenchantment. The union, while profitable to the hotel, has produced an offspring. The Crystal Phoenix, an around-the-clock palace of high-stakes poker tables, glitter, glitz and free food, now knows the Patter of Little Feet.

Time was when *my* little feet were the only ones welcome in the establishment, from the chorus girls' dressing room to the owners' penthouse. However, the newcomer—who has no obvious attractions other than the dubious ability to scream like a harem of Siamese in heat at odd hours of the night—is the center of an epidemic of cooing that leaves myself cold.

I express my distaste by strolling far from my now-unpleasant turf to the Las Vegas Convention Center, which I see by the local rags is hosting the ABA, aka the American Booksellers Association.

I figure on perusing a booth or two, since I always was a bookish sort, having nodded off over many great tomes—including the collected works of Dickins. I like nothing better than curling up on a good book. And I personally know a literary figure or two, the most famous of which—besides Boss Banana, whose memoirs sold quite a few guys upriver—is my hard-shelled pal, archy, whose nightly tap dance on the typewriter keys (he is an old-fashioned kind of guy) brought much fun and profit.

So I decide to broaden my horizons, no easy thing to do in Vegas, which is all horizon, and hotfoot over to the convention center.

I plan to scout the rear service areas, normally deserted at my namesake hour, except for the presence of a few local cats in search of tidbits among the refuse. Even Vegas has its homeless these days, in addition to the usual shirtless.

There are a thousand ways to get into a locked building, especially if you are a stealthy but wiry little guy, and Midnight Louie knows every one. Soon I am ambling through a maze of booths, gazing at piles of books, posters and plastic bags bannered with pictures of every description.

I am vaguely in search of the Baker & Taylor concession, where I am given to understand that a pair of famous felines are on display. Apparently any live acts at a book convention are newsworthy. This duo made all the papers, being official library cats at a little town in the West.

From their mug shots, Baker is a white, gray and what-have-you feline of no distinguished ancestry, and Taylor is likewise. Neither has much to speak of in the way of ears, which gives them a constantly frowning expression. As for tail, I cannot say as I am always the gentleman. Still, a celebrity cat—much less two—is something to see, there being few around since Rhubarb, the long-gone marmalade tom of motion-picture fame. Of course someone has scrammed with both Baker and Taylor for the night; the booth offers nothing but empty director's chairs and slick catalogs. I sniff out the area and am in the process of withdrawing—perhaps the sole individual in history to leave the ABA without a free book—when my nose for news fastens on the dreadful truth that the stale atmosphere is not the only thing dead about this place.

I poke my puss through a curtain, clamber over an Everest of disheveled cartons, dodge several empty Big Gulp–size paper cups and a Big Mac wrapper that has been sucked clean—and find myself nose to nose with a white male sixty-some years of age with specs as thick as the lens at Mount Palomar and no more earthly use for them.

He is supine among the effluvia and deader than a stripper's Monday afternoon audience at the Lace 'n' Lust downtown. I trot around front to catch the booth number. The booth itself is fairly unmistakable, being blazoned with illustrations of assorted bodies in a similar if more spectacular condition of permanent paralysis than the current corpse. There are also depictions of such sinister implements as hypodermic needles dripping blood and embossed silver scalpels lethal-looking enough for Lizzie Borden to be alive and well and using them to practice medicine without a license.

I commit the name bannering the booth to memory—Pennyroyal Press—and retreat to more pleasant venues to await morning and an opportunity to acquaint the authorities with my discovery in a way that will do my duty as a citizen and leave my name off any list of suspects.

Chester's Last Chapter

"Some cat's cutting loose on the convention floor," the guard grumbled, heading for the office coffeepot. "Thought we were supposed to be on the lookout for international terrorists."

"A cat!" Temple's head whipped to attention, abandoning her computer screen. "Where?"

The guard shook his own head, which was decorated by a wilted lei of hair, and donned his cap. Caffeine piddled from the spigot until foam lapped the rim of his Styrofoam cup. "Kitty Kong. Some terrorist."

"Listen, Lloyd, a very valuable cat happens to be missing from an exhibit this morning—two, in fact. We need to corral them before we open the floor to the exhibitors. Where was it seen?"

Lloyd scratched his scalp, almost dethroning his cap. "You office girls are all cat crazy."

Temple made her full five feet one as she stood, slamming the oversize glasses atop her head to the bridge of her nose.

"I'm not an 'office girl.' I'm liaison for local PR for this convention, and I don't give a flying fandango about pussycats on the job unless they're relevant to public relations, so you can bet that corporate mascots like Baker and Taylor are bloody vital to the American Booksellers Convention. Baker & Taylor happens to be one of the country's top book wholesalers."

Temple paused, breathlessly, to dive under her desk and withdraw a formidable canvas bag emblazoned with the words "*Temporus Vitae Libri.*" A freebie from Time-Life Books.

She edged around the desk, frowning. "Now where is this rogue feline? If he's beneath your notice, I'll bag him personally."

Lloyd examined her three-inch heels, her elephant-bladder-size bag and her implacably determined face. She didn't look a day over twenty-one—despite being in imminent danger of thirty; July was her natal month and this was the cusp of May and June—and regretted it bitterly.

Lloyd's head jerked over his shoulder. "Somewhere near the sequined zebra on the stick."

"Zebra on a stick? Oh, you mean the Zebra Books carousel. Damnation"—Temple eyed the silver-dollar-size watchface that obscured her wrist—"the doors open at nine. Good thing book people sleep late. Probably up reading all night."

She clicked out of the office, bag flapping, while Lloyd muttered something uncouth about "modern women" into his scalding coffee.

Lights glared on the mammoth exhibition area, making the booths' glossy posters and book-cover blowups into vertical reflecting pools. Temple threaded the maze of aisles. A few early-bird exhibitors were already at work, unpacking book cartons and readying their wares for opening day.

She bustled past arrays of next year's calendars, juicy dust jackets promising sex and violence in lavish doses, past lush photographic covers on massive art books, past ranks of reading lights and tasseled bookmarks.

She heard Lloyd faintly calling "Miss Barr" and minced on. Few would believe how fast Temple could travel on her upscale footwear; in her favorite Stuart Weitzmans she was even a match for a footloose feline.

"Here, kitty-kitty-kitty," she crooned as she neared the Zebra booths, slipping the Time-Life book bag from her arm in preparation for a genteel snatch.

Nothing stirred but a dedicated exhibitor who was fanning book catalogs on display cubes.

"Hee-eere kitty. Nice kitty."

Zebra Books's life-size papier-mâché namesake glittered, seeming to move in stately splendor amid the eerie quiet.

"Here kit-eee, damn it to—!"

A scream of outrage deleted the rest of Temple's expletive as she tripped on what felt like thick electric cable. She stumbled forward, looking down to see an abused feline tail streaking from the needle-sharp exclamation point of a single Weitzman stiletto.

Lloyd ambled up to announce the obvious. "There it goes."

Temple went after, darting down aisles, careening around corners, caroming off unwary pedestrians.

"The cat, catch it!" she yelled.

Bemused exhibitors merely paused to watch her sprint past. A bald man with a wart on his nose pointed ahead without comment. Temple hurtled on.

A black tail waved from behind a stack of paperback Bibles. Temple followed. The Tower of Babel fell again.

"Baker! Taylor! Candlestick-maker," she implored inventively. "Come back, little Sheba—"

The flirtatious extremity bobbed and wafted and whisked through exhibit after exhibit. Flatter feet pounded behind Temple's—Lloyd and a train of diverted spectators on the move at last. Temple sighted the cat's tail vanishing under a booth's back curtain and dove after.

"Trapped!" she announced, her insteps grinding down heaped cardboard boxes, her elbows dueling the odd umbrella—very odd; who would bring an umbrella to Las Vegas?—and boxing aside rolls of tumbling posters as if they were origami bones.

Her quarry was at last within grasp. Temple tackled a fat black shadow, throwing herself full-length, such as it was, indifferent to impediments, as she handled most situations.

The cat, cornered in the dimness, sat regarding her prone body. Someone yanked back a curtain, admitting a swath of light.

"Don't let him get away," Temple murmured, feeling for her glasses, which had decamped during her flying tackle.

"Oh-my-God," someone said.

Temple patted the assorted lumps upon which she reclined until she found her frames. She assumed the glasses to glare triumphantly at the cat.

"Holy cow," Lloyd murmured behind her.

"Someone help me up," Temple ordered, "and don't let that cat get away."

She had noticed by now that the escapee was solid black; from their publicity pics, Baker and Taylor were particolored. And this animal's large, fully perked ears were nothing like the missing cats' stingy "Scottish fold" earmarks.

The heels of Temple's hands pushed down for purchase. Then she realized that they pressed a man's suit jacket, that her recumbent length was, in fact, badly wrinkling cold-cocoa-colored worsted.

"So sorry, sir. I'll just—" She thrust herself halfway up, palms digging into a hard irregular surface. "Ohmigod." Temple gazed down into a man's eyes. He was in no condition to protest her presence—or that of additional suit wrinkles.

Someone grabbed her elbows and yanked. Upright, Temple stared at what had already mesmerized the crowd, and even, apparently, the cat: a man lay face up amid the booth's backstage litter, a hand-lettered sign reading "STET" askew on his immobile chest.

"Well." Temple turned as the crowd began buzzing behind her. "Lloyd, secure the area until the authorities arrive. And put that cat"—she pointed, if there were any question—"in this bag. Please clear the area, folks. There's been an accident; we need to let the proper people attend to it."

Anyone minded to argue didn't. Temple had pumped her tone with equal amounts of brisk authority and hushed respect for the dead. The crowd edged back. Moments later a dead weight hung from the Time-Life book bag Lloyd slung over Temple's forearm. Bored green eyes blinked from the bag's midnight-blue depths.

Temple went to the front of the booth, the cradled cat swinging from her arm. It weighed a ton. A copper and black Pennyroyal Press sign glinted in the exhibition lights. So did the graphic image of a skull and crossbones rampant over an Rx prescription symbol.

Temple studied the booth's macabre illustrations before glancing nervously at the cat in her bag. Its yawn revealed a ribbed pink upper palate soft as a baby sweater, but its mouth was equipped with rows of sharp, white teeth.

An Editor Edited

Irate book people—editors, sales reps, publishing bigwigs—milled in the aisles, but there was no helping it.

Two rows were cordoned off indefinitely. With police permission, maintenance employees were emptying nearby booths, moving the displays into whatever space could be squeezed from the packed-tight exhibition area. On easels bracketing the cordoned zone, signs announced Keep Out, Filming Area—Temple's idea. Filming was indeed going on, she thought, watching police cameras snap and whir.

Detective Lieutenant C. R. Molina frowned down at Temple. "You were chasing a *cat* when you found the body?"

"We couldn't have one loose in the exhibition area; besides, I thought it had escaped from a booth that features cats."

"Live cats?"

"Well . . . dead cats would be kind of tacky."

"What kind of convention did you say this was?" Lieutenant Molina's skeptical blue eyes squinted at a visual cacophony of illustrations and type styles.

"The ABA—oh, not the American Bar Association. Booksellers. The American Booksellers Association."

"So you found the deceased by accident?"

"I assure you."

"And disarranged the body."

"Hey, he was as stiff as Peg-Board already, the Man in the Iron Suit. Must have been . . . dispatched late last night, but I guess the coroner will determine exact time of death—"

"Where is the cat now?"

"The cat? In the PR office. In a carrier. The cat didn't have anything to do with it—"

"And that's the only reason you were in the area at that time, pursuit of the cat?"

"I'm a PR person. That's my job: to keep things running smoothly. To round up stray cats, if necessary."

"Stray? I thought you said the cat was missing from an exhibit."

"Um, it had 'strayed,' hadn't it?"

"I get the idea, Miss Barr, that you're concealing something again. That's part of a PR person's job, too, isn't it?" Lieutenant Molina prodded with weary logic. "Speaking of concealment, you ever hear from that missing boyfriend of yours?"

"Not a word. Why do you think he's called the Mystifying Max?"

"Not just for a good vanishing act, I'll bet."

Temple said nothing, waiting for the tall police lieutenant to finish eyeing the scene of the crime. Temple *was* withholding guilty knowledge—the continuing absence of Baker and Taylor. But that had nothing to do with . . . possible murder.

"How was he killed?" Temple was unable to resist asking that.

Eyes the color of a midnight margarita iced over. "We

don't know that he was killed; could have been natural causes."

Temple rolled her eyes. "With that sign acting as a tie tack?"

"Who has access to sign materials?"

"Everyone. The ABA centers on the printed word; everybody here wants to leave messages, sign a book, write orders. We're just lucky only the thirteen thousand exhibitors were allowed in today; tomorrow the other eleven thousand hit. Even so, must be twenty thousand Magic Markers on this floor, easy."

Lieutenant Molina's professionally stoic face puckered. Was the homicide detective annoyed because Temple had identified the object used to write on the dead man's chest? Yo, ho, ho and a bottle of Magic Marker ink. "You know what this 'stet' means?"

"Sure. To any journalist or copy editor it's an abbreviation used to mark text. It means, 'Let it stand.' "

Lieutenant Molina waited, tall, patient and as unplacated as an island god.

" 'Stet' means that copy that's been deleted or changed should be restored to its original state," Temple explained further. They turned as one to view the body. "In this case," Temple observed, "ashes to ashes."

"Not quite yet," the lieutenant remarked. "How will you handle the press on this?"

"Discreetly."

"Good luck." The lieutenant grinned significantly and moved on.

Lloyd leaned close to Temple. "That broad sure likes to throw her weight around."

"Any woman who stands five-ten in flats scares the living Shalimar out of me," Temple admitted. She shivered dramatically. "On the other hand, if Lieutenant Molina hangs around we won't have to worry about the air-conditioning breaking down—she could cool the Sahara single-handedly."

"I swear, Temple, you even chitchat like a PR woman, in

snappy press-released superlatives," a familiar voice slipped in. It was not a compliment.

She eyed the approaching Crawford Buchanan, who eyed her back. "And you talk like a DJ, with capital *i*'s every fifth syllable. What brings you here from the Ivory Tower of the *Daily Snitch?*"

Buchanan was entertainment writer for one of Las Vegas's many newsheets, which were heavy on flacking and light on objectivity. He was also a free-lance hiree like Temple, acting as liaison between the ABA's regular publicity force and the mysteries of the myriad local publications. Buchanan was a small man, neat as a wolverine, with permed grizzled ringlets, permanent bags barely upholding limpid brown eyes and spider-silk lashes, and the moral fiber of a sidewinder. Like many Napoleonically egotistical slight men, he figured Temple was just his size.

He ignored her sally to eye the commotion. "Not good for business. Just what the LV C and VA wanted to avoid, T.B." A devotee of Initialese, Buchanan had early on discovered the unfortunate effect of Temple's. So far he hadn't found out that her middle name was Ursula, thank God.

"Well, they can't," she riposted, "not even the Las Vegas Convention and Visitors Authority. You've heard about the eternal unavoidables—death and taxes."

"Better get *that* off the premises." His head jerked toward the body, or rather the figures clustered around it.

"Not until the police are through."

"Maybe you should lean on someone at headquarters, T.B." Buchanan smirked. "You've got such a powerful personality."

"Yeah, and you're Limburger. Why don't you stand over there and drive them out?"

His fingers flicked like a snake tongue across the back of her neck. "Temper, temper, Temple."

"Cut it out!"

But Buchanan had oozed on; he was a hit-and-dodge expert, always cozying up to unsuspecting women. Temple retreated to the ABA public relations office at the facility's rear, anxious to measure damage.

"Well, if it isn't Jessica Fletcher, Junior," Bud Dubbs, the guy in charge of free-lance flacks, greeted her.

Temple flinched. "I thought I was bagging a missing cat; I would have been happy to find just a missing cat."

Dubbs squinted into the cat carrier's small wire door through his half-glasses. Temple'd sent an assistant to buy it once the cat was corralled. "That it?"

"Sort of."

"And the police?"

"Should be out of here in a few hours and we can open up the aisle again."

"What about the bad publicity?"

"Maybe none of the local rags will notice it."

"Think they won't?"

"No . . . but maybe I can defuse it somehow."

"How?"

"I don't know yet."

"Was it murder?"

"The police don't know—or won't say."

"You landed on the body."

"Death doesn't advertise causes . . . except that sign sure looks like somebody enjoyed seeing the guy dead."

"Who was it?"

This was the bad one. Temple moved the carrier to the side of her desk, off dead center. A deep growl remarked on this dislocation. She sat, always feeling more commanding in that position.

"A publisher. Chester Royal, head of Pennyroyal Press."

"A publisher?" Dubbs glowered at Temple as if that were her fault. "A bigwig?"

"Not that big. Pennyroyal Press is just an imprint, a minioperation within a bigger publishing house."

"What's the bigger house?"

"Reynolds/Chapter/Deuce."

"That . . . sounds familiar."

"They all used to be separate publishers until they merged in the eighties."

"What you're saying is this is one hell of a big outfit and it lost an executive at our convention center."

"No, you're saying that. Bud, it's not our fault that out of twenty-four thousand bodies streaming through the security lines one is a murderer maybe, and one a murderee. It could have happened anywhere—San Francisco, Atlanta, Washington."

"It happened here and it's bad press. And tomorrow is opening day when all the booksellers and news-hungry media types come in. You've got to stop this getting out."

"I can't suppress the news, Bud, the public's right to know."

"Public relations is your job. What's the good of doing it unless you can launder what the public has a right to know?" Bud glanced at the cat carrier. "Once the corpse is gone, you better dump this cat."

"I don't know about that." Temple bent to peek into the dim interior. A pair of grape-green eyes regarded her accusingly. "I may have professional uses for this pussums."

Nothing but a Pack of Flacks

Temple slipped down the corridor past Charlton Heston and nodded automatically.

Movie stars' familiar faces bred the notion that one actually knew them, a wholly one-sided phenomenon, unfortunately. She stopped to watch Heston's six feet three inches shoulder around the corner, shrugged and headed for room 208. Amazing, she ruminated, how a murder can alter one's sense of proportion. Heston was en route to the interview room down the hall, where celebrities gathered like an exaltation of La-La Land larks, in high supply given Las Vegas's proximity to Hollywood.

Earlier during the setup period for the ABA's long post–Memorial Day weekend, when Temple's patience had been young and her feet uncallused—just yesterday, Thursday—she actually had been uncool enough to "peek" when a particularly stellar personality was flashing the flesh. Now, she could trip over Charlton Heston, Paul Newman or Sean Penn and she wouldn't care—just so long as he wasn't dead.

Outside conference room 208's nondescript door she paused to contemplate the coming ordeal. Nothing was worse than a triumvirate of PR persons with conflicting goals. A messy murder put a lot of public images on the line: the convention center's, the ABA's and, especially, that of the big publishing house that sponsored Pennyroyal Press. Temple lowered her glasses to her nose, lengthened her neck for an illusion of greater height and charged the door.

Correction, Temple thought as she surveyed the two people in the otherwise empty room: nothing is worse than a trio of PR *women*, definitely the more dangerous of the species. Public relations was one of the rare fields where women could rise to the top; most of them would not settle for less, especially Claudia Esterbrook, the power-suited woman who'd run the ABA publicity circus maximus since the heyday of Messalina. That she didn't show it was only thanks to the gentle art of plastic surgery.

"We don't have much time," Claudia announced. Claudia's lacquered hair was the color of tapioca. It was razor-cut and so were her mandarin-length fingernails. One tapped the table with Freddy Kruegerish emphasis.

"I've got a rock star," she said, "with a mouth that Drāno couldn't fix meeting the press in twenty-five minutes. I've got to be there for damage control."

"This won't take long." Temple clicked toward the conference table and slung her briefcase atop the beige Formica. "We better get our acts together before we rush out conflicting press releases on the Royal Death. That would really prolong the agony."

The mouse-haired woman with a long, sinewy face sitting opposite Claudia Esterbrook nodded. "Lorna Fennick, director of PR for Reynolds/Chapter/Deuce. You're right; if we're not all tap-dancing in time, it'll be Reverb City." From her open patent-leather briefcase she withdrew sheaves of paper and spun them across the slick tabletop.

"Bios of Chester Royal; a history of the Pennyroyal Press imprint; releases on its three biggest authors and a statement from our publisher expressing regret et cetera for Mr. Royal's death."

"Great." Temple grinned as she sat. This was going to be easier than she'd thought. Despite Lorna Fennick's tough-turkey looks, she evinced the hyperactive efficiency of the best of her breed. "Here are copies of the convention center's local and regional press list. That'll let you know who you'll have to fend off."

"Sure." Claudia Esterbrook delicately raked her homicidal nails down her neck. "Something nasty, like murder, happens and we have to fend off the press. Do our regular jobs right—promoting good news, like books and writers—and we can't fill a quarter of the ABA interview room."

"You know why," Lorna put in. "Book reviewers have zero clout because book sections get virtually no advertising support. We'd get more coverage at the ABA if newspapers got more publisher and bookstore ad bucks. Money talks."

"Yeah, that's why our conventions draw so many city-desk types who only want to cover an ABA to flack their own coffee-stained manuscripts, most of which are best suited for use as blotter paper at a puppy academy."

"That's the point, Claudia." Lorna Fennick sipped from a Styrofoam cup. "The ABA does attract members of the press, whatever the motive, and every reporter eats up something meaty like murder, especially at an unlikely place like an ABA."

"I don't know about that 'unlikely' part," Claudia retorted. "You shouldn't be surprised by what happens when egos collide at an ABA. Not two days ago Chester Royal called you a 'ball-busting press-release pusher' to your face."

Lorna flushed. "Chester Royal was rotten to everyone; it was part of his mystique," she explained to Temple. "Some people think that's the only way to express power."

"I take it the victim was a wee bit unlikable?" Temple said as An Awful Thought occurred. "That could prolong the investigation into next week—of the year 2003!"

Claudia sniffed. "Listen, Little Miss Lollipop, Royal even had a run-in with you. Don't you remember? You were in the press room and mentioned that the Vegas papers weren't big on covering culture."

Temple's eyebrows had lifted at the 'Little Miss Lollipop' crack and stayed there. "I remember some guy going into a Geritol tirade about the book business being 'thrills and chills and bottom line, not literature.' I think he called me 'Girlie.' "

Lorna groaned. "That's Chester. Or was Chester. He played professional curmudgeon."

"Heavy on the 'cur,' " Claudia added, scanning Lorna's sheaf of press releases. "Frankly, Reynolds/Chapter/Deuce is lucky to unload the old grouch. I've heard he was getting so senile lately he was deep-sixing the imprint. Mr. Bigwig's regrets are for show only."

"Hardly." Lorna Fennick's voice had turned sharp as filed tacks. "Pennyroyal Press practically invented the medical thriller as a salable subgenre. The imprint is extremely profitable."

"Without Royal?" Temple wondered, looking up from skimming the late Chester Royal's bio.

Before Lorna could answer, Claudia Esterbrook did. "More so, without him. I hear he had the RCD brass by the monkey's marbles. No one had any control, editorial or fiscal, over him or Pennyroyal Press. And PP pulled down a very pretty penny, I hear—or did until lately."

"Does," Lorna Fennick said through her teeth. They were exceptionally handsome, and probably expensive. "We're hardly helping Miss Barr with rumor-mill speculations."

"Speak for yourself," Esterbrook snapped. "Look; I'm outa here. Mr. Razor Mouth is getting ready to spit-polish the podium even as we shilly-shally. You can stay and feed fairy tales to Miss Barr, Lorna. That's all the press sees fit to print anyway."

"Whew," said Temple when the door had crisped shut behind the woman.

"It's a rough job."

"So's mine—now," Temple said. "You're in for a tough time, too. The local police will need a crash course in book publishing to investigate this case. They'll want to know who/what/when/where and why not. It's the last thing your staff will want to deal with."

Lorna pulled out a wine snakeskin cigarette case and lighter and gave Temple a quizzical look. When Temple nodded, she lit up and inhaled until her cheeks were concave.

"Claudia's right," she admitted on a dragonish puff of exhaled smoke. "Chester was a Royal pain. That's between us." Her eyes narrowed. "You ever flacked for a publisher? You have some insight on corporate ins and outs."

"Repertory theater. The same thing: sell arts and entertainment; snuff scandal and any ragged bottom-line stuff."

"Where?"

"Minneapolis."

"The Guthrie." Lorna's murky eyes glinted with respect. "How'd you end up in Las Vegas, for gawd's sake?"

Temple sighed. "A long and personal story. I'm saving it for the movie."

"Anyway, you know how obnoxious these egotistical artsy types can be."

Temple nodded. "The best are usually sweethearts, though."

"Usually."

"Besides, Chester Royal wasn't a temperamental author; from his bio, he was an editor in chief—and more chief than editor nowadays. Wasn't his position mostly business, not art?"

"More people are killed for bottom lines, baby, than art."

"Still, that 'stet' sounds like the last word from an author whose precious prose has been tinkered with. Could any writers on the Pennyroyal Press list harbor a grudge for past indignities?"

"You've got the bios of the best-selling authors. The others have nothing much to gain—or lose."

Temple frowned at the standard press releases—stapled, two-page, double-spaced sheets with small half-tone photos of the author and latest book cover notched into the text. Mavis Davis. Lanyard Hunter. Owen Tharp.

"I've never heard of them," Temple confessed.

Lorna rolled her eyes and inhaled suicidally. "Welcome to the majority of the U.S. population. Most people buy only three or four books a year, including cookbooks, travel guides and horoscopes. Only a tiny percentage of the pop. are regular readers. Divvy that up by reader tastes—literary versus genre fiction like mystery, romance and sci-fi, add nonfiction—and a steady readership of a hundred thousand or so can fuel a middling novelist's career."

"Even a B act in Vegas pulls a bigger crowd in the six weeks during Lent."

Lorna shrugged. "Facts of publishing life. Makes it hard to picture most authors as crazed killers over such meager stakes."

"Aha, but you aren't considering artistic soul," Temple said darkly. "I've known actors who would kill for a walk-on. This bunch, though"—she waved the releases—"looks pretty normal."

Lorna snickered. "Show me a normal author and I'll show you a walking contradiction. Like acting, publishing is built on rejection. A successful author is either someone with incredible luck and an inch-thick skin—or a very long enemies list and a memory to match it."

"This Mavis Davis woman looks just like a nice woman from Peoria, Illinois, should: a fortyish Julia Child coming over with chicken soup."

"Have a chemist check the soup before you sip it. Mavis Davis writes the 'Devils of Death' series." Lorna Fennick warmed to Temple's blank look. "Instructive little tales of killer nurses. Her last one, *Death on Delivery*, was about a serial baby killer. She also features kidnapping obstetrics nurses. We call her the Queen of White-Cap Crime."

"Nice tag line. Is—"

"Yes, it is. You think any publisher would concoct 'Mavis Davis'? We urged a pseudonym, but she wouldn't hear of it."

"What about Lanyard Hunter?"

"The name—or the author?"

"The author. What's his story?"

Lorna lit a new Virginia Slim—her fourth—and studied her copy of the release. "An intriguing case. One of those medical impostors."

"You mean the guys who dress up in lab coat and stethoscope to become fake doctors in real hospitals?"

Lorna nodded. "We don't stress it in the release; we call him a 'medicine buff.' Hunter conned an amazing number of reputable hospitals into hiring him in an even more amazing range of specialties before his deception caught up with him. Chester Royal signed him to write an autobio, but it came out fiction—and this guy knows his hospitals, believe me. Reading his books would convince me to consult a Roto-Rooter franchise rather than a doctor any day."

Temple studied the photo of Lanyard Hunter, a handsome, prematurely silver-haired charmer in his early forties with a chamber of commerce smile. "He's so distinguished and humane-looking."

"Exactly why they should have run the other way when he presented himself as a doctor. He was too good to be true."

"It would take a clever, confident man to do something like that. He would have to feel superior to everyone around him. He would have to cultivate a certain distance that could make it easy to murder."

Lorna nodded soberly. "Lanyard Hunter is fascinating. I interviewed him for that release and if I didn't know better I'd let him remove my gallbladder. But he's made a mint exploiting his knowledge of hospitals, and Pennyroyal

Press gave him lead title status; why kill the giant that let him lay such golden eggs?"

"And this last one—Owen Tharp?"

"The compleat hack. He's written novels in a dozen genres under two dozen names. Owen Tharp's a phony, by the way. His stuff's never lead title, but he's fast, reliable and has a decidedly grisly bent that lends the list a touch of outright horror."

"*Corpus Delicious?*"

"Cannibal morgue attendants."

"*Scalpels Anonymous, P.A.?*"

"Sadistic plastic surgeons who deface their patients and drive them to suicide."

"I do have to wonder now, *are* the people who write these books normal?" Tharp certainly *looked* normal enough—middle-aged, middle-class, Midwestern.

Lorna beamed like a comedian given a straight line. "Are any writers normal? Of course not. They write whatever fantasies are knocking around their brains and get paid for it, if they're lucky."

"There are kinder, gentler things to write about."

"Like what?"

"Uh . . . romance, families, the stock market."

"Kind and gentle doesn't sell. Sex and violence sells. And there's plenty of it in the stock market, in families and between supposedly loving couples."

"If you put it that way, it's a wonder more publishing personnel don't get murdered."

"You sure it's murder? The police haven't said so."

"The body looked like it was left there by someone who enjoyed it. Have the police mentioned how Royal was found?"

"Dead," Lorna said, her eyes narrowing. "There's more?"

"Not yet, but there may be." Temple rapped the press releases from Reynolds/Chapter/Deuce into a neat pile on the tabletop. "Would you ask your people to make themselves available to me? I know the media and police in this town; the more I know, the more I can head them off at the pass—and the presses."

"You really think that there's going to be more, rather than less, hubbub over this?"

"You bet your Lily of France lingerie. Las Vegas is a lot more crime-conscious than it is book-conscious, but then you gave me the sad statistics yourself."

"I'll take cooperation over hanging separately any day. We're all in this together," Lorna Fennick said with a conspiratorially arched eyebrow.

The comment made Temple wonder why an imprint's editor in chief would call his overlord's publicity director a "ball-busting press-release pusher."

"You still here?" Temple was not pleased to find Crawford Buchanan sitting at her desk poking a pencil through the wire grating at the captive cat. It was past six P.M. and the office was otherwise empty.

"We're all in this together," he singsonged back. "Press solidarity. Speaking of which, Dubbs wants to know—any news on the missing pussycats?"

"Oh, God . . . Baker and Taylor. Look, I've been a little busy running damage control on this dead body."

"You mean like that?" Buchanan's lifted elbow revealed the *Review-Journal's* P.M. edition. The headline, "Editor Dead at Convention Center," leaped up at Temple.

"At least the story's below the fold." She leaned over to skim the type.

"Front page, though. Not many details. Went to press too fast. And that Lieutenant Molina's closemouthed. Dubbs took two Ibuprofins this afternoon."

"He should take aspirin," Temple snapped. "At his age, it's better for his heart."

Buchanan spun from side to side in Temple's chair. "A lack of stories like this is even better for his heart, T.B. Hey—ouch! That sucker snapped the pencil right out of my hand."

"Better pick on someone who isn't bigger'n you, C.B."

That got Buchanan out of her chair, but he never stayed angry. He smiled smarmily and rapped his fingers along the top of the cat carrier. "All I can say is, you better uncover those cats and cool this murder, or the Las Vegas Convention and Visitors Authority, not to mention the ABA, will not be pleased with you. Ta-ta."

Temple watched his grizzled mop of curls saunter out of the office, just visible over assorted cubicle tops.

"Shark!" she spit after him under her breath. "Are you okay, kitty? Did the mean little man hurt you? I thought not. Come on, let's hit the road. I'm tired of this place."

New Boy in Town

The cat carrier banged Temple's ankle in four-four time as she plodded through the late afternoon sunlight softening the Circle Ritz's asphalt parking lot to the consistency of a half-baked Toll-House cookie.

Her high heels sank in and stuck at each step, making her feel like a prospector trudging through a desert of hot fudge. She set down the carrier, unlatched the stockade gate, moved the carrier inside, and relatched the gate.

Temple paused to soak up the indigo shade of an overarching palm tree and eye the cool blue apartment pool flanked by yellow calla lilies. Her favorite lounge chair sat empty near the water, just waiting to cradle her weary physique and frazzled psyche in the shade of a spreading oleander bush. . . . Home, sweet home.

Temple had nearly reached the lounge chair before she spotted the stranger six seats over.

"Oh."

He looked up from a Las Vegas guidebook. Born-blond hair, caramel-brown eyes, light tan, bright green short-sleeved shirt, muscles subtle enough to be interesting and a quizzical look—mostly at the cat carrier. "Help you with that?"

"Nope." Temple resented any deference to her petite size. She deposited the carrier on the flagstones and sat primly on the edge of the lounge instead of collapsing full-length as usual. "I wonder if I dare let the poor thing out."

"What kind of poor thing is it?"

"I'm not sure. Black. Feline. Heavy. Has a fearsome yowl."

"A stray?"

"More like an unauthorized intruder. God, what a day!" Even a handsome stranger could not forestall Temple's long-anticipated collapse. She groaned, then wriggled way, way back on the lounger, putting her feet up.

The man came over, encasing her briefly in cool shadow before he crouched beside the carrier. "Take a look at it?"

"But don't lose it. The contents are a material witness in a murder."

"You're kidding!"

Temple shook her head. She debated removing her sunglasses to study her new acquaintance in living color, but restrained herself.

"You weren't kidding." The man hauled a long black boa of fur from the cramped carrier. "He must weigh close to twenty pounds."

"He?"

"Definitely."

"You a vet?"

"I was raised on a farm." He cautiously released the cat to extend a tan hand, accompanying it with a smile that would blind a mole. "Matt Devine. I'm staying here now—I guess. Mrs. Lark was cordial but a little vague."

"Only a little? You must have made a real impression on

her. Hi, Temple Barr. I've lived at the Circle Ritz for almost a year. You'll love it, but you'll have to like 'a little vague' a lot. Say, he is a big galoot, isn't he?"

Temple sat up to inspect the cat, who sniffed long and intently at the heel of her shoe, the aluminum tubing of the lounge chair and Matt Devine's hand.

"Did you mean that," Matt asked, "about him witnessing a murder?"

Temple sighed. "I was exaggerating, a mortal sin for a public relations specialist."

Matt started at her words. Maybe he had something against PR people, Temple thought. A lot of ordinarily nice folks did. PR people as a group were often stereotyped as devious, shallow and phony.

"Actually," she admitted, "Boston Blackie here should get a medal. If he hadn't been AWOL at the convention center, I wouldn't have found the body when I did, chasing him."

"That must be rough, finding a body." Matt had risen to chaperon the cat's explorations around the landscaping.

"It's not in my job description, for sure. Now I'm supposed to downplay the murder before it ruins the whole convention. Damn! This is my first assignment for the convention center; booksellers sounded so stuffy; who'd have guessed? I need a drink."

"Sorry." Matt displayed empty hands and ranged toward the calla lilies, where a black tail was vanishing. "Try Mrs. Lark."

"Didn't she tell you to call her Electra?"

"Yes, but—" Matt bent into the chest-high leaves. "I bet she doesn't want this guy taking a dip in her lily pond, whatever she's called."

"God, no! Back in the hoosegow for him. I gotta get to my apartment and find out if I've got any tuna fish; he can have the run of my place then."

An ungentlemanly yowl from the lilies indicated the cat's capture.

"What does Mrs. Lark—Electra—think about pets on the premises?" Matt Devine wondered.

"It's only for the night. Somebody had to take him, and I was the one unlucky enough to catch him. Lieutenant Molina of Sex and Homicide is looking at me with a gol-darn evil eye. That is not a comfortable place to be, if you've ever met Lieutenant Molina."

Matt smiled at something that amused him, patted the cat's sleek black head and stuffed it through the carrier door despite four black paws and a tail all lashing like octopus arms.

"Don't hurt him!" Temple warned.

"Me, hurt *him?* Have you seen the size of the claws on this kitty-cat?"

"Yoo-hoo!" came a yodel from the apartment building's back door. Electra Lark—or rather the Day-Glo muumuu she wore—soon followed it. She was one of the last living women in America to holler "yoo-hoo" and wear muumuus, separately or simultaneously.

"Either of you play the organ?" The landlady stood panting before them, her hair a picturesque postpunk patchwork of lime-Jell-O green, old-lady lavender and fire-engine red.

Temple just shook her head. Matt looked too dazed to shake anything, which was a real shame in Temple's opinion.

Electra Lark was checking a California Raisin watch on her chubby wrist. "Euphonia's home sick and I've got to do a can't-wait wedding at seven-thirty. It won't seem legal without a march."

"I play—a little," said Matt. He was standing with his hands in his khaki pants pockets, looking adorably diffident.

"Really, Matt? You can play the organ?" Electra vibrated with relief. "Why didn't you say so? I can give you a deal on the rent if you can back up Euphonia. She has four kids." Electra rolled her eyes. "Emergencies are built in."

"I only play by ear, and I don't know *Lohengrin*," he warned.

"Not to worry." Electra's amethyst crystal ear cuffs flashed as she drew Matt's tanned, gilt-haired arm through her freckled, plump one. "Just so it sounds solemn and churchlike."

Temple watched them stroll around the circular building, envying women of a certain age—say sixty-something—who could commit certain liberties with men of a certain attractiveness without anybody thinking anything of it.

Then she kicked herself—figuratively. (The Weitzmans were far too pointed for literal admonishment.) What was she doing—more to the point, thinking? Here one man had left her flat and friendless in Vegas just three months ago; why'd she care if Prince Charming himself moved into the next apartment? Sure, Matt seemed friendly and low-key, but Max Kinsella had seemed a lot of things, also—including too serious about her to leave without warning. Max, who'd charmed her out of the best PR job—position—she'd ever had, the Guthrie, for heaven's sake. Three days and she'd jilted common sense to follow him to Vegas like a Pacific-bound lemming deflected to Sand Central. Max had found the Circle Ritz and charmed Electra into giving them a corner unit. He had even charmed Temple into envisioning a someday-ceremony in the Lovers' Knot Wedding Chapel. . . . That had been Max, an unlucky charm from first to last.

Resurrecting the memories of their intemperate romance and Max's cool departure always pureed Temple's emotions; Temple had been considered sensible until Max. If her Guthrie compatriots could see her now, flacking hither and yon, too ashamed to crawl back to the city she'd forsaken, too stubborn to give up on Vegas and herself just because a man had stranded her there.

Temple concentrated on the pool area's deserted serenity, on putting the past back where it belonged. The Lover's Knot Wedding Chapel faced onto the Strip's twenty-four-hour hullabaloo, but the Circle Ritz gardens, set back from the fevered honky-tonk action, were peaceful and secret.

Temple picked up the cat carrier and went indoors, where a vintage air conditioner kept the lobby temperature a steady 74 degrees during the long, torrid summer. Curiosity overcame her at the elevator doors. She left the case there to dash through the breezeway to the Lover's Knot, trying not to let her staccato heels disrupt the wedding in progress.

The tiny chapel exploded with flowers (mostly recycled from Sam's Funeral Home on Charleston Boulevard; Sam was either an ex- or a would-be beau of Electra's). The happy but hurried couple stood poised in the trellised archway. Ranks of hatted heads filled the pews, but they covered brains of discarded pantyhose and Poly-fil, for Electra fashioned this soft-sculpture congregation one figure at a time with her own talented fingers.

Dwarfing the little Lowery organ on one sideline, Matt Devine sat in his emerald-green shirt and khaki pants, looking like a PGA pro dragooned into musical servitude. Electra's muumuu was concealed by a rusty black graduation robe that gave her a properly clerical look. She nodded once and smugly to the waiting Matt.

The organ huffed into life. Temple listened, first curious, then surprised. Music, marchlike and softly sensuous, swelled into the cathedral-ceilinged chamber. The couple advanced with the traditional nervous stutter of measured paces. Hat brims on the gathered mannequins seemed to nod in approval.

Temple blinked. It had been a rough day. She'd found a dead body, earned a long-distance record for carrying the world's heaviest cat, met a devastating new tenant of the male persuasion just when she was terminally down on the opposite sex and now was melting to the spell of a wedding march she'd never heard before. In a minute she'd be hallucinating the "congregation" humming along in chorus.

She got the hallelujah out of there.

* * *

"Okay, kitty," Temple told the cat on the last leg of her journey. "This is a very special place. It's round, see, the whole building. What we have here is my front door—shhhh; just a minute while I find my keys!—solid coffered mahogany. They don't waste wood like this anymore. Not since the fifties. This was some ritzy place until it hit the skids in the seventies and Electra came along to gentrify it. Now you get to call it home in the nineties."

The door hushed reluctantly open on solid brass hinges; it was that heavy. Temple lugged the carrier over the threshold. Then she was inside, and any of her Minneapolis friends who might have wondered why Temple stayed on in Las Vegas when Max vamoosed would know.

"Nice, huh? I'll let you out, you look around, and then we eat."

This agenda apparently suited the cat. He emerged cautiously from the carrier, putting one massive paw before the other as precisely as a chorine at the Tropicana.

To the left was the odd wedge-shaped kitchen, but after one long whisker-quivering sniff, the cat turned toward the living room, padding silently across the walnut parquet floor.

Temple loved her place, with or without Max. Its decor was a concoction of imagination and serendipity rather than of money and time. The major rooms were pie-shaped wedges widening to curved exterior windows. Vaulted white plaster ceilings seemed to ripple like sand dunes to meet the walls, generating a soft, aquatic play of light. No wonder Electra was a bit mystical after living here for almost twenty years.

The black cat was not interested in mystical or aquatic unless a tasty finned morsel was involved. He headed for the French doors, paws braced on the struts, to size up the triangular garden patio beyond the living room.

"No outside," she told him, setting her apartment thermostat a bit lower for the evening. "That reminds me; I'd better round up a roaster pan or something. Yeah, that's the bathroom, *my* bathroom, so don't get any ideas."

The cat was poking his jet-black nose behind the toilet. He stretched like a ladder against the inch-square tiles of the bathroom walls, reaching for the lone, small window.

"Too high for even you, smarty!"

He agreed, for shortly he was in her bedroom, inspecting her piles of clothes—"So I'm untidy; so what. We're not married or anything." He leaped atop the queen-size bed to recline in the exact middle—"Off! If you're lucky you'll get a pillow in the corner. That's what I tell all my male sleep-overs." His paw edged the louvered closet doors open to reveal a treasure trove of shoe soles. "Sniffing? No monkey business! I'll get you the proper facilities in a few minutes."

The cat stretched up the inside of a closet door, his extended forelegs playfully patting a poster taped to the door.

"Yeah, you got it, bud. My dirty little secret. You are looking at one of the last remaining vestiges of 'The Mystifying Max' in Vegas. Right, worth a good long yawn. What a bore. So predictable of a magician to just vanish, for heaven's sake."

Temple regarded her memento. The Mystifying Max had a look both puckish and lethal; hair so black you'd expect to find it in your stocking on Christmas morning and strong, bony, clever hands. He wore a navy turtleneck and a "now you see it, now you don't" expression, which pretty much summed up their relationship.

She picked up the cat, an intemperate decision. He still weighed a ton. But his eyes were almost as green as The Mystifying Max's.

"I hope you're not two of kind," she murmured into his ample ruff, "and aren't gonna run out on me, too. You I need. Somehow, some way, you're gonna defuse this murder thing at the ABA for me; I know it."

The cat, for all his bulk, remained complacently cradled in Temple's arms, although his green eyes were roaming the Dairy Queen ceiling as if searching for a way out.

Temple tightened her grip. "Don't you do that to me! Don't you dare!"

The Fall Guy

Oh, the personal complications that result from the simple if somewhat unprecedented impulse to do a good deed in a naughty world.

I refer to my subterfuge of allowing someone else to stumble over the body while in pursuit of yours truly. I had not anticipated having to put up with the inconvenience of my own capture. Nor would it be lost on any of my intimate acquaintances that a canvas book bag, however sturdy, is less than sufficient to contain a dude of my fighting weight should I require egress.

But it is my last wish at the scene of the crime to create a scene of another kind, so I go quietly into that good, navy-blue-canvas night.

The portable cell is another matter. Even as clever an operator as myself knows that those steel bars latch on the outside. My particular prison is formed from nubbly plastic in an ugly shade of beige that resembles certain commercial cat foods of my very passing acquaintance. It does not do a thing for my coloring, not to mention a physique that was never meant to be crammed into a cell designed for the wimpy common housecat.

I take all this in relatively decent grace. The Master Plan calls for my swift and discreet removal from any connection—mental or physical—with the *corpus delicti*. As even schemes of mice and men oft gang a-gummy, to paraphrase the Scottish poet, so does Midnight Louie's.

For one thing, I do not count on landing in the custody of a feisty doll like Miss Temple Barr. During my day in stir at the convention center she keeps me close by most of the time. (Who can blame her? She is not an undiscriminating little doll.)

This permits me to hear more than rests easily on my abnormally sharp ears. Although I have revealed the dastardly deed without establishing myself as a suspect, I had not expected my self-preservation tactic to make a sweet-and-tart little dish like this Temple doll the fall girl, so to speak.

It becomes clear, as the voices of ABA and convention center policy growl outside my polyurethane prison walls, that Miss Temple Barr is in worse trouble than myself, her job being that of burying bodies rather than tripping over them.

Although she reacts with enough fighting spirit to see her through a midnight free-for-all behind a mud-wrestling palace, my responsibility in this matter is all too clear: on my honor as a gentleman I am obliged to extract one little doll from one big mess that she would not be in—were it not for her unfortunate attraction to my fleeing form.

My best hand is to keep my cards glued to the chest, sit tight and play dumb. This is where the indignity comes in: I must allow myself to be treated like a domestic pet.

So I submit to being dragged from my cell in the most interesting garden behind the intriguing Circle Ritz without making a run for it. This joint, however unusual, is not up to the standards of the Crystal Phoenix Hotel. Any fool who knows Midnight Louie would know my normal game plan upon release from stir: up a palm tree, down to a rooftop and outa there.

However, I restrain myself and it is a good thing. I have always been a superb inside dude, if I say so myself, and it is when I am wafted by elevator to Miss Temple Barr's charming pied-à-terre, otherwise known as a crash pad, that I get the skinny on her situation.

She is worried; this is obvious when she thinks herself alone and unobserved. (Some of my best pals have said that I ought to go into this psychoanalyzing game. I have a talent for listening to people's troubles—and I even have the whiskers for the job.)

Anyway, this little doll chirrups to herself and me as she goes about her nightly domestic duties, which in clude an outing to the Quik Pik for a bag of concrete makings and an aluminum roaster pan.

The last occasion I see a bag of that size and likely contents, Guido Calzone is preparing a pair of permanent booties and a quick trip to the bottom of Lake Mead for "Noodles" Venucci. As for the roaster pan, certain large fowls of my acquaintance have not fared well in such a vicinity.

Even worse than my speculations is in store, as I discover late in the night, but first the most important revelation. I find it on the inside of Miss Temple Barr's closet door, always a significant location. People tend to stash their dope, as well as outgrown clothes and dreams, in closets. I am partial to such areas myself, mainly because they are cozy, dark and quiet, qualities not often to be found in the same place at one time in a town like Las Vegas.

Anyway, there it is, a poster of this commanding dude resembling a cross between Frank Langella and Tom Cruise. I have not encountered such a piercing stare since I went eye to eye with an ailurophobic pit bull. This particular poster boy has black hair. I have always found the ladies to be especially partial to dudes having black hair, with which I am especially well equipped. It is obvious that my undeniable attractions have led Miss Temple Barr astray, and not for the first time.

I explore my new base of operations while she snoozes in the bedroom. Not a bad pad; I discover several choice corners that are not really corners, more like angles. This appeals to my sense of humor, not to mention self-defense. And the patio outside the living room windows is on the third floor, making it a handy perch for tidbits of an avian nature.

Yes, Midnight Louie could do all right in this joint, and nowhere do I sniff the trail of a yammering human creature who is wet behind the ears and in other more unmentionable places and does not have the inbred good manners or sense to shut up and use its tongue for basic hygiene.

My own natural demands, I admit, compel me to explore the roaster pan, which Miss Temple has wisely tucked behind the bathroom door. This is a cheesy aluminum affair—talk about "tin pan alley"—full up with the worst excuse for sand that I have ever seen—dusty, coarse nuggets of no earthly value whatsoever. When I give them an exploratory paw, a cloud of dust clogs my sinuses and cakes my freshly groomed top coat.

I am even more chagrined when I realize for what purpose this pathetic dish of gravel is intended. I am, however, a good citizen and no litterbug except when forced to it, so I avail myself of the opportunity to mark my new digs.

Later, I slip into the bedroom (I am very good at this sort of maneuver also, and have always been an "upstairs man") and allow my little doll the honor of a warm body to curl up next to. This is not an unpleasant arrangement, especially when she wakes up and makes little manipulations with my ears, my favorite egregious zone. I cannot keep the ladies off me, to tell the truth, and have never been so crude as to complain about this turn of events.

But then, all of a sudden-like, Miss Temple Barr sits

bolt upright, as if she has just taken a stroll down Nightmare Alley.

"Oh, kitty!" she says.

I cringe, which is hard to detect in the dark. No one calls me "kitty" except tourists; even though some twenty million of them mill around per year, I see as little of them as possible. But Miss Temple Barr is not fully house-trained as yet, so I forgive her gaffe.

"Oh, kitty," she coos again, like I say. "What a brilliant idea! You *are* going to help me defuse this murder thing!"

Now she is talking!

Of course I will make every effort to solve the foul deed so that my little doll's job is no longer in jeopardy. I am relieved that she has tumbled so quickly to my unique value, even if it took a dream to do it. I return posthaste to my beauty sleep.

I know I will need my rest because I have a feeling (I am also a tad psychic, did I mention this?) that we are going to have a big day tomorrow.

Authors on Parade

The afternoon edition of the Saturday *Las Vegas Review-Journal* lay scattered on Temple's desk, its second front—the first page of section two—face up.

Also face up was a photograph of the black alley cat, checked deerstalker cap tilted over one ear; magnifying glass cradled between his midnight paws.

The headline on the boxed feature read:

CONVENTION CENTER'S CRIME-FINDING CAT
KEEPS MUM ON HIS OWN MYSTERIOUS PAST

An above-head kicker announced, A BOOKISH SORT, in 18-point italic type.

The local PR office staff had crowded around the first issues of the newspaper when they arrived just past noon—

Bud Dubbs, Temple, the secretaries, everyone but Crawford Buchanan. Even the cat was present, although contained in the cat carrier and, in deference to the headline writer's veracity, keeping mum.

"Fast work." Dubbs, in shirtsleeves, stood cradling his elbows. He regarded the feature story with bemused fondness. "Don't know how you managed it, Temple. This human—or inhuman—interest angle virtually wipes out the shock of the murder."

"I know," Temple purred. She had an earthy, flexible voice that reflected the emotions of the moment. "Smug" would not have been too strong a word to describe her present mood. "Betsy Cohen's their top feature writer," Temple added. "I just hoped she dug cats. But don't forget our feline star. He was an angel; didn't even try to eat the deerstalker. It does work, doesn't it? Now the murder is a footnote to the cat story, and I love the way Betsy portrays this furry fellow as an undercover literary type lapping up ambiance at the ABA."

"We couldn't have bought better coverage," Dubbs agreed, "for an unfortunate, er, accident. Any way you could use this big guy to put out an all-points on the missing Scotties? You know, without letting on that they're actually gone?"

"I'm a publicist, Bud, not a miracle worker. Baker and Taylor may not be eager to announce the disappearance; might cause more problems than solve them. And the missing felines are not 'Scotties,' they're *Scottish fold* cats. That means their ears come pretucked."

"Whatever." Dubbs broadcast his usual air of vague demand. "Round up those cats and I'll forget about you dredging up dead bodies just before the ABA's opening day."

"Body. Singular."

"Keep it that way," Dubbs said gruffly.

The staff had melted away during the discussion, leaving Temple and the cat to absorb Dubbs's directions. The man turned away, then paused. "Better stash that cat somewhere," he said. "Lieutenant Molina is picking you up in a few minutes."

"Picking me up? It sounds like an arrest—or a date. Why?"

Dubbs shook his head, one of his more commanding gestures. "She asked for you. Wants a guide to who's who on the convention floor."

"Rats! *I* don't even know that yet."

"Just help her out. And try to keep it discreet."

Temple sat at her desk to stare soulfully into the baby greens regarding her through the carrier portcullis. "The lieutenant is coming to take me away," she intoned. "Sorry, pal; I'll have to put you in the storeroom again; it's the only place big enough for a roaster pan. Salmon tonight, I promise."

Temple was shoving Louie into the storeroom when she heard the heavy footfalls of the law. She rushed back to find the police lieutenant looming over her desk.

"Cute." Molina's deliberate deadpan tone held no complimentary grace notes. She was staring at the second front feature. "Makes it sound like the force needs a feline division to find its own left foot, much less a dead body. Your creative PR, I assume."

"It beats 'Dead Editor at Convention Center.' "

"Fiction always looks better than truth. That's why so many people turn to crime."

"Hey, don't look at me, Lieutenant. I thought you wanted a guide to the ABA, not a suspect."

"I understand you had a run-in with the victim."

"You must have consulted Claudia Esterbrook. She reminded me of that, too. Except it's kind of silly to kill someone you never met before and whose name you don't even know."

Lieutenant Molina's eyes—an unearthly aquamarine color capable of fascinating if they hadn't been kept expressionless—flicked Temple up and down. Her mouth quirked. "Relax. It's hard to picture you puncturing a man's stomach and ripping up into the heart with a number five steel knitting needle."

"So that's the murder weapon! And, listen. I bet I can do anything you can do."

Lieutenant Molina allowed a tight smile to thaw her professional facade. "Don't get competitive, Barr; this is a murder rap we're discussing. I want you to show me the ropes of this free-for-all."

"It's just a normal convention."

Molina's eyes rolled like wayward blue marbles. "Twenty-four thousand people! You ringmaster this sort of circus all the time?"

"It's my job," Temple said a bit stiffly.

Molina raised a raven eyebrow that needed some judicious plucking in Temple's opinion. "Don't tell me: somebody's got to do it."

"Right. What do you want to know?"

"How this thing is scheduled. What the daily events are. Who here is connected to the deceased."

"Let's hit the floor. First, you'll need a badge." She couldn't help smirking at that, but Molina offered no comment.

Hearing the lieutenant's low-heeled shoes thudding behind her own crisp high-heel taps on the long way to the registration rotunda, Temple mentally toyed with unkind variations on "flatfoot," but kept them safely to herself.

People three deep, many of them women burdened with purses, empty canvas bags and a visible film of genteel perspiration, milled in the lobby.

"Is it always such a madhouse?" Molina wondered.

"Always, but the ABA is one of our behemoth conventions—twenty-four thousand book-loving and -selling souls. We can crash the line for your badge. In-house privilege. Thanks, Carrie. There. Before we face the floor, we better face the press room."

Molina gestured Temple to proceed her.

Their first stop was a quiet room where folding chairs in churchlike order sat slightly askew, as if the congregation had just risen for a mass exit. Temple cruised a long el of tables awash in printed matter along the walls. She paused here and there to snatch up a pair of glossy folders and thrust one of each set at the police lieutenant, keeping the other.

"I don't need all this paperwork," Molina protested. "I've got plenty of my own."

"No?" Temple looked up at Molina over her electric-blue eyeglass frames. "Funny, they're bios on Pennyroyal Press's top three money-making authors."

Molina cracked a folder to study a glossy eight-by-ten photo of Mavis Davis and the accompanying press release. "Any of this information actually true?"

"Enough to fill you in, and I can do more of that, if you'll answer one question."

"Yes?"

"Why me?"

"Why you—why?"

"Why'd you ask for me to lead this little tour of wonderland under glass?"

Molina grinned. "It was either you—or Crawford Buchanan."

"What about Bud Dubbs?"

"He has too much at stake. You *are* a free-lance flack, aren't you? You don't owe your rent to the company store for more than a few weeks at a time."

In answer Temple flipped out her business card, which bore the sketch of a smoking felt-tip pen and the words "Temple Barr, PR."

"Cute," said Molina.

"You don't like me," Temple said. That was a serious offense; most people did. Charm was part of her professional armament.

"Maybe I don't like your boyfriend."

"Ex-boyfriend. And you never even met him. Did you?"

"I'll do the interrogation here, thank you. I find his behavior suspicious."

"I find it actionable," Temple retorted, "but there's no

law against a guy skipping town. It's been three whole months. I got over it; maybe you should."

Something flashed in Molina's icy blue eyes, and vanished. "Maybe you should ask yourself why he skipped. Unless you were part of the reason."

Temple grimaced. "I ate too many anchovy pizzas, all right? Look, Lieutenant. He just left. Guys do that. It wasn't because of me, everything was—"

"Was what?"

"Peachy keen," Temple said through her teeth. "No, he didn't dig the Vegas scene or the way the Nevada heat curled his hair or—something. Besides, I don't see why a Sex and Homicide detective is so interested in a magician who took a powder and vanished. Unless you think my sex life is a lot more interesting than yours."

No flash of distant blue this time. "Depends upon the kind of powder he took. And did you ever consider it might be the Homicide part that involves me?"

"Max? Kill someone? A man who pulls baby bunnies and cockatoos from his coatsleeves for a living? Give me a break."

"It might be the other way around."

Temple frowned. She hadn't expected another grilling on the semiunlamented Max Kinsella. What was the Iron Maiden of the LVMPD getting at now? The answer hit Temple like a block of ice in the guts. She'd never considered that, not even for a minute in the darkest three A.M. brooding session.

"Max . . . dead? No! You don't know how strong and physically fit magicians have to be, how fast, how smart. They are not easy candidates for murder, believe me. You really think that's why Max hasn't shown up?"

"Cheer up, Barr. It's a much more personally flattering reason than the one you've been cherishing for three months."

"What do you know about what I might cherish?" Temple flared, instantly regretting the outburst.

"That's the problem. Nothing. When I questioned you

after Kinsella's disappearance three months ago, you were about as forthcoming as a mob hit man. Now you're stonewalling again on this ABA murder. I am the police, you know. I've got a right to ask questions."

"Not such personal ones. Not in a simple man-missing case." Molina was silent. "What didn't I tell you that you needed to know?"

"Everything. You claimed to know nothing about Kinsella's background, his family, friends—"

"I didn't. Look, Max and I had been together for only a few months. He was a traveling magician, and I don't have much contact with my family, either. I just didn't—don't—know those things."

"And you didn't see what they had to do with his disappearance?"

"I didn't see that our relationship was police business. Max was—is—a free spirit. I knew that; it's one reason I—anyway, he didn't take all of his things, but he never traveled with much. His engagement at the Goliath had ended that night. Isn't it obvious that he just wanted to move on without me and didn't have the nerve to say so?"

"A free spirit. And an emotional coward. And you the soul of stability. Why'd a smart woman like you fall for him?"

"I don't like that question now any better than I did then."

"It wasn't quite as obvious then that Kinsella was playing with fire."

"What do you mean?"

"I'm not at liberty to say."

"But I should spill my guts, sure!" Temple took a deep breath. "I'll say this. Max never did the expected. He liked to surprise people. It genuinely delighted him. That's why he became a magician. He never lost that sense of child's play. Maybe it didn't make him the most predictable of partners, but it sure as hell made life interesting. He came into mine like a white-magic tornado, and I can't say I was surprised when he left in a puff of smoke."

"You forgive him?"

"No . . . but his disappearance wasn't out of character, and it's not as simple as cowardice. Stage magicians take risks; that's part of the performance."

"Sleight of hand and mind." Molina snorted. "Tricks."

"But it takes an athlete to perform them." Temple shook her head. "You'll never understand a man like Max. He doesn't play by the fine print in the book of rules. He laughs at rule books, and steady-job-holding people like us. So he's not dead, if you want my honest opinion, Lieutenant. Death hasn't gotten fast enough for Max Kinsella yet."

"I still think you're covering up something; maybe just the fact that you miss him."

"Think what you like." The policewoman's air of faint amusement cooled Temple's anger—and anxiety—better than a pitcher of ice water. "Listen, Mavis Davis will be meeting the media in about five minutes. Want to get a look at her?"

"Apparently you do."

Temple led them to a pair of seats front row, dead center. "She writes best-sellers about murderous nurses. If you're looking for perpetrators, Lieutenant—and not chasing ghosts—Chester Royal's nearest and clearest experts on murder were his authors."

The press room lunch break ended abruptly. First Claudia Esterbrook charged in, eyeing the disheveled press handouts with distaste and siccing an underling on the mess.

She greeted Temple and the lieutenant with a curt nod and open disfavor. They would file no stories. Her face screwed into its customary expression of impatience when the next persons in the room were Lorna Fennick and the first entrée of the afternoon's media feast, Mavis Davis.

Claudia bustled back out to the hall. In moments she could be heard rounding up reluctant reporters. "Larry, you swore you wouldn't miss the first interview of the afternoon! I'm counting on you; just go right in. Elise—*Graffiti* magazine, isn't it? You don't want to miss Miss

Davis. Come on, now, all of you, and we can get started."

They straggled in, the bleary members of the press, the dapper but bored TV reporters. Their rears had polished the paint thin on the folding chairs so thoughtfully molded to cradle sagging bottoms, and their attentive ears had overdosed on the same questions from their colleagues, the same answers from authors trotted out like trick ponies at twenty-minute intervals.

The morning's sole interesting moments had been Erica Jong's cleavage—and that for only half the press corps—and Walter Cronkite's quips on still-unstable world politics as he plugged his latest tome on sailing ships and squint-eyed old salts.

The media people focused on Mavis Davis with a universally jaundiced eye: a youngish Julia Child without even a chicken wing as a prop to offer the media. Half of them were dreaming over their own book proposals and the encouraging editor, or sales rep, or *friend* of an editor or sales rep, that they had buttonholed earlier on the convention floor, anyway. Claudia kept her whip out—her strident, almost viciously cheerful voice. She rounded 'em up, headed 'em in, plunked 'em down and . . . another four hours of raw hide.

Mavis Davis had been deposited facing them on a tastefully upholstered tweed chair, with a freestanding tweed room divider behind her to which Lorna Fennick was hastily tacking posters of the latest Davis title, *Ladybug, Ladybug*. According to the press release, it followed the medical and off-hours career of an arsonist pediatric nurse. The ladybug pictured on the cover, fully embossed to sensual depth, had a blood-bright shell with tiny black skull markings and wings of red-foil fire.

"People read this stuff?" Lieutenant Molina hissed this in Temple's ear loudly enough to be heard at twenty feet. "It's sick! Gives the wacko element ideas."

Heads whipped around. Claudia Esterbrook glared as her talons scored a glossy folder until the cover stock split.

"You obviously haven't been keeping up with the best-seller list, Lieutenant. Your profession is quite well represented," Temple noted.

"Libeled, you mean," Molina said.

Claudia started the show with a clarion throat-clearing that silenced the well-trained media people. Most were ABA veterans, being book page editors, and knew that Claudia demanded a meek flock in her field. If she found them derelict in their devotion to duty—attending the endless round of programs, interviews, author breakfasts, etc.—she could jerk their press credentials, or at least tarnish them a bit. They settled down, pencils poised and cameras, whether hand-held photographic models or shoulder-high videotape machines, cocked.

Everyone was ready but Mavis Davis, who sat fidgeting with a copy of her novel until the dust jacket crinkled.

"How did you happen upon the idea of writing about lethal nurses, Miss Davis?" came the first, hardly original question.

"Ah—" Mavis Davis was a raw-boned woman whose hair had been crimped into an unflattering greige Brillo pad by the Las Vegas oven. Her figured polyester dress must have acted like a nylon tent, sealing in the heat. Her cheeks were hot spots of ruby-red blusher on a pallor of genuine stage fright. Temple had never seen a person less suited to a public interview. She felt sorry for her.

"Ah," Mavis Davis repeated. Even her voice was unfortunate, an attenuated quiver that couldn't make up its mind whether to sing alto or soprano. "It's the contrast, you see. Behind a calling of mercy, of care and the, the . . . well, you don't expect a nurse to do anything drastic, do you? On purpose, that is. That's the fascination."

"Are you implying, Miss Davis, that there's a feminist undertone to your subject matter; that men are usually assumed to be capable of violence and mayhem, but not women? There've been plenty of villainous doctors in fiction and true-crime nonfiction."

"Exactly," Mavis Davis said eagerly. "Nurses are so innocent, you see; all in white, like brides. And then, their victims, my victims—in my books, that is—are innocent, too. Helpless children. Well, I can't really say why my books are so popular, except that it's a contrast between innocence and evil. And readers always like that."

"But your nurse antagonists aren't innocent caregivers; they're more of the Nurse Ratched school."

"Nurse Ratchet School? I've never heard of—"

"Like the villainous head nurse that persecuted Jack Nicholson in *One Flew Over the Cuckoo's Nest.*"

Mavis Davis blinked. "What an odd title. It's much too long for a book."

"It was a film. And a book before that."

"Oh. Well, I don't know it, young man. Perhaps you could ask me something about one of the characters in my books."

Silence prevailed.

Then a woman's voice lilted from the rear. "What about reality, Miss Davis? Has the death of your editor, the chief of your publishing imprint, Chester Royal, given you second thoughts about the fictional deaths your novels portray?"

"Of course, I'm devas—devastated. I've worked with Mr. Royal from the beginning of my career. Only Mr. Royal has edited my books. I, I don't know what I'll do without him—"

Lorna Fennick spoke up with smooth efficiency. "We will find you another editor as congenial as Mr. Royal, Miss Davis. You are a revered author with Reynolds/Chapter/Deuce. We'll hardly abandon you, no matter the circumstance."

"Still . . ." Mavis Davis smiled weakly. "I'm not a writer by first career, you know. I was a nurse—quite a different nurse from those I write about, I might add. It's hard to—to change horses in midstream—"

Lorna's hands sympathetically clamped the woman's shoulders. "Leave all that to us; we only ask that you continue to create the wonderful stories that you have such a gift for writing. Thank you, ladies and gentlemen; we'll cut this off early. Miss Davis, as you can see, has been deeply affected by Mr. Royal's sudden death. Oh, yes, a few last photos, I'll step back for a moment. . . . There. Thank you all."

"You know who I'd like to see in the hot seat?" came a low male voice from behind them. "The hotsy-totsy homicide lieutenant who's been hanging around this convention. What's the verdict, Molina? Murder?"

C. R. Molina turned and fixed one eye on the local newsman behind her. "Come to the police briefing for that, Hentzell. There's so much fiction floating around here, you're likely to confuse it with the facts, as if you aren't liable to do that anyway."

"How to win friends and influence people," Temple whispered to an unheeding world.

"What was that?" Molina had turned on Temple with dispatch.

"You'd make a horrible PR person."

C. R. Molina looked momentarily abashed. Then the instant passed. "It's my job to uncover what people want hidden, not to help them hide it."

"You really think hiding the truth is what PR is about?"

"Isn't it?"

"No more than police work is about civic politics and corruption. Sure, PR has a downside. Most of the time it's a necessary link in the vast chain of communications that the modern world depends upon."

"You believe that?"

"Why not?"

Molina regarded her piercingly. "Maybe you really don't know anything about Kinsella's vanishing act."

"Does that mean that you think I'm naïve?"

Molina shrugged. "Your profession requires looking for the silver lining. If you'd seen some of the things that I have in this city—"

"You mean on the force."

"That, too. But I grew up in L.A. and came to Las Vegas as a teenager. Neither place is Kansas, Dorothy."

"I once was a big-city TV reporter, Lieutenant. I've seen more than the merry old land of Oz in my time, too."

"Maybe." Molina consulted the Timex on her wrist. "When can we catch the next Royal author?"

Temple squared her shoulders. "Follow me."

Molina did. After the stone-faced security personnel at the portals eyed them both in the name badges, they were admitted to the vast exhibition area where Chester Royal had set up his inadvertent last stand.

Crisscrossing hordes flooded the exhibition floor. Everyone was draped with canvas saddlebags choked with books that swung erratically, bruising shins and hips of brushers-by. Dismayed yips punctuated the din.

"Who are all these people?" Molina demanded in exasperation after they'd progressed only three jam-packed aisles in five minutes.

Temple unleashed her best informative downpour. "Only about six thousand are booksellers—owners of independent bookstores and small chains, and buyers for the big bookstore chains like Waldenbooks, B. Dalton's and Crown. More than thirteen thousand are publishing personnel—editors in chief, subsidiary rights heads, senior editors, publicists, PR people and the all-important sales reps. The reps are the ones who actually sit down to flash the fall covers past the booksellers and take orders. What happens here determines what you'll find on the bookstore shelves up to Christmas."

"I go to the library," Molina snarled, resisting the pulse of free enterprise throbbing all around her.

"Librarians are here, too. They're part of the miscellaneous five thousand. Purchasing librarians, book reviewers, oh . . . everybody."

"And authors."

"Of course, but only selected authors. The ABA isn't open to anyone outside the trade. If the publishers let all their authors in, the place would be swamped. Plus, authors don't sell books, except indirectly or in their own imaginations. Above all, the ABA is a marketplace. Think of this as a trade show."

A man in a gorilla suit passed them, escorting a girl in a metal bikini. Molina stopped dead. "There's nothing genteel about this scene; it's like any big convention, except for the book fever."

"There's nothing genteel about publishing, from what I hear," Temple said. "It's a multibillion-dollar entertainment business, with an iron-clad bottom line now that movie and oil companies own most of the publishers."

"What about ivory towers, men of letters and women of blue pencils—?"

"Are the police anything like their stereotypes—men of steel and long, blue lines?"

"Of course not. I see." Molina said the last two words as if they closed the subject, and her mind, forever. "The ABA is a perfect environment for murder, then; the high pressure point of the entire industry. Victim, suspects and perpetrator all obscured in a sea of"—Molina looked around piercingly—"bound galleys and free Winnie-the-Pooh posters."

C. R. Molina having a revelation standing in her conservative khaki blazer and skirt amid a tide of book-happy conventioneers was a sight to cherish.

Temple mushed the lieutenant onward through the mob. "Think of it as a convention of strippers or bookies and it'll all fall into place. These are book people—most of them utterly respectable and perfectly nice—but they're *people* first, and murder will out, even at an ABA."

Writers Anonymous

"Now there's a man who could murder."

"That a professional opinion?" Molina asked.

The police lieutenant was still somewhat dazed by the lines of people—four across weaving in and out like human plaid—blocking the long tables of authors signing their books.

Temple shrugged off the question. "Your press release describes Lanyard Hunter as a 'medical buff' and medical suspense novelist. *She*"—Temple pointed unpolitely, but in this mob, who would notice?—"says he masqueraded as a doctor for years. He'd know how, and where, to plant a knitting needle in an editor's heart."

"That horse-faced woman hovering over Hunter, she was in the press room with Mavis Davis."

"Lorna Fennick, PR director for Reynolds/Chapter/Deuce."

"And you think because this"—Molina consulted the press material—"Lanyard Hunter was devious, and loony enough to pose as various doctors once, he wouldn't stop at homicide now?"

"Look at that wavy silver hair, that air of benign attention, those slick, reassuring aviator bifocals. Was that man born to pull wool, or what?"

"You oughta know," Molina cracked with a sideways glance and a veiled reference to Max. "How'd this Fennick woman beat us here from the press room?"

"She knows the ropes. She probably dumped Mavis Davis at the RCD booth and raced here to offer aid and comfort to Pennyroyal's star author. Signing a few hundred books ain't pickin' cotton, but it's close to it."

Molina nodded. "Too bad Hunter didn't have his autograph session *before* Royal was murdered; I'd never suspect him of having the strength to wield so much as a tweezers afterward."

"Was that . . . humor, Lieutenant?"

"Naw." Molina gave a discouraging shake of her head and heaved an unconscious sigh.

Temple nodded. "Now, if we only could find Owen Tharp."

"Owen Tharp. Another author?"

"Not really. A pseudonym, but you've got his picture—yup, that's him. I don't know where we'll find him; he's not scheduled for an interview or a signing, but Lorna said he was here."

Molina's sharp blue eyes scanned the mob. "How about—there?"

"Where?" Temple went on tiptoe to strain in the direction Molina was looking, but saw nothing.

Moments later the lieutenant was striding through the press of humanity, her impressive physical presence clearing an automatic path. Temple clicked after, feeling a bit like a glum pet Pekingese.

On the sidelines, positioned to watch Lanyard Hunter sign every hardcover, lounged a man of middling height and age. About fifty, his hair blended brown and gray into a peppery mix. A stocky build and air of contained energy advertised three-mile runs and oat-bran muffins. He'd ditched a mustache and cut his hair since the press kit photo, but Molina's professional eye had ID'd him in an instant.

Temple examined a grudging flare of respect, then stifled it as she spotted a too-familiar shape melding with the inky shadow at the pillar's foot. Yikes! She must've left the storeroom doorknob unturned so the cat could shoulder it open again. The police detective was too intent on human prey to notice the feline, which was fine with Temple. She was getting tired of apologizing for the cat's peregrinations.

"Mr. Tharp?" Molina said briskly. "Got a few minutes?"

The man spread his hands. "Lady, I've got a few hours, seeing as how my publisher hasn't seen fit to schedule me for one of these hosanna sessions."

"Lieutenant," Molina corrected impassively. "Las Vegas MPD. I take it you worked for the late Chester Royal."

Owen Tharp straightened to give himself as much height as he could manage toe to toe with the long Amazonian of the law. He was so mesmerized by the police presence and its personal implications that he failed to notice when Midnight Louie ingratiated himself against his trouser legs by rubbing back and forth. Temple chuckled and felt much better; at least someone else felt intimidated by Lieutenant Molina.

"Sorry, sir," Tharp said. "I mean, ma'am. Being a writer isn't exactly 'working for' an editor, or even a publisher. We're all free-lancers, at bottom. Certain publishers buy certain of our books, and that's the extent of it."

"And they put them out under certain names?"

"Sometimes."

"What's your real name?"

Tharp's cocky smile became both gentle and bitter. "Would you buy Indigo Atwill? Two hundred thousand historical romance readers did. Maeve Michaels? Sean Owen, then? Kevin Gill? How about Owen James and Jesse

Wister? It's bad strategy to use the second half of the alphabet for an author's last name, but I have an affinity for bad strategy. I see, Lieutenant, that none of my aliases rings a bell—good for my continuing freedom but bad for my writing career. No wonder I'm out here in limbo while the sainted Lanyard Hunter, who under his own name sat out three years in Joliet, basks in the adjacent limelight."

"Are you saying Hunter has a record?"

"I'm not saying anything. I am merely venting a bit of authorial bile. I presume that an autopsy of the late lamented Mr. Royal has returned a verdict of death by unnatural adventure?"

Molina regarded the writer with polite wonder until the man shook his head as if emerging from a mental fog. The black cat, unacknowledged and perhaps miffed, stalked behind the pillar and vanished. Temple hoped he was heading to the storeroom like a good kitty.

"Sorry." Tharp offered a final head-clearing shake and a wry smile not without charm. "I was talking like a character out of Christie, wasn't I? I'm a natural mimic. My personal, as well as my literary style adapts to suit the subject matter. How can I help you, Lieutenant?"

"If you didn't work for the late Mr. Royal, how would you describe your relationship?"

"I wrote books; he bought 'em. I could always churn something out when one of his prima donnas was overdue. Or when one of theirs required a complete rewrite. I was Royal's safety net. He could always take my stuff and ram it through with just some copy-editing.' Course, that wasn't enough for Pennyroyal Press to pull me out of third-lead position or onto the best-seller list."

"Lorna Fennick said you were one of the imprint's best-selling authors," Temple put in.

Owen/Tharp/Gill/Michaels/Et cetera regarded her pityingly. "Production. None of my titles sold that much, but I sold 'em a lot of my titles. It adds up. But the big-buck advances, the sure thing, no, that's never been my role."

"I'm puzzled," Molina began, surprising Temple, who'd

never expected to hear her admit any such problem. "You say the other authors turned in unpublishable work? Not big sellers like Hunter and Davis, surely?"

Tharp snorted with gusto. "Are you kidding? They were the worst of the wimps. Look, I'm a writer. Day in, day out; trends in, trends out. In the late sixties I wrote Gothics; in the seventies it was historical romance; the eighties were Westerns and male adventure, and horror; now I've hit this medical gore vein, excuse the expression, and at least Owen Tharp earns some royalties even. But Hunter, he's a medical con man, an obsessive, if you wanta know the truth. Sure, he knows the underbelly of a hospital, but pacing, story, structure—phooey! And Davis is just a Kankakee nurse with a weird sense of horror who wrote this strange little book which somehow found its way to the Pennyroyal slush pile and, bingo, she's a star. Editors always like writers they can remake better than ones they have to take as is, because they know what they're doing."

"Slush pile?" Molina inquired faintly.

Temple was feeling beneficent. "Unsolicited manuscripts, sent without benefit of agent or introduction. Some best-sellers have been plucked from the slush pile—"

"And a few million haven't," Tharp finished.

"How long have you been in Las Vegas, Mr. Tharp?"

"Lieutenant. Lieutenant." He looked down. He looked up. The only place he didn't look was at the thick, twisting line of Lanyard Hunter fans, all bookstore owners likely to order mega-amounts of the new fall title. "I've been here since Tuesday. I like to play the slot machines and a little craps. I coulda killed Chester, easy. Anybody could have, that late and that lonely. But I didn't. Without Pennyroyal Press, I wouldn't have the modicum of success I do; I'd be writing porn or Ninja Turtle novelettes. He never axed my stuff, wasn't any fun in it. He never owned me enough to push me to the top. It was a comfortable arrangement for us both."

"Now that he's gone, you might be given first-title status."

"Lead title, it's called. No, it doesn't work that way. Now he's gone, the whole imprint could be cannibalized and I could be out a gravy train. I had no reason to dust the dude, honest."

Molina remained silent but skeptical.

"Oops, I'm sounding like Sam Spade or something. Sorry. Habit. Anything more?"

"Not for now."

"Good. I'm gonna hit the slots. The odds are better there."

Tharp pushed off the pillar he'd been upholding and melded with the crowd. Temple regarded Molina expectantly.

"Thanks for the tour," the detective said absently. "I'm going to have a long talk with Hunter about his white-coated past as soon as the signing is over."

It was a dismissal, which Temple acknowledged with an internal clench of disappointment. Asking people personal questions was a stimulating pastime. She'd hoped to eavesdrop on more of Molina's interviews. But she gave way gracefully.

"I'll introduce you to Lorna Fennick, the PR director. She'll arrange everything with Hunter."

"Oh, good, Temple!" Lorna greeted the pair as they approached the besieged autograph table.

Lorna took the introduction of Molina calmly and bent down to pass the police officer's request to Hunter. He showed no alarm. Sterling-silver hair only enhanced youthful features. His light gray eyes flicked up from the flyleaf he was inscribing in a flowing hand, resting on Temple with interest.

"It'll be another fifteen minutes, Lieutenant Molina," Lorna said. "There's a private area in the RCD booth where you can talk."

When Molina nodded and resumed her place at the pillar until the signing ended, Lorna clutched Temple's wrist to detain her.

"Listen, Temple! I had to leave Mavis Davis in the green

room. She is not in good shape. Chester's death really ripped her up. And the stress of the mass interview . . . I shouldn't have left her, but I had to get Lanyard set up and I can't leave until everything's squared away, including this police interview all of a sudden. Be a doll and baby-sit Mavis for me. You know."

Temple did know, and nodded. She also did a mental jig of glee. There was nothing she'd like better than to sit down with a distraught Mavis Davis and ask a few uncensored questions. Waving a cheery goodbye to the unimpressed Lieutenant Molina, Temple skittered her way through the throngs. Even as she kept one eye out for the delinquent black cat, a thrill of intuition and excitement zinged from her toes to her scalp. Temple scented something electric in the convention hall's chill, icily conditioned air, a hot lead scintillating like heat lightning in the distance.

She almost forgot that her feet hurt.

Feline Follies

"There you are, T.B.!"

Temple stopped dead amid a maelstrom of passersby. "Amazing. Twenty thousand people and *you* find me just like that."

Crawford Buchanan produced the expression he expected to pass for a smile. "The Baker & Taylor people want to talk to you pronto."

"Hasn't Security explained that they're looking into it?"

"Apparently B & T places more faith in you, T.B., for whatever reason."

She eyed her watch. The tempting Mavis Davis would have to sit unconsoled for a few minutes. Certainly a suspect-starved cop like Lieutenant Molina would not let a proven medical con man like Lanyard Hunter slip away without at least a half-hour grilling, so there should be time to placate Baker & Taylor and still interrogate . . . comfort the Davis woman.

"Well, don't thank me," Buchanan whined as Temple sped away on winged Liz Claiborne pistachio-colored heels.

Baker & Taylor—the wholesaler—occupied a handsomely accessorized string of booths directly off the Rotunda, which was the entire vast length of the exhibition area away. Temple finally sighted their mock-mahogany-paneled pillars towering above surrounding exhibits. Rich tones of emerald, wine and teal fostered the impression of a well-to-do library. Amidst all this tasteful opulence sat the *pièce de résistance,* all forlorn.

Baker and Taylor—the actual felines—had, for their first in-*purr*son ABA appearance, been provided with a royal setting. An eight-feet-tall display case was painted all around with a waist-high trompe l'oeil mural of bookcases holding forthcoming fall titles.

Above that, a large custom Lucite habitat had showcased the famous pair for their public. Inside were cat beds shaped like easy chairs. Chintz draped the "windows" on all four sides; carpet-padded ladders climbed to an upper reach of painted library shelves equipped with such apparent feline classics as *The Brothers Katamazov, Ben-Purr, A Tail of Two Kitties, Androclaws and the Lion, The Feline Comedy* and, of course, a complete set of Lilian Jackson Braun's *The Cat Who* mysteries. Perhaps the most poignant—and properly prophetic—title was *The Cat Who Walked Through Walls* by Robert Feline.

An enclosed area entered through a curtain no doubt housed the sanitary facilities.

Although the cats in question were absent in body, they were well represented in the booth—glossy calendars and posters pictured them perched on towers of best-sellers, in round spectacles and assorted bookish poses. Despite their stardom, Baker and Taylor were short-haired, sensible-looking felines with large patches of pepper-and-spice-seasoned white fur. Their undersize ears—a trademark of their unusual breed—were tucked neatly to their sagacious Highland heads.

The booth contact person was a sleek, reassuringly friendly woman Temple's age wearing—since Baker and Taylor's absence had been discovered early yesterday morning before Chester Royal's removal—a now-constant frown of anxiety.

"Miss Barr! Have you heard anything?"

"No"—Temple swiftly consulted the name tag depending from the lapel of a teal silk blazer—"Miss Adcock, I haven't. To be quite honest, I've been caught up in the other crime."

"Other crime? Oh, the murder." Emily Adcock absently jabbed the ballpoint pen behind her ear more firmly in place. "But what about the cats! I've had a chance to ask everyone who was on duty when we were setting up the booths. Nobody took the cats home for the night, as I'd hoped some misguided animal lover had done. Good grief—this cat palace is equipped with every comfort known to exhibit engineers. Baker and Taylor are library cats. They're *used* to mingling with the public. They like the attention. They wouldn't run away!"

"How did they become corporate cover cats?" Temple asked.

"The sponsoring library got Baker on its own, and wrote the company, which gave them a grant a couple months later to purchase Taylor. These cats are *famous* among librarians and libraries everywhere. If anything's happened to them . . . who could have taken them?"

"Have you talked to Mr. Bent?"

"The convention hall security chief? Yes, he was most cooperative. He agreed that the cats couldn't have escaped without human aid. The display area is secure. It might be malicious mischief. He's sparing what staff he can to search the facility, including the air vents. But who would hear a 'meow' in this mess?"

"It's terribly distressful, but if you don't want to involve the police—"

Emily Adcock shuddered in her lightweight blazer. "Lordy, no! Not . . . yet. Not when it could be an accident or a prank. Did you see the *Review-Journal* with that cat story on the second front? Think what the press could do with this! 'Double Trouble: Cats out of Bag at ABA.' 'Major Book Distributor Loses Catty Corporate Mascots.' No, thank you."

One PR woman's publicity coup could be another's *coup-de-grâce* Temple mused. "I don't see what I can do."

Emily Adcock wrung her hands despite sizable diamond solitaires on the third fingers of each hand. "Just make sure that your security personnel takes this matter seriously. I'm just a PR free-lancer like you. My goose will be chopped liver if Baker & Taylor loses its namesake cats, not to mention that everyone's grown terribly fond of them. Such good-natured creatures. I never would have suggested that they appear in person if I'd suspected—"

"Mr. Bent will find them if they're hiding out in the building. And if their absence has a more sinister cause—"

"What do you mean?"

"Catnapping. Surely you've considered that?"

"No! Who would do such a thing?"

Temple extended a forefinger and began ticking off possibilities down a descending ladder of digits: "A business rival, to embarrass the company. An animal rights fanatic, to protest using animals to sell products and services. An off-beat criminal who wants a ransom. A cat hater who'll send them to an experimental laboratory." Temple was about to start on her other hand when Emily Adcock clutched it.

"Stop, Miss Barr! You have such . . . an active imagination. No more, please. Those possibilities alone are sufficient to cause a sleepless night."

"Those are just off the top of my head, of course." Temple sighed. "My immediate problems with the Royal death are almost over. I promise that Baker and Taylor—cats and company—will be my next priority."

Next, after a previous priority was settled.

Temple raced for the interview area green room, checking her wristwatch. The show-and-tell act was over for the day. If she was lucky, she'd have Mavis Davis all to herself.

"This is so kind of you, Miss Barr." Mavis Davis gazed around the cocktail lounge of the Las Vegas Hilton. Like most Vegas hostelries, the Hilton flooded its restaurants and bars with air-conditioning and dim nocturnal elegance from dawn to dusk to dawn again. Despite the crowd and the noise, the place felt cozy, dark and intimate, perfect for breaking off a love affair or confessing to murder.

"Think nothing of it, Miss Davis. And call me Temple, please. Lorna was sick at having to desert you, but the signing was scheduled and then the police lieutenant wanted to interrogate Lanyard Hunter afterward—"

"Oh, dear." Mavis Davis shivered, but Temple doubted she felt the frosty air-conditioning. Although the Hilton was next to the convention center, the walk here had been long, hot and dry. No walk in Vegas is brief, simply because its buildings are so sprawling.

"You haven't been . . . interrogated yet?" Temple asked.

"Me! No. Why should I be?" Mavis Davis looked truly appalled.

"You might have some notion or unsuspected information about the murder."

"Miss Barr—Temple. I write about murder. I don't think about it in real life. I'm a nurse." Mavis Davis sipped her Rob Roy, which Temple had never seen ordered before.

"I'm a PR person, but I've sure got murder on the brain now. Doesn't it intrigue a writer to have the real thing fall on her doorstep?"

"No! My books are stories, that's all. I know my hospitals, and I've seen death. It's not dramatic, and it's always so disappointing. We always hope that we won't lose."

"Except for your homicidal nurses."

"Yes, but they're—well, a few in real life have been so deranged—but mine are made-up."

"You aren't basing your novels on true crime cases? How

refreshing. These days truth is more shocking than fiction."

"I did try using actual cases for inspiration, but Mr. Royal discouraged me from doing that, I don't know why. But I always listened to him—oh, dear! Who'll tell me what to do now? My next book is due in only ten months!"

"You'll have to carry on as best you can without him. How did you happen to start writing, anyway?"

"Goodness, that was something I always did, from the time I was little—I'd write and nurse baby-dolls. My foster parents still have all my dolls with their bandages and slings and—oh, my, so much slapdash Mercurochrome on them they look like Indian chiefs!" Mavis smiled maternally. "And my 'scribblings' drawer was full of doggerel and notebooks."

"So why'd you become a nurse first?"

Mavis sipped her romantically named drink, her lips pursing at a taste more tolerated than savored. "Practical. Girls like me were terminally practical in the sixties, my dear. Teachers or nurses, those were our career choices, and only if we couldn't catch a husband first. Obviously, I 'caught' a nursing degree and—later, the writing bug."

"And you lived with foster parents, so you don't even know why you gravitated toward nursing and writing?"

Mavis Davis lowered her unfortunate voice. "Maybe that's why I did. Mother and Father Forbes would never talk about my parents. Adopted or fostered children in those days weren't encouraged to wonder about their origins—and it was probably for the best. But some Forbes cousins used to giggle about it in front of me when I was a teenager. My mother died having an illegal abortion when I was three, you see. Nobody would talk openly about it, but everybody knew, even me eventually. That's why I never knew anything about my father. And why I went into nursing, I think."

"To make sure that women would never have to undergo the trauma of abortion without a caring attendant?"

Mavis Davis regarded Temple as if she were mad. "Heavens, no! The Forbeses were Roman Catholic, and that's the way I was raised. My mother may have been young and desperate, but she was also desperately wrong! The Supreme Court decision legalizing abortion coincided with my first nursing assignment, but I only worked in hospitals that resisted abortions—or at least gave staff a choice. Mostly I worked in maternity wards, and those are such happy places." The joy on Mavis's face reflected hundreds of unclouded, socially sanctioned births.

"Isn't it hard, then," Temple asked delicately, "to write about made-up medical horrors?"

"No. It's make-believe. A scary story. I feel so . . . free when I'm writing one of my naughty nurse thrillers. Because I know it's not real. Readers love them. I cherish this secret fantasy that someday my real father or someone who knew him will read one of my books and recognize some family trait in my photograph and write the publisher . . . an awful lot of people read these things, you know. Maybe a million." Mavis laughed with harsh suddenness at her million foolish readers—and her own poignant little fantasy. "I honestly don't know why my books fascinate the public. I don't even know why Mr. Royal bought my first book."

"How long was he your editor?"

"Twelve years."

"And you still called him 'Mr. Royal'?"

"He was older," she began.

Temple studied the woman's plain but unlined features. "Considerably older than you—sixty-six, the bio said."

Mavis pursed her lips over a sip of tricked-up scotch. "Young people in my day and place were trained to respect their elders. I may be an adult now, but Mr. Royal seemed so much older—and he was the head of Pennyroyal Press. I never would have felt right about calling him Chester. Nor, I think, would he."

"What did he call you?"

She looked down at the soggy napkin on which she was restlessly turning her glass. "Mavis."

"I wish I'd known him. You know, I don't even know if he was married."

"Oh, yes."

"Really. To whom?"

Mavis Davis looked confused. "Well, I don't know to whom at present. I'd heard he had several wives."

"Several? A sorry little weasel like him?" Temple suddenly realized she had somehow identified the late Mr. Royal with the very live and loathsome Crawford Buchanan.

Mavis blinked.

"I know he's dead and all that," Temple backpedaled quickly from her apparent lack of sympathy, "but I'm the one who landed atop the corpse. It was not that of a Romeo I'd care to meet—dead or alive."

"I can't say. I never thought of Mr. Royal in that way. To tell you the truth, I was in awe of him."

"Why?"

"He made me rich and famous."

"But you wrote the books."

"But he published the first one."

"And built Pennyroyal Press on it, from what I can read between the press release lines."

"Oh, no. I'm sure my little book had nothing to do with that. Why, he could hardly afford to pay me three thousand dollars for it, and it was years before he could pay as much as ten thousand dollars. I had to keep nursing for seven years before I could afford to quit. Quite biblical, don't you think?"

"But—" Temple searched her memory for the press release's boastful statistics. "*Now I Lay Me* had fourteen printings and almost made *The New York Times* best-seller list. Your next books did better."

Mavis simpered modestly. "Mr. Royal never grew tired of pointing out how lucky I was to have sold to Pennyroyal my first time out. It took quite a lot of work to rewrite the book; he sent it back four times and had to fix some parts himself. I am—was—a rank amateur, Temple. I owe everything to Mr. Royal. Or did." Her face blanched, if not quite with grief, certainly with a spasm of personal loss.

Temple eyed the chaste white-wine spritzer before her, the prudent PR professional's choice when conducting business over cocktails. She caught the eye of a skimpily skirted waitress. "A gin and tonic, please. And another Rob Roy."

"Oh, no, really—" Mavis protested without conviction. Her face had sagged, first from heat and now from the uninhibiting tide of alcohol. She resembled a tired housewife who'd been prevailed upon to baby-sit the grade school soccer team. Temple felt a wave of guilt that she drowned in a swallow of gin as soon as it arrived, which was very quickly, this being Vegas. Teetotalers don't up the house take.

"I'll miss him," Mavis said bleakly. "I'd gotten so used to him telling me what to do. He took such great pains about it. I know they say they'll get me another editor, but—"

Her hand made a white-knuckled fist of pure fear. Temple expected to see the tail of a handkerchief trailing from it, Mavis Davis was that kind of old-fashioned, naïve woman. There was nothing old-fashioned about the raw edge of her nerves, her desperate lack of confidence.

"Tell me something, Mavis—I can call you that?"

"Yes," the woman said with pathetic eagerness. "I'm really all alone now. I don't think—they—know how much Mr. Royal did for me."

"Or *to* you," Temple muttered into her gin. "Mavis. That first book, did you write the whole thing all by yourself when you sold it?"

Mavis nodded.

"Did you have a literary agent?"

Mavis shook her head.

"Do you have one now?"

Another nod. "Mr. Royal said I really should have, after the third book. He recommended someone he'd known for years."

"But your advances didn't crack ten thousand dollars until the seventh book."

"No . . . why?"

"Well, what did the agent do besides get a cut of your money?"

"He handled all the business stuff that gave me a headache."

"You mean selling foreign and film rights, that stuff?"

"No. Those were handled by Pennyroyal Press. I was lucky the house had such a big stake in my outside rights, it made them work harder to sell them, my agent said."

Now Temple's knuckles had whitened on her glass. She didn't know much about publishing, but she knew enough to see that Chester Royal had taken shameful advantage of Mavis Davis. The question was, could Mavis Davis, mistress of the Maniacal Nurse Novel, have really been naïve enough—even to this moment—to never suspect it?

The right—or wrong—answer to that question could spell a motive for murder.

Chapter 9

Lost and Found

"I saw you at the Hilton lounge. Some people have all the fun."

"I guess you'd know about that, Crawford."

Temple swung her heavy tote bag to the desk. The nice thing about working late—six P.M.—was that the ABA PR office was pretty much cleared and no one was around to hear Buchanan's charge that Temple had been drinking on the job, even though advertising and PR had invented the three-martini lunch.

The usual notes on incoming calls and current crises sprinkled Temple's desktop like a giant's dandruff. First she had to remove her new paperweight: the black cat (an enterprising rascal) had returned to the office all by himself for some serious grooming. With apologies—to him—she swooped the cat into the storeroom, hoping Buchanan would lose interest and leave, which he did while she was gone. Temple returned to her desk, sank onto her chair and began shuffling memos. Then she pushed her glasses atop her head, cradling her face in her hands. Her eyes refused to focus. It'd been a helluva day. Forget the messages tonight; she'd just scoop the cat into his carrier and head for home, sweet home.

"Excuse me," a female voice said pointedly from the doorway.

Temple forsook her "Abandon Hope" pose and took in the visitor—visitors, plural. A man stood on the threshold, too, a darkly handsome man. The woman was petite, blond and looked as though she meant business in a Dresden kind of way.

What now, Temple wondered.

The woman marched to Temple's desk. "We saw this in the evening edition."

"Oh, the cat story."

The man had followed her. "The story's wrong. We know the cat. It's not a stray."

"Not a stray? You mean it's . . . your cat?" Even Temple heard a rising note of denial in her voice.

The couple was too busy exchanging mute, consulting looks to note Temple's fraying control.

"Not exactly 'our' cat," She admitted.

"It's the house cat," He said.

Temple just stared at them.

He recognized an opening and uncorked a 150-watt smile. "Our 'house' happens to be the Crystal Phoenix Hotel and Casino on the Strip. Louie hangs out there, always has since before we reopened the place. I don't know how he got way over here, but—"

"Louie?" Temple interrupted.

"Midnight Louie," the blond woman elaborated. "The cat."

"And who are you?" Temple said.

A tanned hand extended. "Nicky Fontana, and my wife, Van von Rhine. She manages the Crystal Phoenix. I own it."

"And Louie is the house cat," the woman said firmly. "When we saw his photo, we thought we'd better bring him home."

"Home." Temple didn't know why thinking was so hard; maybe it was trying to find believable excuses for the cat's supposed absence, like she'd sent him to the pound, or a Hollywood animal trainer had already claimed him or—"He's in the storeroom. I'll get him."

They followed her to the storeroom door. Maybe they didn't trust her; maybe they were just eager to see . . . Louie. Stupid name for a cat, Temple fumed; why not Whiskers or Schwarzenegger if they wanted a really dumb name?

The cat unloosed a long *rowwwwl* of welcome. Temple watched it stalk past her, pause, then thread itself around Van von Rhine's legs before giving Nicky Fontana a greeting nip on the knee.

"Hey, those are my best Italian silk-blends!"

Van von Rhine squatted before the huge cat. "Louie! You're famous now, but how on earth did you get into the convention center? Where have you been all week? We missed you!" She looked up at Temple through limpid blue eyes. "I really did panic when he hadn't been seen for a while—imagined he'd been run over or worse. I guess it's from having an infant around. Mother's nerves."

"Father's nerves," muttered her husband, "aren't too calm at the moment, either; must be those nighttime serenades. We're sure glad we found Louie. We'll take him from here. He eats a ton, not to mention weighs one. Thanks for looking after him."

"Sure." Temple's weight shifted from foot to foot. Her precarious high heels felt like true needles, as if they would puncture the floor and drop her another six inches. The cat obviously knew the couple, was glad to see them, glad to be out of the storage closet, her apartment, her life, the limelight even, who knows what a cat thinks? Temple knew what she thought. That it was ridiculous for an almost-thirty-for-Christ's-sake career woman to be standing in front of strangers with a sock-size lump in her throat.

"Wait!" she said past the sock. "The cat's been really important to the center. The publicity he got took the spotlight off a rather unfortunate event here. I'd like to keep him a while, until I'm sure we won't need him any-more."

"You don't understand," the woman said gently. "Louie's not a pet. He adopted us, to tell the truth, and the whole hotel to boot. Everyone from bellboys to visiting celebrities expects to see Midnight Louie around."

"He's an alleycat, Miss Barr," the man added with a glance at the nameplate on the desk. "He needs to come and go as he pleases. Sure he'll cadge what he can from the staff or raid the carp pond in the hotel gardens if he can get away with it, but he's not really domesticated. He's not used to being"—Nicky Fontana eyed the empty cat carrier with distaste—"kept. It's not fair to him."

"Did I say that? No, of course not." Temple's voice sounded forced. "I understand." A sinuous form wove against her legs. She bent down to stroke the glossy black fur. "Well, Louie, thanks for helping save the day. Take care of yourself, you big lug."

Temple straightened and turned quickly to get the car-rier.

"Naw—we won't need that," Nicky Fontana said. "It won't fit in my 'vette. Louie'll ride in the rumble seat, right, fellah?"

Temple turned back to see the cat occupying most of Nicky's arms, being borne away like a big, black, furry baby.

Van von Rhine's blue-sky eyes had clouded with know-ing sympathy. "Don't worry. I'll call and let you know how he's doing. You can always come to visit him."

"I will." Temple saw them to the door, the cat's green peepers regarding her soulfully as its huge head lolled over Nicky's elbow. Louie looked supremely comfortable.

Temple closed the door as soon as polite goodbyes had

been said. She couldn't stand to watch the couple shrink down the hall, even the big black form of Midnight Louie shriveling at last.

"Dumb name!" She kicked the wastepaper basket, paused, then bent to stuff papers, paper clips and candy-bar wrappers back in one by one.

Finally all that was left to do was to collect her purse and go home. On the way out she hesitated. A stack of second fronts sat on the secretary's desk, ready for clipping and saving. Trust Valerie to remember.

"Well." Temple slipped a copy off the pile and stared at the too-cute pose of the recently reclaimed Midnight Louie. "I guess our sleuthing days are over, Sherlock."

She wasn't burdened by a cat carrier and its eighteen-pound resident when she arrived at the Circle Ritz, but Temple felt as if she were. The June heat welded her linen blouse and skirt to her body and turned her pantyhose into steaming spandex long johns. The sky was the deep, dark blue of Lake Mead, and the distant ruffle of burnt sienna mountain ranges shimmered blue-purple in the heat.

Temple parked her aqua Geo Storm next to the Ford Escort that had taken the last shaded spot, unfurled her cardboard sun-shield over the dashboard and trudged to the building's rear and through the wooden gate.

She scraped a lounge chair into the palm tree's shade and collapsed with a vehemence that made the lounge frame squeak for mercy. At her size, she didn't often make such a big impression on inanimate objects.

"Another bad day?"

A familiar head had popped over the pool's old-fashioned tiled edge. Temple mused darkly on the likely trustworthiness of men who could look attractive even with their hair wet.

"Where's the cat?" Matt Devine asked next.

"In the afternoon edition of the paper."

Matt cocked an eyebrow and hefted his chest out of the water by bracing his elbows on the edge. "That's bad?"

"That's good." She sighed.

Matt pulled himself all the way out while Temple tried not to watch. She'd once attempted to exit a pool the hard way and had ended up clawing at the concrete like a drowning lemming.

"Mrs. Lark made lemonade—want some?"

"Thanks."

The glass—a tall, thin tulip-shaped vintage number with Saturn-like silver rings around the top—was stippled with water drops, and so was Matt. A delicate blend of jasmine, chlorine and sweat perfumed the air. Bees hummed in the oleander bush. Matt pulled his lounge chair into the shade beside Temple.

"How'd the cat make the daily news?" he wondered.

Temple unenthusiastically produced the second section she'd grabbed at the office. Matt carefully dried his hands on the towel draping his lounge chair and took it.

"Cute story—takes the heat off the news of the murder at the convention center. Your idea?"

She nodded disconsolately.

"Why so glum? Looks like your strategy worked."

"Too well." Temple sipped the lemonade—tart the way she liked it—and smiled just a little. "This couple turns up from the Crystal Phoenix down the Strip and claims the cat is some 'house' stray they've had around for years. So . . . bye, bye, Midnight Louie."

"Midnight Louie. Yeah, he's the rambling, rogue feline type, all right. And you'd gotten attached to the cat."

"Maybe I have a tendency to get inappropriately attached."

Matt smiled at Midnight Louie's likeness. "So do most people. Animals seldom make that mistake, and certainly not cats."

"I was getting used to the clump of his big paws around the place. When you live alone . . ." She let it trail off, aware she was dumping her bad mood on a mere acquaintance.

"Have you always lived alone here?" There was a disingenuous tone to Matt's voice that in no way could be mistaken for a flattering personal interest in her answer.

"No," Temple said.

"I'm not used to living alone, either."

Curiosity killed the cat, she reminded herself, too downcast to inquire further into *that* intriguing confession.

"That's why I like Mrs. Lar—Electra's place here," Matt said. "It feels like a community . . . I don't know—like a campus dorm or something."

Temple nodded. "Electra has a way of making her tenants feel at home, just like she makes the soft-sculpture people in her pews seem almost real. She even names them and accessorizes them down to their pinkie rings with estate-sale finds."

"If only all congregations were so attentive." Matt smiled wryly. "Just what are Electra's ministerial credentials?"

"Frankly? The Church of Barely Respectable Mumbo-Jumbo. Some mail-order ministry that believes in assorted paranormal phenomena. Las Vegas boasts twenty-five wedding chapels, and half of the officiators are women, but they're all nondenominational. Luckily, you don't need establishment credentials to marry people in Las Vegas, just a state license."

Matt shook his head and sipped lemonade.

"Churches can be . . . funny things," Temple found herself musing out of the blue—out of her prolonged blue mood, rather. "Religion can be dangerous."

Matt kept a blandly neutral face. "What do you mean?"

"Oh, I heard something awful today from one of the ABA authors. This very out-of-it middle-aged lady writes novels about murderous nurses—medical horror, they call it. Anyway, she just told me her mother died from a botched illegal abortion back in the fifties."

Matt winced. "Ugly. But it happened."

"The fallout is that the people who reared Mavis—she was only a little kid—were Catholic, so Mavis feels she must morally condemn her own mother, who was probably just a terrified teenager. No wonder her novels depict berserk nurses—women who should nurture but who kill instead—even babies. We sit here smiling at tacky Las Vegas ministers, but so-called 'respectable' religion can be a lot more lethal, if you ask me. And if Mavis's mother hadn't been so ashamed of being pregnant, maybe she wouldn't have tried an illegal abortion."

Matt nodded soberly. "I take it you're not Catholic?"

"Me? I'm not even a good atheist. Whatever you believe about abortion, that's . . . politics. What's really sad is to see a grown woman who believes that her mother was a monster rather than a victim. And now Mavis is another victim, but she doesn't see it, probably because she has such low self-esteem as the daughter of a 'bad' woman."

"How is Mavis a victim?"

"That murdered editor at the convention center was the Rasputin type. He convinced his authors that their writing success depended on him. Mavis was his biggest patsy from what I can tell. He exploited her shamelessly; even now that he's dead, she's so sure that she needs him that she may never write again!"

"That's not religion gone wrong," Matt said. "That's ego."

"But the shame Mavis was made to feel for how her mother died makes her a perfect victim for everyday, secular exploitation. Do you see what I'm saying? Chester Royal manipulated her like Silly Putty. And if Mavis ever really saw how she's been used—all her life—well, that's when people get murdered, isn't it? When someone near them *sees* for the first time what's really been going on."

"Most victims don't turn victimizer," Matt argued. "They strike out at themselves, if anybody."

"Somebody struck out at Chester Royal with a number five knitting needle."

"And you think it could be this Mavis—?"

"Davis," Temple put in glumly.

Matt looked confused.

"Mavis Davis. That's her name." Matt was right. Temple

did think that Mavis was capable of killing Chester Royal, and a knitting needle was the kind of flaky, genteel weapon a genteelly flaky person like Mavis would use. "And this Big-Girl-Lost routine of hers could be an act."

"Whoa—if you're going to play detective, you can't get depressed every time you discover that someone is a good candidate for the role of killer."

"I *was* trying to play detective," Temple admitted, "and I'm too involved for it. One last reprise. You make a good shrink. Are you?"

He laughed hard enough to break Temple's gloomy mood.

"I mean it," she prodded. "I'll bet you majored in psychology in college, right?"

Matt's laughing face smoothed to neutrality. Temple felt like she'd stepped off the edge of a pool and only then noticed there was no water in it. "More like sociology," he said cautiously.

"Close." Temple knew she'd been prying again. "Sorry. PR people are naturally curious."

"Like cats."

"Yeah." She scraped a high heel across the hot cracked concrete rimming the pool. Louie was another reason for her flagging spirits. Matt's toffee-brown eyes were watching her, warily. Temple wondered if he'd resurrected the subject of Louie's loss to distract her from himself—from talk of college majors. Could that be? Maybe he hadn't gone to college and was sensitive. Time to leash her curiosity and back off before Matt got spooked.

"What exactly do you do at your job?" she heard her irrepressible public self ask, even as her sensible private self urged restraint.

Matt smiled a rueful smile that Temple liked very much. "I'm a telephone hot-line counselor."

"Aha! Shrink!"

"Not really. I'm not . . . degreed."

"But you're a great listener. Sorry I was religion-bashing. You must've had some church exposure in your wild-and-woolly formative years, as the sociologists say," Temple speculated. "You play a mean organ. That was a wonderful wedding march you did for Electra. I peeked in. What was it?"

His smile tiptoed around a mouthful of tart lemonade. "It's not a march, and it's not normally played at weddings."

"But it was perfect! Slow and dignified and tender. I'd love to get it on CD."

The smile had expanded into a grin. "Ask for Bob Dylan at the audio store."

"Old Gravel-larynx? You're kidding!"

"Swear to God. It was 'Love Minus Zero—No Limit.' Listen to it. Even the lyrics are hymeneal."

"Huh?"

"An old Greek word for 'marital.' "

"Oh, as in the Greek god of marriage." Temple felt a flush coming on as she connected the god Hymen with the adjective made from his name and certain gynecological terminology also derived therefrom.

"Were you a classics major?" Matt was asking innocently, as if his mind had eluded the natural but racier connotations.

At least he was interested. "Communications. I did some TV reporting, then ended up in public relations at a repertory theater company in Minneapolis. You tend to learn Greek gods' names when the director favors five-hour revivals of Aeschylus. Generally in the form of ancient curses. But that melody is really Bob Dylan's?"

"Really." Matt pressed his hand to his heart.

Temple eyed the Devine physique. Talk about Greek gods. . . . Great-looking, good-counseling Matt. Honestly, this guy was too good to be true. Well, Max had seemed pretty spectacular at first. The trouble was that Max had seemed pretty spectacular at last, too. Damn Max. Damn runaway cats. Damn hope springing eternal. . . .

"Thanks for the lemonade," Temple said, standing. "I

better see what that half-full open can of tuna is doing to my refrigerator."

"Electra probably wouldn't have wanted to set a precedent with pets, anyway."

"Midnight Louie is not a 'pet,'" Temple announced loftily. "He is his own person, free to come and go, as I was informed today. And I guess he's gone—from my life, anyway."

"Maybe you could get another cat. Mrs. La—Electra—seems something of a pushover."

"You noticed that, huh? No, I work such long hours sometimes it really wouldn't be fair. All's for the best. I should be glad my brilliant idea for an article not only cooled the ABA murder, but got M.L.—as my associate Crawford Buchanan would say—a home."

"Too bad about the murder. I don't blame you for getting down about it." Matt's brown eyes narrowed against the surrounding sunlight. "An ugly thing: one human being feeling such hatred toward another that he—or she—would actually end the other person's life. Have the police any theories?"

"They don't exactly consult me, although I spent half the day in the custody of Lieutenant Molina of LVMPD Sex and Homicide."

"Why was he bothering with you?"

Temple smiled. Matt Devine's laudable care with the gender of the possible murderer had fallen victim to the automatic assumption that a sex and homicide detective must be male—but then, maybe C. R. Molina was, in a way.

"Lieutenant Molina needed a tour guide to the American Booksellers Association convention. I learned more today about publishing than I want to know—and discovered even more reasons why an author might want to ax an editor than the ordinary reader would ever suspect. Remind me never to get the book-writing bug."

"You're not getting seriously caught up in the case?"

"No, I'm a definite fringe element, but I can't help noticing things."

"Leave it to the police; noticing too much might get dangerous."

"Yeah, but it's that communications major of mine. I have this insatiable need to know—and tell. Besides, people naturally seem to confide in me."

"Not always an easy position to be in."

"No." Temple thought of Mavis Davis mauling her cocktail napkin not two hours before. "No."

She couldn't sleep that night. First she'd had a hot idea—she was always getting hot ideas after hours—and had consulted with Electra, who'd been only too happy to volunteer her talented fingers for a worthy project. Then Temple had returned to her apartment and a sultry night alone. Visions of Matt Devine backing up Bob Dylan on an organ, wearing nothing but a pair of bathing trunks, revved her active imagination, along with scenes of Midnight Louie's presumed triumphal welcome back into the bosom of the Crystal Phoenix.

And then there were the trio of authors she met that day. She hadn't had a chance to talk to Lanyard Hunter, but he was scheduled for an interview tomorrow—today—and she probably could catch him then. . . .

Could Mavis Davis really have smitten down Chester Royal? She was a sturdy-looking woman. A nurse would know how to manhandle large, inert bodies—and Chester Royal had been small-statured. Like Owen Tharp; no wonder they got along! Was Royal as controlling of Hunter as he was of Mavis Davis? Was it because she was a woman; or did Royal keep all his authors terminally insecure?

Temple had seen stage directors like that: men (and they always were; few women directed even nowadays) who used their entrée to the artistic ego to twist it, to find and manipulate the self-doubting child that lurks in every adult. Such men were vicious egotists who claimed credit for their victims' talent even while bending it past the breaking point.

No passion was more terrible than that of an artist who has given all and been betrayed. Temple had seen normally rational theater people ready to kill a klutzy critic for an undeserved insensitive review—could writers be any less intolerant of meddling with their words?

Temple shivered in her hot, limp sheets, under the lazy breeze of the ceiling fan's Plexiglas blades. It clicked ever so slightly as it turned, sounding like the snap of distantly chewed gum.

The night was warm—Temple tried to keep utility bills down by running the air conditioner on "tepid" after the sun went down—and somehow sexy. God, but she missed Max sometimes! He'd left enough of his things behind to haunt Temple: a foot-wide swath of his clothes now huddled in the dark against the closet's most inaccessible wall. In the linen closet, a box of magician's implements—handcuffs, trick boxes and lurid chiffon scarves—gathered dust and would convince any stranger who stumbled across it that Temple favored kinky sexual practices. Speaking of which, Temple hadn't yet had the heart to sweep the Vangelis CD's off the bedroom shelves—Max had liked to make long, lingering love to those slow, swelling organlike chords. . . .

Molina's questions had evoked a new, terrifying scenario today. Max was gone because he was dead? No. Not Max. He was definitely not a victim—of anything, including too nice a conscience. Whatever Molina thought, Temple's ego was not so in need of soothing that it would console her to know that Max had left—had left her—because he literally couldn't come back.

That led Temple into her favorite bedtime fantasy. Max coming back. What Max would say, how he could possibly explain—and if anyone could, Max could. What Temple would say. What Max would do. What Temple would do. Oh, shit—!

Lord. She'd forgotten the cat box, such as it was, in the

bathroom. Had to get rid of that. In the morning. Which should soon be here. Great, another night down the tubes.

And then—what? A sound. A . . . soft, rasping sound. At her window. *Noticing too much might get dangerous.* The latches in this place were a joke. Nobody'd been worried about personal security in the fifties; besides, Superman—the comfortable old George Reeves rerun one—could always fly to the black-and-white TV rescue.

She listened. Silence. And then that determined brush, a motion repeated again and again. Deliberately. Against the shell of Temple's apartment. *Brush, brush, brush.* No trees or branches lay against the windows or walls. Las Vegas had zip for trees or bushes unless they were expensively watered, and Electra could only afford to nurse the greenery around the pool.

Temple's bare feet touched the bedroom floor. The wood parquet did nothing to cool their burning soles. She moved softly through the familiar demidark, wishing for a weapon, wishing for Max, who'd always been a two-edged sword.

In the living room, the handsome rank of French doors leading to the patio looked like nothing but glass and frame and flimsy struts. Had she even locked the doors for the night? Sometimes she felt so safe, she forgot.

Brush, brush, brush.

Stop.

Nothing.

She had moved. She had been heard.

Her breathing resumed. She could hear her lungs expanding. *Brush, brush, brush.* Too regular to be inanimate.

Maybe it was Max. Coming back. Be just like him, a surreptitious entry in the night. Surprise.

Brush, brush, brush.

Temple plucked an Art Deco ceramic peacock from an end table. The tail would make quite a bludgeon. She hushed toward the doors, feeling naked in her thin T-shirt, feeling cold in the warm, still room.

Brush, brush, brush.

The patio was terra incognita, a distorted landscape of folding chair and prickly pear. The sound was just outside the third door.

Temple edged nearer. She had to see.

A bit of shadow broke off from the night. She had to know. An insane—inane?—need to know.

The shadow stretched up, up, up, lengthened itself against the fragile, breakable glass. It reached the knob, a lever-type French latch. The latch vibrated to a blow. Temple lifted her plaster peacock.

The shadow yawned. Moonlight reflected from a diamond of tiny shark's teeth.

"Louie!"

Temple unlatched her patio door. The shadow fell lazily inward and commenced to scrub its furred sides on her calves.

A Little Night Music

You hear it here first.

I am free to come and go. And if anything is free, I take full advantage of it. I am not born and bred in Las Vegas for nothing.

As fond as I am of Mr. Nicky Fontana and his lithesome wife, Miss Van von Rhine, they are prone to understatement under stress. I have been free to come and go since I was a pup, figuratively speaking, and my dear mama batted my face and nudged me in the direction of the refuse containers behind The Sands.

Lest you think my dear mama was lacking in maternal sentiment, you should know that I was one of seven and we all got the heave-ho early in life. That is because our dear mama was something of a *femme fatale* and had no access to population control devices in those days when I was born.

So I have been slipping in and out of where I should and should definitely not be since I was knee-high to a police dog—and the police dog none the wiser.

Miss Temple Barr's delicate French-style latch is kid's play to me, especially with the door unlocked and a terra-cotta pot to stand on. Speaking of which—kids, that is, in the human form, not the goat edition—that is why I show up here again.

In the long, jostling ride back to the Crystal Phoenix in Mr. Nicky Fontana's custom-painted Corvette convertible, I am held in close communion with my two friends. It dawns on me that despite the scent of desert rose upon the Las Vegas breeze, Miss Van von Rhine's ever-present aura of Opium and Mr. Nicky Fontana's devotion to Russian Leather, a distinct odor of Essence de Diaper Pail yet pervades this formerly loving (to me) couple.

Anyone who might think that some soft spot in my ticker has led me back to Miss Temple Barr in her hour of need should keep in mind that Midnight Louie is a fall guy for neither man nor woman, and nothing human. *¿Comprende?*

I simply see that my previous carte blanche run at the Crystal Phoenix must yet be shared with that abominable yowling, crawling intruder, and this is not to be tolerated. I require persons about me with the same level of intelligence, not to mention manual dexterity.

There can be no attempt to dissuade me with any argument that the Abomination "will grow up." It is well documented with such creatures that this "growing up" takes an insufferable amount of time—not to mention money. I may have nine lives, but I am advanced enough along my longevity graph to avoid wasting any of them in fruitless endeavors.

I must admit that my reception at the Circle Ritz is all that I hoped for.

"Ah, Louie," Miss Temple Barr murmurs in dulcet, rapt tones, much as Leslie Caron must have chirped off camera to my (some say) handsome human soul mate, Louis (pronounced "Louie") Jourdan, in *Gigi* in their heydays.

Miss Temple Barr clasps me to her bosom. She fondles my head and cradles my weary body—it is a long trot from the Crystal Phoenix to the Circle Ritz.

She wafts me to the kitchen and casts slightly stale refrigerated tuna before my nostrils. She reconsiders and opens a fresh can of room-temperature sockeye salmon. This chick has possibilities.

She strokes me from dome to gehenna and back again. I am one purrin' kitten. Also, lately I have been pondering the advantages of acquiring a retirement condo far from the Strip's hurly-burly (mostly burly, when one considers the local "muscle").

Anyone can see it is clearly to my advantage to take an interest in the doings of Miss Temple Barr. I do not wish to gain an undeserved reputation for becoming a sentimental slob in my old age, but I am, as the top dogs at the Crystal Phoenix say not eight hours earlier, free to come and go.

And I foresee that matters of a mysterious nature will come and go around Miss Temple Barr for some time. She is, if I may be allowed to say so, as curious as a cat, but shockingly naïve and in desperate need of seasoned guidance. Like mine.

And she smells good.

Catastrophe . . .

Temple awoke to find the black cat sleeping on her feet. This gesture of affection was wasted in the hot afterglow of a long, tossing Las Vegas summer night.

Midnight Louie, however welcome back, was hot, hairy and weighed about eighteen pounds. Come to think of it, Temple had only to add a zero to Louie's avoirdupois and she'd have a pretty good description of the nocturnal presence of the Mystifying Max.

"Bastard!" Temple growled at the morning and Louie, following this undeleted expletive with an unexplained shiver.

"Guess what I'm going to do at work today," she told the cat, extracting her numb feet from its warm underbelly. "I'm going to find out more about Pennyroyal Press and the late Chester Royal—just for the heck of it."

The cat apparently approved of her resolve. He ate his

seven-ounce can of spring-water-packed albacore tuna, from a fishery that abided by the new Geneva conventions for the preservation of dolphins. Then he freshened his whiskers and was waiting, sleek and expectant, by the door when Temple charged out of her bedroom dressed and ready for battle.

"Why not?" she asked nobody rather pugnaciously. "The convention center has *thousands* more square feet than the Crystal Phoenix, even if none of it's that upscale. You can rule the roost—and the rats to boot. Come on."

She was not surprised when the cat trotted out after her like a dog. Midnight Louie was obviously a feline of great enterprise and intelligence. First she stopped at Electra's penthouse apartment one floor up to collect the surprise package that had been a-borning all night.

Electra, an insomniac who welcomed nocturnal projects, was baggy-eyed but not too worn to fail to admire Midnight Louie rubbing demandingly at her ankles. Apparently she had no objections to his presence. Readily abandoning his new fan, the cat followed Temple to the car.

After Temple had stuffed Electra's huge paper sack in the Geo's rear area, Louie hopped into the front passenger seat and braced his huge front paws on the dashboard like a pro. The Storm whipped through Vegas's sparse morning traffic. Folks who'd been up until two and three in the morning weren't out puttering around at 7:30 A.M.

When Temple and Louie slipped into the nondescript rear employee entrance to the mammoth convention center, Lloyd pushed his cap back on his balding cranium and narrowed his eyes to miniblind slits.

"Look, Lloyd. Midnight Louie's a VIP around here now. Famous detective cat. You read it in the paper. He can come and go as he likes."

"That official?"

"It will be as soon as I talk to Bud."

"Humph."

"Humph is right! If the Crystal Phoenix can have a house cat, we can have one, too. He might become a valuable convention center mascot, like Baker and Taylor. Any news of the missing duo?"

Lloyd shook his head as he inspected the contents of the huge paper bag Temple carried. His eyebrows lifted almost to the brim of his ebbing cap.

"I swear that there are no hidden explosives, Lloyd. Terrorists wouldn't pick Vegas to make a statement and there aren't any incendiary books out this year, except maybe the new Pee Wee Scouts kiddie title. The one a couple seasons back that told kids there was no Santa Claus raised more of a ruckus than Salman Rushdie."

When Lloyd finally nodded her in, Temple, bag and cat obliged him.

The office was still empty, but Temple made a quick call to Cyrus Bent, the security head, and told him her needs. Within twenty minutes she was meeting him at the Baker & Taylor booths. Within five they had managed a semiofficial break-in to the cat castle. Within eight they were out of there with an empty paper bag, mission accomplished.

"I hope those people appreciate your efforts," was Cyrus Bent's parting sentiment. Most men in private security were like stateside leftovers celebrated in song during World War II: either too young or too old. Bent was on the old side of that statistic, which meant that he knew that good security included being secure enough to bend a rule.

"Hope so," said Temple, saluting him as she raced down the long exhibition floor toward the offices.

Once there she showed Louie his food bowls in the storage room—a source of much interest—and a new permanent site for the previously floating workplace litter box—a source of great disdain. She left the storeroom door open as a sign of Louie's new status.

When Valerie came in, Temple's word processor was chuckling with rapid-fire releases. Her messages would have to wait a little longer. By the time Bud Dubbs arrived at 9 A.M., Louie had selected Crawford Buchanan's desk as the most congenial resting spot. Buchanan scowled in at 10:30; by then Louie's presence was *fait accompli* and Buchanan was in serious danger of being supplanted as the office layabout.

"Get that monster off my desk!"

"Why? Every time he switches his tail he clears off two months of outdated clutter."

"I hate cats!"

"You would."

"What's that supposed to mean?"

"It takes a certain discrimination to appreciate a cat like Midnight Louie. Gosh, that's a great name—I'd wish I'd known it before the *Review-Journal* article ran."

"A disgusting name, surpassed only by its possessor," Buchanan snarled. He was in a vile mood.

Just then Emily Adcock from Baker & Taylor came charging in with an exultant look.

"You found the cats!" Valerie guessed.

"Not quite. It's either the most astounding thing . . . or—" Emily Adcock focused on Temple, who had not said a word or moved a muscle—"*you* did it! What a wonderful idea!"

"I didn't do it personally," Temple said.

"It certainly takes us off the hook and makes the setup look intentional."

"What is this wonder?" Bud Dubbs asked on his way from the coffee maker.

"You'll all have to stop down and see it," Emily went on. "When I came in this morning, there in the pathetic, abandoned cat display were the dearest stuffed versions of Baker and Taylor you ever saw!"

"My landlady does soft sculptures," Temple explained. "She stayed up all night to do them."

"But it was your idea," Emily Adcock repeated.

"I figured that a faux Baker and Taylor were better than no Baker and Taylor."

"A brilliant idea." Emily smiled broadly. "I feel so much better with *something* on display. Now all we can do is hope the real B and T show up."

She left looking vastly relieved.

In her wake, Buchanan fidgeted under all the good vibes flowing in Temple's direction. He scowled at Midnight Louie, who was now grooming himself on the floor. "Could have killed two birds with one stone if you'd put this black brute into the crystal cage instead."

They regarded him as if he had proposed barbecueing Baker and Taylor. Temple answered. "Louie doesn't look anything at all like a Scottish fold cat. His ears are all wrong."

"Fix 'em," Buchanan said. "I've got a nail clipper with me."

"Boo, hiss," Valerie put in.

"I wouldn't mess with that old boy," Bud advised. "He looks big enough and mean enough to clip *your* ears before you'd lay a fingernail on him."

Louie yawned and shut his eyes.

Temple saw a verbal opening and darted in. "Say, Bud, that story was so cute. Why not keep Louie on as a mascot through the ABA? It might focus attention off the absent cats. Okay if he hangs around?"

"As long as he doesn't make any messes."

Buchanan headed for the men's room. "Great. This place'll smell like a tuna factory in two days."

"It does already," Valerie said. "You guys always order tuna salad from the Pita Palace. It's pretty ripe by the time it gets here."

Temple finally began flipping through messages from late Saturday. One was actually in an envelope. She tore it open. The last time she'd seen her letter opener was when she'd used it to cut a loaf of zucchini bread Bud's wife had sent in. Besides, her nails were long, strong and lacquered Aruba Red. They could open nonscrew-top beer bottles and type at 105 words a minute.

The envelope was standard business issue, midget-size. An ink smudge decorated the corner where a stamp would be had it been mailed. Temple felt uneasy as she withdrew the note-size sheet of paper.

Typed letters uneven in pressure and alignment skipped across the page.

"IF YOU WANT THEM CATS BACK, PUT $5,000 IN A BROWN BAG AND LEAVE IT AT 10 A.M. MONDAY BY THE THIRD GODDESS ON THE LEFT IN FRONT OF CAESAR'S PALACE. OTHERWISE, THEY IS STEW MEAT."

. . . And Apostrophe

"Would you like a drink, Temple?"

"Yes. A stiff one. I've got to come to grips with an extremely delicate matter after lunch." Temple winced, recalling the urgent message she'd left for Emily Adcock to meet her at two P.M. Passing on the "stew meat" threat would be no fun.

Lorna Fennick grimaced sympathetically. "Me, too."

"Now it's catnapping."

"Cat, not kid?"

Temple nodded as the waiter placed before her a cool white gin and tonic featuring Bombay Gin's lethal Sapphire brand. Anything purportedly good enough for Queen Victoria's menstrual cramps should do the job. "This is for our ears only, but Baker & Taylor lost their mascots to an ambitious animal-grabber."

"I wondered why they made such a big deal in their ads

about 'meeting' Baker and Taylor at the convention, then put a couple of stuffed shills in an elaborate display case. Of course, Baker & Taylor always invites booksellers to 'meet' their mascots at the convention, and it's always in purely photographic form. Importing them in person was a great publicity stunt."

" 'Was' is the operative word. It's a shame, but I'm not going to let this latest crisis interfere with keeping on top of the Royal murder."

"Speaking of which." Lorna pulled a canvas book bag up from the floor, the Time-Life, Midnight-Louie-toting kind. "Here's a bunch of titles by Pennyroyal's Top Three. I even found some of Owen Tharp's other pseudonymous efforts knocking around. I thought you could use a crash course in the Pennyroyal medical thriller."

"Thanks a million," Temple said, eyeing the bag. As she took it, the unexpected weight nearly jerked her arm out of its socket, recalling her first fond moments of custody of Midnight Louie. "These will be great. And I deeply appreciate your arranging for Mr. Big to drop by our lunch table later, Lorna."

The Reynolds/Chapter/Deuce PR director sipped her murky orange Manhattan and nodded soberly. "We could have *had* lunch with him, except that ABA meals are working occasions. You'd be amazed at the megabuck deals that go down at this superficially innocuous convention. He's eating here anyway, and if you recognize his lunch date, don't let on! The deal isn't signed yet. But he will stop by for a few minutes. He wants to insure that Chester Royal's death causes as little scandal as possible."

"Don't worry. I don't know the name brands in publishing. I'm too ignorant to blow a deal. Trust me."

"I do, that's the funny part. Emily at Baker & Taylor thinks a lot of you."

"You know her?"

"We behind-the-sceners responsible for making the ABAs run smoothly year after year get to know each other."

"How did Lieutenant Molina's grilling of Lanyard Hunter go yesterday?"

"I wasn't invited, but Hunter was in a vile mood afterward."

"So was Molina, probably. This is definitely not her normal turf."

"I don't blame the lieutenant. How's she going to nab a murderer in four days flat with twenty-four thousand strangers in town?"

"Somehow I don't feel too sorry for her."

Lorna Fennick laughed. "No, I wouldn't want to negotiate a deal with that one."

"Did you? Ever negotiate a deal, I mean?"

"Some small ones. I started as an editorial assistant and worked my way up to editor."

"How'd you get into public relations?"

Lorna looked uneasy. "I didn't have the stomach for nitty-gritty editorial matters. It can be a frustrating, petty business. Now, what did you want to know about my liege lord?"

The waiter descended. To save time Temple ordered the first thing that popped into her mind—tuna salad. Lorna had some nouvelle concoction with chard and assorted alien vegetables whose repugnant appearance was exceeded only by its outrageous price.

"Tell me about an imprint, Lorna," Temple suggested after forking her tuna salad. The sight and smell repelled her for some reason. "How is one born, how does it grow, how is it grafted onto a big mother of a plant like a major, multislashed publishing house?"

Lorna turned her Manhattan glass until the cherry pointed Temple's way. "It's like this. Some enterprising person—an ex-publishing executive or even a rank amateur like Chester Royal—begins packaging a certain kind of book. That means he finds the authors, edits the books, commissions the cover design and hands the house a ready-to-go book. They print and distribute it. If, as in Royal's case, the book is a medical thriller when the only solid-gold practitioner in the field is Robin Cook, and the packager attracts aspiring med-thriller writers, he's on his way to a stable of authors. Say his books do well for the big publisher who buys them. When they do spectacularly well, the publisher grafts the imprint and its founding editor onto the corporate tree. Then you have Reynolds/Chapter/Deuce/Pennyroyal."

"So Chester was a big success story."

"Yes, imprints are becoming more common. The system allows the little guy to take the risks and prove a product's durability. He must have a good track record at finding authors who perform at a predictable level of success. Then his promising small company is acquired by a big company that can increase his business effectiveness."

"Only this business is books, and artistic egos are involved."

"And a product's marketability is less determined by statistical consumer need than amorphous factors like trends, luck and instinct."

"Vegas is a perfect location for an ABA, then. From what you say, publishing is a crapshoot."

"But a classy crapshoot, Temple. Some book people cringe at the idea of having an ABA in a crass commercial arena like this town. It's the antithesis of publishing's Manhattan roots. Yet they must. This convention center is one of the few in the country big enough to handle a display and crowd of this size."

"So what was Chester Royal's story? How'd he happen to hit it big—and get hit?"

"He stumbled across Mavis Davis, number one. She was a long shot for established publishers, who turned down her first book in droves. But Royal with his medical background saw something there, and the rest is history."

"Medical background?"

"He trained as a doctor, even practiced briefly, I guess, decades ago. That's what he had that regular editors didn't; firsthand knowledge of the field. Apparently it was a magical combination in medical thriller fiction."

"About Mavis Davis—"

"She's having a nervous breakdown over Chester's death. I know."

"From what I can tell, she was hooked on him as her editor. There's something almost sinister about his influence over her."

Lorna's mouth quirked, and she took a long swig on her drink. "Listen. A lot of us at RCD-about-to-be-slash-P didn't approve of Royal's methods, but we couldn't argue with his bottom line. His imprint was essentially independent although RCD distributed his list and shared the profits. He got plenty out of it personally, believe me. More than the old buzzard deserved. He ran his own fiefdom, but he had a compulsion to handle his authors with an iron hand. He underpaid and overedited them into numb obedience and, frankly, that's why his bottom line was so attractive. This is a business, Temple, it's not an experiment in the nobility of the human spirit. Sometimes the meanest bastards make the most dough."

"Owen Tharp seems rather realistic—and bitter—about the system. Yet he got along with Royal."

"Some writers did. A lot didn't."

"Couldn't the unhappy writers just leave the imprint?"

"Sure, they left, but Royal kept pulling new gullible ones from his slush pile. His madness had a method: to prove that his judgment, not any particular writer's talent, was the cornerstone of Pennyroyal Press's success."

"And was he proving that?"

"What do you mean?"

"Was his bottom line still firm? How long could he afford to alienate his more independent authors? How long could an abused writer like Mavis Davis remain productive under such pressure?"

Lorna shook her head, her expression troubled. "Temple, it's the real world. Jobs are being lost out there, paperback books are being returned in huge percentages, publishing houses are going under."

"Exactly. How could a heads-up company tolerate an ego mill under its wing? The law of diminishing returns holds true for paperbacks, too. Maybe nobody was admitting it, but his bottom line was crumbling. Claudia hinted that Reynolds/Chapter/Deuce was ready to dump Royal, if it could, for running his own imprint into the ground. Those whom the gods would destroy they first make mean."

"He was mean," Lorna spat out suddenly. "He was a mean, small-souled man. Why do you think he kept Mavis Davis down on the farm? Ex-*Doctor* Royal despised nurses; he didn't want them to benefit at his expense. Everyone knew that her terms were worse than simply being a shrewd deal for the publisher. Other houses tried to lure her away, but she was so brainwashed into thinking she needed Chester Royal . . . I don't know if she'll ever write another book, now that he's dead."

"Then she wouldn't want him that way, would she?"

"Mavis? A suspect? You're dreaming."

Temple shrugged and watched as a man angled toward their table, keeping his eyes on Lorna. She didn't know what a prince of publishing should look like, but this one was tall, bald and wearing rimless spectacles.

Lorna rose as he neared the table. "Temple Barr, this is Raymond Avenour, publisher and CEO of Reynolds/Chapter/Deuce."

"Thank you for your time," Temple said, shaking hands with the CEO as he sat.

He shrugged. "Anything I can do to help, as I told the detective in charge." A flash of instantly charming smile. "I've discovered that there are a lot of bright, attractive professional women in Las Vegas."

Temple, who seldom bothered to protest the rote male gallantries common to the PR business, blinked as she realized what the man had said. She'd couldn't quite put herself and Lieutenant Molina under the same umbrella, however flatteringly it was extended. She wondered what the blunt-spoken detective would say to such a remark.

But Temple didn't carry a badge as backup, so she just got down to business. "Since I've had some experience in cultural PR, the officials are relying on me to offer some guidance to the book field. I confess, Mr. Avenour, that I'm confused."

"What about?" he asked with another perfectly charming, perfectly bland smile.

"This imprint business. If Pennyroyal Press was an imprint of RCD, why wasn't it included in the corporate name?"

"It would have been." Avenour rebuffed an approaching waiter with a brisk shake of his head. "The matter was under discussion. The lines of control within an imprint and from it to the overall corporate entity are delicate and must be clearly defined."

"It was a power struggle, then?"

"No! No." Avenour gave a genial laugh. "You ever seen a book publishing contract, Miss Barr? They're legal-length pages—and pages—of fine print on the simplest one-book deal. To unite separate publishing entities requires a whole telephone book of fine print and more lawyers than a Trump bankruptcy. The process is closer to a royal wedding than anything so crude as a power play."

"But what if RCD had doubts that Chester Royal had all his marbles together? He was getting older and had been set in his ways for years. He was losing promising authors."

Before Temple even finished talking, Avenour's head shook as briskly as it had when warning off the waiter. "Authors can be bought back if they're important enough. The point is, Royal built the imprint. He could run it as long as—and how—he wanted to. If he ran it into the ground, Pennyroyal Press would go under. Reynolds/Chapter/Deuce would be protected, you can count on that."

The publisher was rising, fanning a palm to keep Lorna seated for his departure. "I hope I've dissipated your confusion, Miss Barr. Call on me for clarification anytime." He spoke with such careless cordiality that only a fool or Crawford Buchanan would take him literally.

Soon after Temple said goodbye and raced off; somehow she didn't have much of an appetite. She left Lorna nursing a third Manhattan. A PR director's life was no bed of roses.

Neither was Temple's.

When she got back to convention central, Emily Adcock was waiting by the press room door. A sprinkling of media types—their numbers lessening visibly as the convention lengthened—sat respectfully while a pop-singer-turned-kid's-book-author tried to say something profound.

"*He* wrote a kid's book?" Temple asked with some wonder. According to the tabloids, the singer had acquired the usual accouterments of success—drug and alcohol addiction and scandals involving underage females, and possibly males.

Emily Adcock nodded. "If it's got a brand name, it's probably written a book, or at least has a byline on one. Celebrity books sell, even if they're mostly written by open or covert co-authors. I expect an unauthorized Bart Simpson bio by Kitty Kelley out any day. What's so urgent?"

"Come into my parlor." Temple led Emily to the office storeroom.

"Ooops." Midnight Louie was in the act of using the litterbox. He regarded their arrival over his shoulder with a glassy green glare. Temple pulled Emily around a pile of copier paper boxes. She dug in her ever-present tote bag until she produced a manila mailing envelope and tweezers.

"What on earth, Temple—?"

"Listen, this is the best I have for police lab equipment." With the tweezers, Temple withdrew the white envelope and notepaper. "This was on my desk this morning—don't pick it up. The police might want to dust it for prints."

Emily read the message in an instant. "This is awful! Baker and Taylor kidnapped and potential 'stew meat.' Who would do such a rotten thing?"

"From the syntax, an idiot after a quick buck, but that may be done to mislead us. It's no local operator. He'd know that Caesar's Palace has no apostrophe. Ungrammatical as it is, that's Las Vegas. You're sure no business rival—?"

"Baker & Taylor doesn't have any. Look. The two biggest national wholesalers are Ingram and us. Traditionally, we supplied libraries and Ingram handled the independent bookstores; you know, the local Book Nook and Cranny. Lately we've expanded our focus into the bookstores as well—"

"Aha!"

"But that doesn't even border on cutthroat competition. Bottom line or not, there's some gentility left in the book business yet."

"Well, it's time to call the local police. This looks like a rinky-dink operation. They don't ask for much money—but it's still kidnapping of a sort, and serious stuff."

Emily clapped a well-manicured hand to her forehead; even that broad gesture didn't completely obscure her worry wrinkles.

"Temple . . . no. I can't. It was my idea to bring the cats here. I just can't embarrass the company that way. I—we've got to get them back."

"How? How are you going to get the money so fast? How are you going to deliver it with any personal safety? How can you be sure you'll get the cats back, or that they're not stew meat already?"

"I don't know! Temple, help me!"

Temple thought. From the background came the rhythmic rasp of litter being pawed over the scene of the crime. How would she feel if Midnight Louie were in danger? How much would she herself do to avoid the humiliation of reporting a catnapping to someone like Lieutenant Molina?

"We'll hire a P.I. Vegas is full of 'em."

Emily moved her hand from brow to mouth, a wary expression in her eyes.

"He can deliver the ransom without risk to either of us," Temple explained. "We can watch, maybe, and spot the crook. The big question is, how will you get the money?"

Emily shut her eyes. "My American Express Gold Card."

"You could lose it."

"As long as I find the bloody cats. Temple, I just couldn't face losing those cats, professionally or personally."

"It's not your fault, Emily. Who'd think somebody'd bag 'em? That's really odd—a murder and now a—"

"Well, well, well. Sorry, didn't see a Ladies' Room sign." Crawford Buchanan was leaning in the doorway in an ice-cream suit, eyeing Emily Adcock with his usual predatory smirk. She was too distraught to notice.

"We're leaving." Temple stuffed the manila envelope back in her bag and grabbed Emily's wrist.

The woman's hand was cold and limp with anxiety; she numbly followed Temple into the office. Buchanan remained in the doorway, forcing them to brush by. A moment later Midnight Louie swaggered past his pantleg, leaving a swath of long black hairs on the pale fabric.

"Alleycat," Buchanan hissed, kicking at the cat. Louie leaped away like a heavyweight boxer avoiding a gnat.

Temple and Emily had forgotten both man and cat.

"We've got till tomorrow. It's Sunday, but I'll find a P.I. somehow," Temple promised quietly. "You get the money."

"What kind?"

"Small denominations, unmarked bills, like they say on TV. If we want the cats back, we don't want to rile the napper."

"I don't even know how to get *marked* bills. Oh, God, Temple! I hope we get those cats back."

"They also say on TV that kidnappers are notorious for not keeping their word once they've got the money."

Emily smiled wanly. "It's a mess, but thanks, whatever happens. You've been superb."

As Emily hurried away, Buchanan sidled up. "What're you girls up to?"

Temple eyed the ream of typing paper cradled in his arm.

"I didn't know you were fetching your own paper these days, instead of using mine."

"You're out, for some reason."

Temple shook her head and stalked off. Midnight Louie followed.

Enter Ingram

The lady said it herself; she requires a private eye.

So I leave Miss Temple Barr paging morosely through the Las Vegas Yellow Pages, which offer every service that can be sold and quite a few that should not be, and am on my way.

I exit the convention center by my secret route; I can only say that it involves air-conditioning ducts and certain adept but undignified motions on my part. It is the usual hot, bright day outside, but my tootsies flat-foot over the heat-polished parking lot asphalt as if treading black satin sheets.

I have not had an assignment of an investigative nature for some time. Such is the way of things. A fellow begins to be taken for granted when he is about the place day and night. And my past exploits around this town remain unsung, no doubt due to the lack of a good press agent.

That celestial masseur, the sun, beats hot hands on my head and back until I reach the Hilton and slip into the shade of its extensive, also expensive, landscaping. A noxious scent of cocoa butter and human sweat slaps my sensitive nostrils like a fly swatter. Tourists splash in the huge chlorinated pool and soak up ultraviolet rays and frozen margaritas. But I walk soft and I walk silent and nobody notices me unless I want to be observed.

I can move when necessary, and I know where I am going: to check out a reliable source of mine. If any foul play of a feline nature is abroad in this town, this gent will know about it.

Soon my hot-trotting feet have slipped the surly bonds of the Strip's endless asphalt. I approach a modest shopping center not far from downtown. Like most desert burgs, Las Vegas is laid out plain, not fancy: the long angled line of the Strip, otherwise known as Las Vegas Boulevard, shoots as crooked as Saturday night dice from McCarran International Airport to Downtown.

Otherwise, a few north-south avenues and a lot of east-west cross streets divvy up the four-square monotony of town planning. Except for the angling Strip and Highway 15 that parallels it, the street layout resembles a tic-tac-toe board, which may be why some call the old place ticky-tacky.

Once away from the Strip and Downtown, where all the high-rise neon sprouts, tourists express surprise at the city's modesty. Few buildings hit three stories; most houses are one-story bungalows with rocks on the roof. You heard me, stones are a roofing material of choice. Maybe the people who like to live here—and a lot do—have just got rocks on their heads.

In fact, were it not for the unique drawing card of legalized gambling, you might say, one would not find so much as a spitball out here. I might say more, but it does not become me to disparage the place of my birth.

My destination comes into view: the Thrill 'n' Quill bookstore, which occupies a modest storefront. I pause to review the tomes displayed in the window. Although the menu here is murder and mayhem, it is more tastefully presented than on the front of the Pennyroyal Press booth at the ABA.

Thrill 'n' Quill book covers feature tangled gardens and shadowy figures, lengths of pearls and open bottles of sinister prescriptions, a lot of letter openers—or are they daggers I see before me?—and the occasional depiction of a noble feline, usually in silhouette. (I am getting to an age where silhouette is not always my best angle.)

The most ignoble feline of them all reclines in the window, white-socked feet tucked under his bib and a look of complacency on his tiger-striped mug.

I pace back and forth on the hot sidewalk to indicate my interest in entering the establishment. He yawns, showing not very white teeth. That is how the domestic life degrades an ancient breed; not enough natural fiber in the diet to keep the physique sleek and the teeth lethal.

In his own sweet time the lout at last rises, stretches and bounds down into the shop proper. I race to the door with high hopes and corresponding cries. Soon there comes an urgent call from within, then another. Shortly thereafter, the door opens, but instead of yours truly strutting in, a firm foot in high-top Reekbok (at my nose level it does) bars the way.

"Stay out, you old reprobate," a reedy male voice admonishes.

In a moment my acquaintance sallies out, whiskers smooth and houndstooth-checked collar turned around so the rabies tags chime at center throat. It is enough to make a red-blooded street cat puke.

Ingram, however, as this guy is known to his intimates, is a savvy sort about some things, for which I am willing to put up with a lot of hogwash. We ankle over to a shady spot around the side, which Ingram first dusts with his tail before sitting. I have never seen such a fastidious dude in my life, but then a bookshop existence does that to some. I remind myself not to spend much time around the ABA, in case this sort of thing is catching.

I fill in Ingram on the missing fancy cats. He has heard

of these Scottish-fold geeks (apparently the Thrill 'n' Quill also stocks books on related subjects) and, in fact, reveals that a mug shot of the pair adorns the bookshop bulletin board.

I say I already know what these missing persons look like, I want to know where they might be at.

Ingram spreads his rear toes and examines one neatly clipped nail. Then he commences to tell me he has not heard a thing. If they are on the town they are keeping a low profile, says he. Nobody has reported a midnight serenade with a Highland skirl to it, and nobody's domestic life has been interrupted by the appearance of foreign suitors. So Ingram tells me.

I suggest that these out-of-town types might have been surgically prevented from that last sort of thing.

Ingram eyes me slyly through his amber peepers and begins one of his more boring lectures, to the effect that not all felines are rabble-rousing ladies' fellows like myself. He remarks that, given my aggressive amatory proclivities, it is a miracle that my ears do not have a decidedly Scottish-fold look by now.

"Listen," say I, "I know how to keep my ears pinned back and outa the way in a set-to. Now are you saying you do not have a clue to the absent Baker and Taylor?"

Ingram admits as how he sees one of my ex-lady-friends lately, purely on a platonic basis, he adds. This particular acquaintance is just out of the hoosegow, otherwise known as the Animal Pound, and mentioned that a couple of out-of-towners had gotten rounded up.

Scottish folds are out-of-towners, all right. I inform Ingram that this is not much of a lead and inquire as to the appearance of this so-called pal of mine.

Ingram is not flattering. Two-tone low-life with a grizzled mug and a tail kink, says he.

Sassafras, say I, that being the name of the cat in question, not an expression.

Ingram yawns again. He is openly dubious about Sassafras being a genuine nomenclature and implies that my friends trade names as often as they switch humans and in general are a promiscuous lot.

I am forced to growl my disagreement. Ingram can be a schnook with whom I find my temper growing short. I point out that "Ingram" is a somewhat less than riveting moniker also, and that his usual ready rumor-mongering has come up pretty thin soup. He gets on his hind horse and says that he is named for a major wholesaler in the book business and that Thrill 'n' Quill owner Maeveleen Pearl has a computer that instantly connects her to Ingram Central and takes the name quite seriously, or she would not have conferred it upon him.

Further, it has been a slow week, Ingram admits, rising to rub his chin on the corner of the building. He complains that he does not get as good info with The Substitute on duty while Maeveleen Pearl is trudging around with loaded book bags at the convention center. She returns every night with bound galleys, catalogs and more posters of Baker and Taylor. It is obvious by now that Ingram does not care if those two bozos ever show up again, in person or not.

I glimpse the green-eyed demon in Ingram's expression, even though his eyes are old-gold-colored. If one is a bookstore mascot it would no doubt be a trifle aggravating to find some outside pinup boys tacked to every wall. Me, I would not give you an empty Tender Vittles bag for any of them, including Ingram, but there is no accounting for tastes.

I bid Ingram an insincere goodbye and pace back to headquarters, pondering. No matter how I shake it, an unauthorized call on the city pound is in order, if only to eliminate possibilities. I am not overjoyed. I also have not failed to note what number falls on this chapter of my reminiscences. It does not look good for Baker and Taylor. Maybe not for Midnight Louie, either.

Behind the Eight Ball

Temple ripped a page from the D section of the Las Vegas Yellow Pages, folded it into quarters, and skidded her rolling office chair to the wall where her tote bag rested.

It took her a minute to contemplate the jam-packed but admirably organized contents for a place to stash this most precious cargo of the moment. Suddenly she was aware of being alone in the office—and of being intently observed.

Living with Max had cultivated that sixth sense. She'd often pottered around the apartment in happy self-absorption only to feel the abrupt pull of someone's utter attention.

Temple would look up, or around, and Max would be staring at her with the sphinxlike intensity of a cat, as if he were dreaming deep, dark dreams just as she happened to cross his focal point. Or he'd arrive in a room unheard and unseen.

At first, Temple had decided that Max liked surprising people, that the lax attention span of most people was one of the bridges to his magic. Later, she suspected that he'd been training himself, training her, to heed stimuli only heard or seen half-consciously. Either way, goosebumps blossomed on her forearms as she looked up.

Claudia Esterbrook stood in the doorway staring at Temple's Stuart Weitzman kicky black-patent-and-hot-pink heels as if the ABA PR woman were the Wicked Witch of the West browsing for something in the way of ruby-red slippers.

The shock of seeing her wasn't as bad as if it had really been Max, but was still unpleasant. Claudia's face had dropped its professional perkiness. The flesh had curdled, sagging and hardening. Claudia stared at Temple and her high-spirited shoes as if they embodied everything that she saw slipping from her own life.

The insight was fleeting. Then Claudia's face and voice sweetened. She stepped into the room and might never have posed unhappily on the threshold.

"Breaking news on the Royal death," she announced.

"They haven't found . . . somebody?"

Claudia measured Temple's surprise, her ebbing vulnerability, and loosed her most impervious smile. "Oh, they've found somebody—not the killer. More like one of Royal's victims. A wife, ex variety. Right here at the ABA. That Lieutenant Molina did some biographical backtracking. It leaves us PR people looking like horses' derrieres—or like we've got something to hide. Here's an addendum to the group press release. A postmortem statement from the ex–Mrs. Royal."

Temple slipped the twice-folded Yellow Page into the tote's side pocket. Some instinct told her to keep Claudia from seeing it. She took the sheet of scanty double-spaced type Claudia offered and skimmed the contents.

"An editor at Cockerel/Tuppence/Trine? Why didn't she come forward immediately?"

"I imagine that's what Lieutenant Molina wanted to

know. She also wanted to know why Lorna and I didn't tell her."

"And?"

"We don't keep track of everyone's exes. With the musical chairs at publishing houses today, it's tough enough to keep tabs on who's in whose job, much less who's in whose bed."

"Or out of it. So when Molina asked you about this Rowena Novak, you cleverly scurried over to CTT and got a statement. Great thinking. The ex-wife wasn't too shook up, I suppose?"

"About the death—hard to tell. About Molina's interrogation, probably. That lieutenant means to find the murderer before we all pack up on Tuesday."

Temple nodded. "Thanks, Claudia. I doubt I'll be involved in any more PR on the case, but it's good to be up-to-date. Now, I've got an urgent errand to run—" Temple left the release on her desk and headed for the door.

"Oh," Claudia called after her, "got to change some kitty litter?"

Temple whirled in the doorway and studied Claudia, noting the same bitter expression she'd observed earlier. Then Temple blithely shook her head.

"Nothing so important—just a shoe sale at Pay Less. 'Bye."

In five minutes Temple was at the Cockerel/Tuppence/Trine booths on the crowded exhibit floor, eyeing name tags.

"Miss Novak?"

The woman nodded. She was plainer than dry toast, a spare, Persian-lamb-haired woman of forty-something with eyeglass frames that echoed her jaundiced skin tones. Trendy shades of chartreuse and rust underlined her enduring homeliness.

"Can we . . . talk? I'm Temple Barr. I'm assisting with public relations for the convention and also helping Lieutenant Molina with orientation."

"I've talked to Lieutenant Molina, and Claudia Esterbrook."

"I know, but I hoped you might spare a few more moments. The police don't understand how an ABA works. They need a translator, and it's my job to get the information out and the facts right."

Rowena Novak's big-boned face screwed tighter, then she sighed. "All right. The refreshment area should be quieter with the lunch rush done. I could use a soft drink."

"Fine. I'll buy."

They threaded through the crowds, Temple making sure that her catch remained in tow. As the woman had said, seats were available in the vast eating area. They shuffled through the cafeteria setup, Temple suddenly ravenous after her nonlunch. She splurged on a sweet roll and gaped when Rowena Novak ordered an honest-to-God Coke, no diet version.

As they hunched over their trays at a round white table, people came and sat and left all around them. In one way it was the worst site for a probing interview, in another the best. The casual atmosphere and crowds made it seem that nothing serious could be said here, so of course it would be.

"What do you need to know?" Rowena Novak took a quick sip of her Coke.

"It's still hard to explain to Lieutenant Molina what an imprint is, how someone gets started in the business. You were married to Chester Royal for—?"

"Seven years, an appropriate number, like a plague of Egypt."

"Was that before—or after—the formation of Pennyroyal Press?"

"Oh, before. Chester was writing nonfiction then."

"Really?"

"That's how I met him. An agent was enthusiastic about a proposal of his. Of course in nonfiction the author's salability is as important as the book's."

"You mean, whether the author's good-looking, articulate, will do well on media tours, that kind of thing?"

"Exactly."

Nothing more was forthcoming except another of those tiny, birdlike sips. Temple munched a mouthful of sinfully sugared pastry. How to keep the interview going before Rowena Novak suddenly finished her Coke and walked away?

"So Mr. Royal, Chester, went from author to editor. That must have been after you'd married."

"Yes. He became interested in the other end of the business after we'd met and begun—I suppose you'd call it dating."

A flicker of disgust in those ocher eyes told Temple that despite the woman's enviable composure, much that was unpleasant lurked beneath.

"I understand Chester Royal was the marrying kind."

"If you're asking which wife I was—it was number three. And Chester was not so much the marrying kind as the exploiting kind. If a woman came along he could use, he married her. At least he did when he was younger."

"He didn't marry Mavis Davis." Temple issued a frank glance.

Rowena's mouth quirked. "No. He'd figured out how to use women without marrying them by then. He owed it all to me."

"Did you tell this to Lieutenant Molina?"

"No."

"Why are you telling me?"

"Because you're asking the right questions. I have nothing to hide about our lives together, about what he was. I don't even hate him anymore, I just understand him. I probably understand—understood—Chester better than anybody. I taught him all he knew." When Temple stared at her incredulously, she added, "accidentally, of course," and went on. "I'd never been married before, but I was no kid. I might have resisted Chester, but he was so fascinated, so enthralled by my work. At the time it seemed to mean that he took me seriously. What he took seriously was my work; he took my work."

"Took your . . . work? How?"

"He absorbed it. He became what I was."

Temple, still confused, searched for the right next question.

"Have you ever been betrayed in love, Miss Barr?"

It was a no more personal question than Temple had been asking. "Yes," she answered with fierce honesty. "I think."

Rowena laughed, a pleasant sound and an expression that did pleasant things to her plain face. "I can't say I was disappointed in love, but I was betrayed in my judgment. I failed to see that it wasn't I to whom Chester was so earnestly attracted, it was something I had."

"What?"

"Power."

Temple didn't know what to say. Claudia's press release had described Rowena Novak as a senior editor at Trine Books, not a bad position, but certainly not one that would put her into a corner office in Manhattan.

Rowena's fingers, sallow and ringless, moved up and down the sides of the oversize Styrofoam cup as if they were caressing Baccarat crystal. Her face softened with rueful recollection, reflected a sadness at the ways of the world, at what she had been and Chester had done.

"He saw me edit, that's all. He saw how careful I was in phrasing revision letters to my authors; he saw me worry when I couldn't offer them the money and support I thought their work deserved; he saw them trust me and depend on me. He saw how a good editor—and I was, am, a good editor—nourishes the literary ego, encourages it to stretch to produce the book it hopes to. He was fascinated by how my authors confessed their troubles—money, marriage. Writing books is a long, lonely business. Authors hope to find an editor who will listen through it all, though they seldom do today. Editors are itinerant midwives now, sometimes leaving a house in mid-contraction, unable to invest their own ego in an author or a work they may never see through to the end."

"And Chester took what he saw you doing, twisted it, and became a bad editor."

"A destructive one, rather. He didn't do it consciously. You must remember he had started as a doctor, in the days when physicians were demigods. Patients came to him with their ills and insecurities extended, like an aspiring writer presenting a sickly manuscript. Through all the years, he had missed that position of power, of judgment."

"Then why did he quit practicing medicine?"

"He had to. Can't you guess?"

"No," Temple admitted.

"Malpractice. He lost the suit, lost his license. Lost his power. He never really found himself again, until he met me and saw that there was another way to wield power over people's lives and make money at it. Best of all, he discovered the medical thriller, so he could have it all back in a sense."

"You give me the shivers. He sounds like a villain in one of his own books."

"Oh, no." Rowena smiled. "No. You will find few villainous doctors in Pennyroyal Press books. Only Owen Tharp could get away with doing that occasionally, for some reason. What you will find in a Pee-R Press book are whining, incompetent, crazy, homicidal nurses. You will find demanding patients and pompous, worthless hospital administrators, especially if they're women. But you will rarely find ignoble doctors."

"Remind me to skip reading a few. Claudia said Chester called Lorna Fennick a 'press-release-pushing ball-busting broad.' He hated women?"

Rowena nodded. "So deeply that he didn't consciously admit it."

"Why?"

"Only Chester really knew. He seldom spoke about his family, but I gather that he felt humiliated in grade school by the women teachers."

"That warped him on women for life?"

"Maybe." Rowena smiled. "I remember him grumbling more than once that a man used to be able to get away from women in medical school. . . ." She sighed. "He never had been a prepossessing man; dates couldn't have come easily when he was young. Maybe that's why he went through five wives later: to prove he could do it. After our marriage, I realized that he feared losing part of himself in the face of women's competence. That's why Lorna couldn't work for him for long."

"Lorna Fennick worked for Chester Royal?"

"She was his editorial assistant when he first began packaging for Reynolds/Chapter/Deuce. She never married him, but she's another victim of the Chester Royal School for Women, as is Mavis Davis."

"What about his male authors—did he abuse them, too?"

"A raging thirst for power will consume any kind of fuel, but, no, it never bothered him to see another man get ahead as much as it did a woman."

"Not much question why he was murdered."

"No. Somebody'd had enough."

"Not you."

"I'm glad you didn't make that a question. Not me. I studied the situation the way I would the structure of a novel. I understood why he became skewed, how my own flaws had made me so useful, so usable. That common book of ours is long out of print. It's old, cold type; the acid in its pages has already consumed it. And now Chester himself is dead matter."

"What does that mean, exactly?"

"A manuscript that's been turned into type. It's redundant."

Temple grimaced at the aptness of the phrase in the current case. "Why didn't you come forward when he was killed?"

"Why should I? I'm two wives back. I don't care, and neither did he."

"Your detachment is admirable," Temple said, wondering if Max would ever fade as docilely into her past. "From what I've grown to know of Chester, he'd be a horrible doctor. It's lucky that he was forced out young. What was the malpractice suit about?"

"A woman died—in childbirth, I understand."

"Childbirth, but—*he* was an ob/gyn?"

Rowena nodded sadly.

"That doesn't make sense, not with his fear and hatred of women! I mean, babies and the wonder of birth and all that."

"I can see you've never had a baby."

"No. Have you?"

"Yes. Very young. I gave it up. That's past history. It had nothing to do with Chester. Nothing to do with this."

"I'm sorry. And you've never looked back—?"

"Never." Rowena's face tightened. "Having babies isn't all pink and powder; it's also pain and helplessness. A woman is absolutely dependent on her doctor. He sees her at her worst, bloated, swelled-of-belly, fearful; he examines her in what could be called the most passive position imaginable.

"You're too young to have heard the horror stories: often ob/gyns dictated when and how many children their patients had, even after the birth-control pill came along; you still can't get it without a prescription. Your doctor determined when you had your baby; if it was inconvenient for him, as it was for the charity doctor who delivered me, he had his nurses pin a woman's legs together, maybe so he can drink two more martinis at his dinner party before going to the hospital. A doctor can make a woman patient feel weak, and stupid and worthless. And such doctors often did. Ask any woman over the age of thirty-five."

"It really was the bad old days, wasn't it?"

Rowena Novak nodded, her face wry. Temple couldn't tell if it had been soured by memories of that long-ago, ignorant pregnancy and the shameful way it had been treated—or recollections of the late Chester Royal.

"When I finally found out," Rowena said, her voice slow and firm, "about his malpractice problem, that's when I left him."

Temple sat in her idling Storm, the ventilation fans on high and the flimsy Yellow Page trembling in her hand.

It was four o'clock. She had already visited neighborhoods of Las Vegas she had never known existed. And she still didn't have the private detective she'd so blithely suggested to Emily Adcock.

What she had was a problem.

Private investigators either came in the form of firms, in which case they would hardly countenance dropping off money to catnappers without police knowledge, or they were the lone wolves of legend whose shingles hung on disreputable buildings in decrepit areas. Temple wouldn't trust $5,000 cash to any one of these sleaze-os.

She began to see why so many private-eye novels opened with a woman in trouble (in this case, unfortunately, her) consulting one of these lone strangers in some down-at-the-windowsills office.

This one—her last chance—worked out of his home in a neighborhood where cars rusted like modern sculptures in sandy driveways and the rocks on the roofs were matched only by the gravel in the front yards. Joshua trees and cactus crowded around the low-roofed, one-story crackerboxes provided a sort of prickly shade.

Temple got out and locked the car, then approached the house. If she were lucky, E. P. O'Rourke would not be in. Sunning lizards scattered at her approach, pausing only to rear tyrannosauruslike on their leathery hind legs and watch her with bright black eyes.

The ground felt like the bottom shelf of a red-hot oven as the heat rose to meet the blazing overhead sun halfway. Temple felt sweat blossom on her face and limbs and as swiftly evaporate. It was not an unpleasant sensation, rather like being steam-ironed, she imagined.

Several nearby houses looked deserted, except for one

four doors down, from which the drumming bass of a rock station drifted. Spanking new Harleys tilted at rest near its weathered side doors. In the distance a dirt bike droned soft and loud like a circling hornet.

Temple knocked on O'Rourke's screen door, which was wearing so little forest-green paint she expected it to flake loose at her blows. The door beyond it was solid wood except for a small black diamond of glass high above the knob.

It jerked partway open.

A man stood against the deep shadow within, a slight, wiry fellow with eyes squinting against the daylight. "Yeah?"

"Mr. E. P. O'Rourke?"

"Yeah?"

"I'm interested in discussing an investigative job."

The eyes looked her up, then down. The door swung open, baring more interior darkness.

Temple swallowed, then opened the rickety screen door. Entering houses in torrid climates was like plumbing the dark secrets of some ancient tomb. Windows were few and kept shaded. The visitor always blinked blindly on the threshold until the eyes adjusted to the abrupt dimness. In the meantime, E. P. O'Rourke could conk her on the head, rummage her tote bag and ravish her body.

Temple discounted her last foolish fear as her vision adjusted. E. P. O'Rourke was as stringy and desert-baked as beef jerky, with a shock of white hair and eyebrows in odd contrast to his seamed bronze skin. And he was about sixty-five.

"Come on in," he said, turning.

Temple followed. Like most desert houses, this one offered a right-angle corkscrew of turning halls and boxy dim little rooms. In five steps she had lost the direction of the front door, which O'Rourke had shoved shut before preceding her into the house.

The air inside was hot and damp. She heard the drone of

an old-fashioned water-cooling air-conditioning system—suprisingly efficient but invariably dank.

O'Rourke stopped in a room almost completely occupied by a huge slab of desktop. The surface was bare except for a black billiard ball that had been drilled into a pen rest and a free-form olive-green ashtray dusted with ash residue. No butts. He slipped into a battered leather office chair behind the desk and indicated a seat.

"What brung you here?"

"I read your entry in the phone book."

"I mean, what problem?"

"First I should ask you your qualifications."

O'Rourke shrugged. He was wearing a short-sleeved peach polyester shirt and, she thought, jeans and tennis shoes. At least no one would hear him coming, if his joints didn't crack. Light filtered through the dusty blinds along one high, long window. O'Rourke's hair was ethereally white in the hazy illumination, and his eyes gleamed baby-blue.

"I been in the merchant marines, but that was before you was born. I knocked around a bit. Been in business in Vegas for nineteen years. Worked for Brink's before that. Been around, that's about it. Now, what can I do for you, girlie?"

"You're no relation to Chester Royal, I hope?"

"That dead'un at the convention center? What's this got to do with that? I don't mess with homicide cases."

"Nothing. This is cats."

"*Cats?*" He spoke as if she'd named an alien being.

"Pet cats. Two are missing. What is your fee per hour?"

"Pet cats are missing all over the world. Nobody seeks professional help for it. Fifty dollars, plus expenses."

"There wouldn't be expenses. It's a simple . . . drop."

"Drop, missy? Where'd you get that lingo?"

"TV."

"Don't have one. Hasn't been anything good on since Sid Caesar."

"Before my time," she shot back. "Are you bonded?"

"Are you kidding?" He paused to groom an unruly eyebrow with a forefinger, the way another man might stroke a mustache. She would have sworn he looked mischievous. "My word is my bond."

"Are *you* kidding?" She shifted to rise and leave.

"Look. You don't get a license unless the police say so."

"You got a license?"

He pointed to the wall beside her, where a cheap black frame defined a document. Temple rose, got out her glasses and took her time deciphering the cursive script in the dim light.

"I don't know, Mr. O'Rourke," she said, resuming her seat, "there's money involved."

"Eightball," he said.

"Huh?"

He gestured to the shiny black ball on his desk. "Eightball. It's what everybody calls me."

"Isn't an eight ball supposed to be unlucky?"

"Only if you mess with it too early in the action. If it's last on the table, the way it's supposed to be, it's lucky for the winner. I usually last to the end at whatever I do," he said, with an emphasis both crisp and salacious.

Temple, surprised, laughed. She would bet that Eightball O'Rourke would be no one to tangle with in a barroom brawl if he had a broken bottle in hand, and as for his endurance in other pursuits, she wasn't about to challenge it.

"How much money," he asked genially, "and what's involved?"

"It's ransom money."

"A kidnapping?" He whistled through teeth so white and even that they had to be false. "I don't usually send folks to the cops, but even if it is only cats—"

"The ransom is five thousand dollars. That may not seem like much for a kidnapping."

"That's considerable for cats," he admitted. "You want I should tail the napper when he picks up the cash?"

"I want you to drop off the cash so that I can tail the catnapper."

"You got this backward, miss. Tailing's the hard part. You could drop the cash and know it's done and let me do the walking. That's what you use the Yellow Pages for, isn't it?"

"If you think that's best. We could meet before the . . . drop and I'd give you the ransom money then."

"And give me my money, too. Then. Heck," he said when she hesitated, "if you aren't sharp enough to make sure I drop the dough, how were you gonna tail a kidnapper?"

"I was hoping it would be somebody I'd recognize."

"Don't they all."

"How much is this going to cost?"

Eightball O'Rourke eyed the big round schoolhouse clock on the wall. "We talked a half hour here, say another couple hours before and after the drop. Hundred fifty dollars flat unless your napper takes off for the Spectre Mountains and I gotta trail him."

"It could be a her," she said.

"Don't matter. Either sex trails the same."

"One thing. Is there anything you can do to ensure the safety—and safe return—of the cats?"

"Nope." Eightball O'Rourke rose and extended a hard, dry palm for a farewell shake. "Not a damn thing."

Hunter on the Prowl

Temple returned to the convention center after five P.M. for the second night in a row. This time she found the office empty and Midnight Louie lounging on her desktop grooming his expansive, jet-black belly.

"Hey, guy. Where you been all day? Enjoying the convention center?"

The cat looked up, impassive, and began taking long licks at his copious chest hair. His feline face had that vaguely withdrawn look that some people interpret as superiority to other beings.

Temple shrugged. Louie had already demonstrated that he had his ways in and out of the mammoth convention center, as well as around it. She wouldn't even be surprised to find that he had beaten her back to her apartment one evening, and was waiting on the patio outside the French doors, bored as you please. Louie was abstracted at the moment. He accepted her strokes of greeting with a short "merow" and a narrowed glance. Perhaps he was just tired, as Temple was.

She sat at her desk without bothering to drop the tote bag. A minute to compose herself and then she had to hustle Louie down to the car, red-hot by now after roasting in the peak afternoon sun. Then they'd go home to a chill, refreshing tuna dinner: raw from the can for him, salad for her. Cats left a lot of half-full cans of tuna sitting around going stale. Better that she eat it than that Louie should suffer from refrigerator-mouth tuna, at which he always turned up his jet-black nose.

"I'll eat the lettuce," she told Louie. "I've got to watch my figure even if you don't."

Approaching feet echoed down the hall. They stuttered to a pause, then rounded the corner into the office.

"Temple! Thank God you're still here!" Lorna Fennick cried rapturously.

"What now?"

"Lanyard Hunter wants to talk to you."

"Haven't you got that backward?"

"No. After his media interview this afternoon I mentioned that you wanted to speak with him. He immediately asked if you were 'the cute redhead' he kept seeing with me. Naturally, I said yes. He said dinner tonight would be fine. I think he likes you."

"Oh, Lord. That's all I need. A mashing murderer."

"Temple, you don't think—?"

"No, I'm just tired and irritable and surprised. Why'd a famous author want to waste time on me when he could be wined and dined by his publishers and assorted hangers-on?"

"Look, this is Sunday evening. After tomorrow, it's virtually over. Maybe he's just attracted to you."

"Why? I'm not a hospital."

"That's below the stethoscope, Temple. Aren't you PR woman enough to take advantage of an interview you wanted when it drops into your hand like a plum?"

"More like a plumb bob," she complained. "That's what I don't like. Hunter is playing too easy to get."

"Well, *you* don't have to."

"Okay, what's the deal?"

"You pick him up here at six-fifteen. Take him wherever you figure is the best setting for prying information out of him."

"Are you suggesting I use my feminine wiles?"

"I'm suggesting you use your public relations savvy."

"Okay. I gotta scram this place, then get Louie home and . . . sob, freshen up . . . to get back here in"—Temple consulted her watch, whose minute and hour hands seemed to have shrunk or stretched to a matching length—"fifty-five minutes."

At that she fished her car keys from her tote bag, drew the handles over her shoulder and swooped up the lounging Midnight Louie in one uninterrupted motion.

" 'Bye," Temple called to Lorna through the key ring between her teeth on the way out. "And thanks. I think."

Not even Wile E. Coyote can move faster than a PR woman on the run. Crisis is the profession's middle name. Temple's aqua Storm darted like a dragonfly through the five P.M. traffic, its glittering sides snaring reflections of a searing red sun melting like strawberry syrup over the chocolate ice-cream peaks of the western mountains.

At the Circle Ritz, Temple sprinted for her apartment, Louie's legs dangling like furred pendulums from under her arm. The cat was plopped onto the parquet and presented with a fresh mound of tuna before he got his sea legs.

Temple showered before he finished it. She was redressed, remade-up and ready to rush into the torpid evening by the time he had finished his postprandial ablutions and had settled by the French doors, keeping one sleepy eye cocked on the patio.

Temple sped from the bedroom, cramming necessities from her tote bag into a small, dressy purse. Her flame-colored floaty dress was a tribute to the heat, the sunset and

Lanyard Hunter's apparent weakness for the color crimson.

After waving goodbye to the cat and turning her air conditioner up to 80 for the evening, Temple slammed her mahogany front door locked. She was back in the car, the air-conditioning on Max as in maximum, or Max the bum, her shoulder-length red earrings swinging maniacally, at one minute to six P.M.

By six-twelve, she was in the long line of vehicles queuing up the semicircular drive at the convention center's Rotunda entrance. Lanyard Hunter's silver hair and patrician height were readily recognizable. So was Lorna Fennick, to whom he was talking as they waited. Temple zoomed the Storm to the curb, waved at Lorna, who waved back as she spotted her own ride, and leaned across the seat to open the door.

Hunter bent down with a charming smile. "Miss Barr, I presume. Lanyard Hunter. I wouldn't want you accepting a strange man in your car without a formal introduction."

"How thoughtful. Do come in, Mr. Hunter. I thought we'd dine at Dome of the Sea at The Dunes, unless you hate seafood?"

"Perfect," Hunter said obliquely enough that the comment could apply to anything, including the driver. "After all the bloody beef dinners it takes to maintain the strength to deal with one's publishers, I'd prefer something subtler."

Temple lifted an eyebrow and eased the Storm into the traffic. She'd be willing to bet that she was "something subtler" than Lanyard Hunter expected.

The geodesic Dome of the Sea restaurant offered an aquatic dimness into which it was possible for the neon-weary diner to sink like a peaceful pearl. In tanks surrounding the upholstered banquettes, tropical fish massaged illuminated azure waters to the accompaniment of a harpist plucking liquid melodies.

"Very nice," Hunter said, the object of his compliment again ambiguous but his eyes resting exclusively on Temple. He had a compelling, platinum-gray stare that sliced past normal social barriers as intimately as a hot scalpel.

Temple took refuge behind a long, glossy menu specifying double-digit prices. A slice of the adjoining casino was visible behind Hunter. One of the many crystal-hung chandeliers haloed his dramatic silver locks like a diamond-toothed circular saw.

He's no angel, Temple reminded herself, but a skilled and shrewd con man equipped with the smarmy charisma and florid handsomeness of a televangelist. She'd had enough of the type, plus Hunter was a little past her age limit. She was apparently not out of his.

"Charming," he murmured again.

"Thanks so much for making yourself available, Mr. Hunter," she said briskly. "I'm sure your insight will be helpful in creating a correct picture of the late Mr. Royal's achievements. It's a big responsibility to generate an obituary on a stranger, and an out-of-towner to boot."

"Lorna said you wanted some information, but could we order drinks and appetizers first?" He regarded her with an understanding tolerance, well aware that his practiced charm made her nervous.

"Certainly. Everything, of course, will be on my PR tab, so order as lavishly as you wish." That ought to reestablish control, Temple thought. Independent career woman picks up the check.

"I will." Hunter's smile broadened into an amused grin. "And the bill is mine; I insist. Experience before beauty."

She saw little point in playing the liberated career woman in the face of Hunter's determined role of gracious host. Temple smiled back and proceeded to order a martini, the crab pattie appetizers, lobster, a twice-baked potato with cheese and shrimp sauce, and a Caesar salad.

"That's a little rich for my blood," Hunter commented. "High cholesterol."

"Mine's one hundred sixty-eight. How's yours?"

"Well enough. I'm curious; how can I help you with anything involving Chester Royal?"

Temple's martini had arrived, brimming a stemmed glass almost wider than it was tall. She managed to lift it without spilling and sipped the level down.

"I've heard fascinating things about you, Mr. Hunter, your medical savoir faire included. Surely you, more than anyone, would know how Mr. Royal made such a success of the medical thriller books he packaged."

"The public fixates on physicians, Miss Barr. May I call you Temple? Doctors are perceived as benign, all-powerful beings who reveal little of themselves while probing into their patients' most intimate matters." Hunter paused, while Temple considered that the foregoing wasn't a bad description of the Hunter modus operandi either. "We all fall into their hands sooner or later," he went on, spreading his. "The medical establishment is a perfect environment for exploring our most irrational fears of death—and sometimes of life."

"Don't some people hate their doctors?"

"Only if they've been mistreated—misdiagnosed or overmedicated or ignored when a genuine problem was present. Otherwise, they're ready to canonize them."

"And you? Do you admire doctors also? Is that why you tried to ally yourself with them?"

"No doubt the ever-efficient Lorna has mentioned my medical 'record.'" He paused again, as if to consider a revelation. He spoke more quickly, without the ever-present smile. "My . . . mother became seriously ill when I was only in my teens. I matriculated in medicine because of it. I became fascinated by the milieu. My pretending to be a doctor was simply a youthful enthusiasm—and proved to be the perfect education for my current career."

"Why were you compelled to masquerade as a doctor? Why do others do it?"

"I can't speak for others, Temple." Analysis rumpled Hunter's smooth face. "And I don't characterize my exploits as 'compelled.' It was a . . . hobby of mine. I functioned quite well as a doctor, as well as my peers did. What tripped me up was the constant record-keeping this society is addicted to, not any mistake on my part."

"What specialties did you practice? Family physician? Pediatrician?"

"No, no! Nothing so pedestrian. Once I was an oncologist. I was a surgeon another time."

"But people's lives were at stake! And you knew you were a fraud."

"I knew I had no medical degree. And how many real M.D.s are frauds? Medicine wouldn't be any fun if people's lives weren't at stake. We wouldn't worship Dr. Welby and Dr. Christian and Drs. Kildare and Casey without something vital in the balance—our lives."

"You wouldn't have enjoyed the masquerade if that same vital something wasn't at question?"

Hunter's dove-gray eyes narrowed. "You make me sound quite bloodthirsty, Temple. I was younger then." His glance softened as his tone sharpened. "Young men like risk. They race cars, they chase other men's wives, they practice medicine without a license. It is much the same thing. We all thrive on excitement."

Temple couldn't miss the throbbing challenge in his voice. This man intended to devour life. To him, living dangerously included pursuing his spur-of-the-moment attractions. And she could be the current one.

"Do you miss it?" she asked quickly.

"The charade, you mean?"

"Yes. The thrill of the deception, the intricate creation of the believable persona and a paper trail to back it up. The innocent stupidity of everyone around you. The feeling of being so secret and so special."

Hunter set down his fork, forsaking his fillet of sole. "How well you put it." His gaze grew even more intense. "I'd almost think you had an appetite for that sort of game. You know the rewards well."

"PR is a game, too, sometimes," Temple said, attacking her lobster. "You try to find out what people don't want to tell you, then turn around and try to keep other people from finding out what they most want to know."

"Is that why you're playing gumshoe?"

"I'm not."

"Nonsense. I must say I much prefer you to that overgrown police detective."

"Lieutenant Molina seems highly competent."

"I wonder if that's what it will take to unravel the murder of a complex man like Chester."

"You're a complex man," Temple objected. He smiled again, as if she had just conceded a point in a chess match. "You must be to have done what you did, then make a writing career of it. Chester Royal, from what I've learned, was the antithesis of complexity. He had very simple needs: to feel powerful, to make others, particularly women, feel his power. I don't think I'd have liked him if I'd known him."

"A mutual distaste, I'd think." Hunter laughed. "Yes, Chester had a rabid dislike of women. He always felt they were trying to take things from him—his stature both physical and figurative; his sense of superiority; his money. Must have been embittered by all those wives—and divorces."

"But I understand that his fear of women goes back to his medical days. And he was a gynecologist!"

"Most male gynecologists are Roman Catholic, did you know that? It makes sense, a very baby-directed religion by virtue of its proscriptions against both birth control and abortion. Chester was not RC, and I understand he was not averse to performing the clandestine abortion now and again, before it was legal in any sense."

"Surely only doctors compassionate to women would do abortions in those days."

Hunter smiled sadly. "Do you know what abortions by medical doctors were like then—often sans anesthetic? No time for recovery rooms and other niceties. I suspect Chester did them for money, period, and to thumb his nose at the system . . . and to rip fetuses untimely from wombs. He and his many wives never had children, you know."

"You really think he was that kind of monster?"

"Many of us are that kind of monster, Temple. I never hurt anybody during my bogus medical career. I have an IQ of one hundred seventy-eight, did you know? I can't say as much for many of the genuine doctors I practiced alongside. I've always meant to do a medical exposé, but Chester channeled me into fiction. I think he feared that if I did a controversial book, it would draw attention to his less than glorious past."

"Or maybe he didn't want you running down his ex-profession."

"True. Chester was old-fashioned in more than wanting to keep women in their place; he wanted control. He wanted all his authors as off balance as cats on a hot tin roof. Everyone around him was a possible enemy: the woman who would henpeck him, the man who would outperform him in any arena. He loved to put his authors through hell, playing on their insecurities. He wanted me to rewrite *Broken Bones* five times."

"Why put up with it?"

Hunter shrugged. "I knew his type from my medical masquerade days. I simply hired a ghost writer to diddle with the ms. over and over until Chester decided he had put me through enough."

"So you were never taken advantage of editorially, or fiscally?"

"I'm no Mavis Davis, no." Hunter grinned to observe Temple's surprise. "I knew Chester's game; I didn't let it get to me. And he'd made the mistake of breaking me out early; there was no way he was going to nickle and dime my agent to death at that late date."

"You seemed to have used him, rather than vice versa."

"Exactly. I had good training for it in the hospitals. And after."

"You're referring to—Joliet, was it?"

"The games played there make those of editorial ego

very small potatoes indeed. Speaking of which, are you really going to eat all that? It's the size of a wooden shoe."

Temple forked into the tuber in question. "You bet. I've been on a strange diet lately—tuna fish—and it's time to make up for it."

Temple spent the rest of the evening inquiring politely about Hunter's novels. Most offered unlikely scenarios about heroic physicians foiling near-future plots dealing with corporate clones, sinister truth serums and genetically engineered plagues created by global conspiracies.

Temple could see why spinning such farfetched tales would satisfy Hunter's con-man instincts. He could play the doctor every day in his novels, and be the hero as well. She could also see why patients trusted him and women would find him attractive, even if they suspected his sincerity. If you're going to be sold a bill of goods, the salesman had better be smooth.

"What will happen to your books now that Chester Royal's dead?" Temple polished off the last of her potato just before the waiter cleared the table.

"Nothing. Even if Pennyroyal Press breaks down, any major publisher would be pleased to snap up myself and Mavis Davis. Even Owen Tharp."

"What about the others on the Pennyroyal Press list? The writers who were just beginning?"

Hunter shook his head as he finished his expensive white wine. "Nothing. They'll go on clawing in the melee and living on thin air as they always have. But the top authors won't have to worry. Survival of the fattest."

"Maybe one of the thin types did it?"

"Kill an editor in chief? Most of them haven't even figured out the score yet, much less become ready, willing and able to kill the umpire."

"Then, no matter how horrible Chester was to his writers, none of them had motive to kill him, since it would only hurt themselves?"

"Yes, that is the Gospel according to Lanyard Hunter. Of course you must take into account that I'm a very slippery fellow." Again the concentrated, intimate stare. Temple fidgeted, then fought off the spell and returned to basics. "Is that your real name, Lanyard Hunter?"

"As a matter of fact it is," he said complacently. "Though nobody believes it. That's the best kind of lie: the truth that nobody takes seriously. It will never catch the teller and it will seriously mislead everybody else."

"I take it these are the con man's rules to live by?"

"Call it what you will—it works. Doesn't it?"

She ignored his question, although it had crossed her mind to wonder if his lovers really called him 'Lanyard' in bed, one of those uncensored idle thoughts that one disowns faster than a Freudian slip. "Who do you think murdered Mr. Royal?"

"I haven't the slightest idea, and I don't care."

"Then why take the time to spend dinner being questioned by me?" Too late did she recognize that as a provocative question under the circumstances, or considering the company.

Lanyard Hunter bounded into her opening with relish and a seductive smile. "Because, my dear Miss Temple, I happen to enjoy intelligent female company, especially when it's as attractively wrapped as you. I noticed you at the ABA right away. Besides, there's only one thing a reformed con man can do, and that is to watch others play the game. I am breathless to discover whether you or Lieutenant Molina will find the culprit first."

That touched a nerve. "I'm not competing with her; I'm just doing my job. At least it started that way." Temple remembered that the onerous duty of ransoming Baker and Taylor would occur first thing on the next day's agenda. She either had to be up early—or up all night. . . .

The waiter had slipped a salver, bearing the usual coy bill peeking out of a leatherette folder, next to Lanyard Hunter. Hunter's forearms rested on the table as he leaned closer for the kill. His compelling eyes fixed on Temple with a flattering, unmistakable intent. At the same time, his expansive elbow had unobtrusively nudged the check tray to her side of the table. Temple blinked, feeling like a robin who had been hypnotized by the world's largest worm. The rat was going to take her at her word, stick her with the check and seduce her into the bargain, if he could! Lanyard Hunter was the Total Con Man. All of his promise and promises, especially romantic ones, were bogus. He could even be the murderer. No thanks.

"Speaking of my job," Templed segued as smoothly as a con lady, "I'd better get you back to your hotel. You must be exhausted after two days of the ABA."

"The night is only postadolescent," he suggested in a baritone that could have seduced a Barbie doll.

Temple smiled. She was small but not that small. And not born yesterday. Or desperate. "My internal clock is on senescence," she answered blithely. "I've had a long day, and I need my duty sleep."

On that note the evening ended. Hunter never tried to beat Temple to the check. In no time flat she was pulling the Storm under the Las Vegas Hilton's scintillating entrance canopy.

"Would you like to come in for a nightcap?" he asked.

"The only nightcap I want is flannel and at my apartment," she said firmly.

"Are you sure?" Lanyard Hunter's well-manicured hand had materialized warmly on Temple's knee.

"Thanks, but I live with someone who might not understand."

"Oh, who?"

"He's a . . . big black dude. Some people think he throws a lot of weight around in this town."

The hand vanished. Its opposite number was fumbling with the door latch. "An enjoyable evening," Hunter said as he hastily left the vehicle. "Thanks, and give my regards to your, er, friend."

"Oh, I will," Temple promised with a perky goodbye wave. The Storm took off like a hot aqua bat out of hell.

* * *

The moment Temple unlocked her big front door, the apartment felt wrong.

One thing was the heat. It prowled the darkened rooms like an invisible black panther. Its hot breath caressed her face first, then lapped down to her feet.

Even after the tepid air-conditioning of the common areas, the marble-faced lobby and the wood-paneled hallway, this hothouse atmosphere felt unnatural, or rather, as natural as all outdoors. Far too hot for 80; more like a sizzling 90 degrees.

Temple waited while the unfamiliar hulking shapes turned back into her furniture. She slipped out of one high heel, bracing herself on the kitchen divider wall, then another. The shoes toppled onto bare parquet with a soft snick. She'd been meaning to get an entry area rug and now it was too late. Now she'd be murdered in her own apartment! Maybe not.

She was alarmed, no denying that. The more you took a place for granted, the more you noticed when it altered, even slightly. Why would her air-conditioning have gone off—and hours before, to judge by the temperature now?

The pink neon clock on the black-and-white kitchen wall, so bland by day, broadcast an eerie *Miami Vice* glow over the counters. It reflected rosily, like a frivolous vigil light, on the living room's sculpted white ceiling. A vigil light betokened a presence. Temple wondered whose.

She debated retreating. Yet the place was so still. Empty. Utterly empty. The parquet felt warm under her silent stocking feet as she skated across it, afraid of slipping.

The living room opened up before her, a book too dimly lit to read aright. A gap in the French doors was instantly evident, like a dog-eared page. One of the doors was ajar on an acute angle, admitting the heat of the night, and a grinding chorus of distant cicadas that she hadn't noticed at first.

A heavy scent of jasmine and gardenia also rolled in like fog from the patio. Temple paused at the living room wall, her fingers reading the braille of the thermostat's raised plastic letters. The tiny marker was parked in the Off zone—but what burglar would turn air-conditioning off?

She shuffled further into the living room. Then she stopped. Something was missing. The cat should have sensed her presence by now. Louie should be stalking from some favorite retreat, or thumping down from atop the refrigerator, merowing for food. He should be wreathing her ankles, even in the dark, no challenge for his superior night vision. Where was the cat?

Temple back-shuffled as silently as she had entered, and slipped out the front door, never turning her back to the room. Once in the hall with its feeble wall sconces and dull rose carpeting, she raced flat-footed for the elevator and hit the Up button.

It took forever to come. She'd never noticed before how the gears clanked and squealed, how blasted loud the ancient mechanism was! It arrived empty. Temple darted in and pushed the P button. Inside, the car was richly paneled, like the exterior of a coffin. It jerked upward with the unholy racket of an unoiled guillotine being hoisted for the fatal drop.

A clanking stop almost persuaded Temple's heart to imitate it. She tore for the coffered double doors opposite, pounding them with both fists.

They sprang open. Electra Lark stood there with her hair in stiff peaks resembling properly beaten egg whites. Little papers pressed onto her scalp. One egg-white peak was stained blood-red.

"Temple! What is it? I'm doing my hair."

"God! I thought you were being scalped." Temple scampered over the threshold and shut the doors behind her. "Someone's in the building—or was. My apartment air-conditioning is off, one French door is wide open and the cat's gone."

Electra whipped the hand towel from around her neck, thinking. "The maintenance man is gone for the night. It's too bad that nice Matt Devine isn't here."

"He isn't?" Temple hadn't considered that there might be advantages to being a damsel in distress.

"Works nights." Electra sighed. "We'll have to be liberated ladies and do it ourselves. I'll get a flashlight. We don't want to give the intruder any more to see by than necessary, if he's still there."

Temple nodded, and Electra vanished into her kitchen. Temple had never explored the inner depths of Electra's quarters, but she glimpsed an odd green crystal ball on a huge claw-footed brass tripod in the living room—atop a blond TV cabinet from the fifties. A shadow flitted away as Temple strained to see into the half-glimpsed rooms; probably a phantom of her unsteady nerves.

"This oughta do it." Electra reappeared, waving an old-fashioned, silver-metal-barreled flashlight that reminded Temple of ancient Eveready battery ads. She just hoped a black cat of her acquaintance, her brief acquaintance, had the same nine lives the Eveready cat always did.

They rode down the two floors in silence; the elevator did not. Temple had left her door unlocked, so they entered immediately on a well-oiled hush of hinges. Electra switched on her beam; the click sounded like a cocking revolver in the silence. A sickly circle of light piddled on the parquet.

Electra and Temple followed the yellow ick road to the French door.

"Oh!" Temple's gardenia plant lay roots up, its terra-cotta pot smashed. Otherwise, the patio was untouched and deserted.

"Better check out the other rooms," Electra ordered. "I hold the flashlight out to the side, see, in case they're armed. That way, they shoot at the light, but they don't hit the torso or anything vital."

"No, just me," Temple hissed, walking as she did to the right and behind Electra.

Each room proved empty, even when Temple put on the overhead lights and they inspected corners and the shower stall.

"I'll check these closets," Temple said quickly as Electra was about to jerk the Mystifying Max poster into the hard glare of her flashlight. Temple poked the light into the interior nooks and crannies.

"Sure a lot of shoes in there," Electra noted.

"But not much else. No Midnight Louie, either. Electra, he's gone!"

"Now, now." Electra Lark left it at that. She was not a believer in false sentiments.

Temple checked her watch. Only 10:27 P.M. She could hardly call the police about a door they would say she'd left unlatched, or an air-conditioner they'd assume she'd left off. Or a missing cat who'd never been domesticated in the first place.

Some of her belongings looked vaguely disarranged, but who was to say that wasn't the vanished Midnight Louie doing some creative nesting? Who was to say that the wind hadn't blown the door ajar, and that the vagabond cat had leaped out when opportunity knocked?

"What a shi—shazam of a day." Temple locked the errant French door.

"Will you be able to sleep, dear? I mean alone."

"I've managed it so far," Temple said ungraciously, "although I turned down an offer tonight that begins to look better by the millennium."

"You keep this flashlight tonight. I'll have Mr. Marino check your thermostat and the door in the morning. We can reach you at the convention center these days, I suppose."

"Not until almost eleven," Temple said. "I'll be running an errand first."

Compared to this unsettling night, a rendezvous with a catnapper was beginning to sound like the answer to a maiden's prayers.

The Ultimate Sacrifice

It is a far, far better thing that I do than I have ever done. It is a far, far better rest that I go to, than I have ever known. I quote, of course, from the immortal Who the Dickins. To which I say, baloney! There is one thing for certain that it indeed is: the biggest gamble of my career.

No, let me be utterly honest. It is the biggest gamble of my life. Perhaps I should say lives, though I cannot be sure how many of these I still possess, having never been one to keep count.

I can count days and hours, however. Where I am now, the sun does not shine, but the people provide a convenient reckoning of the passing hours by coming and going in eight-hour shifts around the clock, just as they do in the hotels and casinos and jails.

This is no hotel or casino, but that does not mean a guy cannot gamble his life away here in a very few hours.

It is dark now, which would be comforting were it not for the insistent whines of those loudmouth losers in the adjoining cell block. What a bunch of lily-livered squealers. I have never had much time for dogs.

Yes, you have apprehended correctly. Midnight Louie is in stir. Not only that, my cage is located on Death Row. Oh, it is not so labeled, but I am not born yesterday.

I have much time now to meditate on my past life, or lives, and my many sins of commission and omission. I am outside the Sirocco Inn when Gino Scarletti buys it—not the inn, the farm, otherwise known as six feet of dirt, downward. But the cops never hear a peep from me; I am still light on my tootsies even if I acquired some pinchworthy inches lately, and I rabbit that one.

Did I ever mention how I single-handedly save the Crystal Phoenix from utter destruction at the hands of a mob of crazed killers? No? Good.

I am also the silent type—it does not pay to know too much in this town, as I say before and will again. Mostly I mull how my last life now hangs by the fragile thread of a certain little doll's ardent regard. I am not the first dude whose well-being depended on some dame, and, frankly, the record is not good.

Some may wonder how a savvy sort like myself has landed in such a pickle. It is, like the foregoing Dickins's *Tail of Two Kitties,* a long, sad story, and no consolation to know that Baker and Taylor lounge not five cells away, together still, but not for long.

How it all comes down is like this:

After I find that know-it-all Ingram and learn that the able Sassasfras believes a pair of Scottish type to be languishing in the city pound, I decide to check it out for myself. Sassafras is one sharp old doll, having been put in the pound—and been bailed out by her delinquent owners—more times than she has had kittens or cannipation fits, which is to say a lot. If she says they are having scotch with their soda water at the pound these days, those fancy cats are there.

The first snag is when Miss Temple Barr, whose education on a gentleman-about-town's needs is still in the formative stages, locks me in her apartment for the night.

Now this is a swell place with many amenities, but a dude has gotta do what a dude has gotta do. As soon as she exits for what is obviously a hot date, probably with the snake-eyed Svengali on the poster, I hone my neglected housebreaking skills. Ingram tells me that many people nowadays are interested in what they call "polite procedure," so I will describe the method of my egress, since I am nothing if not polite.

First I study the terrain for any discreet exit available. The air-conditioning vents, besides being mostly in the ceiling, are also covered with screwed-on grilles. I am not particularly adept with screws.

Next I practice jumping up to the thermostat and moving the dial with my right mitt. I have not been required to exert myself to this extent of late and am soon huffing and puffing. Once I manage to move the mechanism, I am ready to tackle the Big Outdoors. Miss Temple Barr's apartment features French doors to the patio that open with a lever rather than a knob.

It will take some superfeline leap to tilt the balance on one of these numbers from the floor, cold, but to my recent good fortune Miss Temple Barr's dietary regimen has done nothing to reduce my fighting weight—normally about eighteen pounds.

Since the French latches are lower than the thermostat, I am now in fine shape to bound up and put my mitt to the metal on the way down. After five of these love taps, the latch clicks. Then it is but a matter of hooking my nails under the door and pulling until it cracks open. After which, I nose through, inspect the patio for any pausing tidbits, leap up to the edge—accidentally overturning a pot containing a rank-smelling plant—down to the top of the umbrella table on the patio below, where I rip some canvas to break my fall, then bound to the chair and so on down to the street. Those patios and French doors could not keep out a tumbleweed.

My journey to the target structure is unremarkable.

Suffice it to say that I know my way around every over-baked square foot of this tortilla-flat town. Even at night the asphalt warms my toes.

I take a sudden chill, however, when I glimpse the animal pound silhouetted against the moon-silvered clouds. Too many of my kind have been snuffed there, for no greater reason than they were considered homeless. I would not wish such a fate even upon a dog. There are also rumors that certain of my kind are singled out for shipment to laboratories, where scientists see no harm in experimenting on any species on earth so long as it is not their own.

Yet there is no help for it. I creep closer, keeping to the shadows, my ears flat so the delicate pink lining does not pick up a stray streetlight, and my mouth shut so my teeth do not betray my approach. (I have been told that I sport quite a dazzling set of incisors.)

At a rear window I hear the heart-rending cries of my captive kind, plus a lot of yammering from the idiotic dogs, who will raise about the same ruckus for a simple rabies shot as they would for the end of the world.

I hoist myself up, but all I can see is a slice of the main cell block. The mewling of the infants is the hardest to take. I must admit that I have not spent much time around the young of my kind, but they produce a united wail that comes close to the outcry of a human newborn of my (fortunately) temporary acquaintance.

In this unsung cacophony I detect a foreign element and pick out the unmistakable brogue of the Highland twosome. I am brought abruptly back to earth, mainly because the grip of my claws has given out.

What to do? It dawns on me rather swiftly that the missing Baker and Taylor have likely been deposited in this Auschwitz-on-the-Mojave since sometime Friday. They have less than twenty-four hours of survival left, unless someone does something about it.

I pace the ground outside their prison. I sit and muse upon the moon when it coasts free of some passing clouds. I weigh options. I clean my ruff and box my ears, hoping for some stroke of genius to strike.

Nothing occurs. Only one course remains. This will have to be an inside job. I do not kid myself; even a dude of my weight, finesse and manual dexterity has never broken into—or out of—an animal pound cage.

I will have to go undercover, allow myself to be captured and do what I can as an inside man. If all else fails, I have one card up my sleeve. Maybe, just maybe, the little doll I left lonely at the Circle Ritz will tumble to my possible whereabouts and ride to my rescue. Hell, she can even walk. If she is fast enough, we might even spring Baker and Taylor.

If she is not, give my regards to Broadway.

Missing Purrsons

Eightball O'Rourke was waiting for Temple and Emily Adcock next to the equestrian statue of Julius Caesar that stood, appropriately, kitty-corner from Caesars Palace.

At a distance, the famous hotel and casino glittered frosting-white in the hot sunlight. An endless driveway from the Strip bracketed fountains that led to a reproduction of the headless Winged Victory statue. A semicircular facade of columns fronted the hotel proper and framed a line of oversize marble goddesses, replicas of world-renowned statues. Cars swept up the curved approach—Mercedes, Cadillacs and costly custom jobs wearing more chrome than paint.

The scene at the foot of Caesar's statue was more humble. Emily had brought the money, neatly wrapped in brown paper. Temple was impressed by the solid brick formed by $5,000 in small bills.

She didn't try to pay O'Rourke by check, but handed him three fifty-dollar bills.

"This is our money, Mr. O'Rourke," Emily said after the terse introductions. "Mostly mine. I've got to get those two cats back. What are our chances?"

He stuck the parcel in the crown of the Western hat he carried. "Not good. Odds is never good on kidnapping. Too easy to lose the object of the game once they've got the cash. Kidnapper don't care, and if the victims is cats, well—some folks don't care for cats. Usually crooks. Hell, crooks don't care for their kinfolk or womenfolk. Why should they care for cats?"

"There's no guarantee, then?"

"Nope. But I'll do my best to make the drop so it looks like this here young lady done it."

"Me?" Temple said. "If I've got to be involved, why pay you?"

O'Rourke flipped up the rear skirt of his shapeless polyester-knit sport coat to reveal the gun butt in the back of his jeans. "I'm muscle."

"*You*'re muscle!" Temple snorted impolitely. "Even I can see your bald spot when I'm wearing my Charles Jourdans."

Eightball O'Rourke most likely had no idea that Charles Jourdan French pumps were not only expensive, but arch-breakingly high-heeled. However, he immediately absorbed the gist of her words.

"I'll do my best to tail the wrong-doer, ladies. More than that you cain't ask in kidnapping. If those cats are safe, the napper's the only one who can lead us to 'em. Now, you with the stilt shoes, wander along the road there behind me and make a big deal of stopping to fix your heel when you reach the third statue of whazzits from the entrance. If you got the ransom note, they expect you to show some interest in this-here drop."

"It's Venus," Temple said. "The statue. Then what?"

"Then amble off. Speaking of statues, you know what happened to Lot's wife."

"Salt?"

O'Rourke nodded soberly. "Enough for a whole box of soda crackers. Don't look back."

Temple had not expected to play a part in this drama, if only a walk-on. Even at ten on Monday morning, tourists were trickling out the doors and hoofing up the long expanse of curved front walk, just as Temple was doing behind Eightball O'Rourke.

While Temple watched, Eightball suddenly paused, whipped an automatic—camera, that is—from his coat pocket, planted a booted foot on the raised concrete rim and shot the facade of Caesars. He doffed his hat, swept his sleeve over his brow and bent as if to adjust his boot. Though Temple didn't see it, this had to be the moment when he placed a plain brown paper parcel (chock-full of some very fancy green paper) at the feet of the proper goddess.

Eightball strolled on. By the time Temple reached Venus, her watch said three minutes to ten, the assigned hour of delivery. She peeked over the whitewashed rim. A brown parcel lay at the goddess's bare feet, which matched most of the rest of her.

Temple sat on the rim and fiddled with her shoes. She twisted to regard the larger-than-life-size looming goddess, which for some reason reminded her of Lieutenant C. R. Molina, and trailed a hand over the edge until she touched the package. Then she rose, shook her apparently pained foot and gamely limped into Caesars Palace.

Then it was through the crowded lounge area, along the marble-paved Appian Way mall of exclusive shops, out a side door, then around to the back and a rendezvous with Emily at the statued Caesar's feet.

"Well?" Temple was, justifiably, breathless.

"I don't know. I watched, but . . . Several people came along after you stopped. Couples, a street person in a wheelchair, a really pitiful man—Lord, he can have the money if he found it; um, some kids."

"Did you see O'Rourke again?"

"No."

"That's either very good or very bad."

"What do you mean?"

"Either he's an expert tail and even we couldn't detect him, or he took our fee, made the drop and went home to twiddle his thumbs."

"I had to try, Temple. Surely if they've got the money they'll release the cats. Maybe Baker and Taylor will suddenly show up at the ABA in time for the last day."

"Maybe," Temple said. "Does it really end tomorrow? I can hardly wait." She bent to fuss with her left shoe. Somewhere on her circuitous route, she'd picked up a genuine grain of sand.

The Pennyroyal Press press kit came in a copper-colored folder with the imprint's logo embossed dead center: a coin depicting, not the familiar profile of Lincoln, but a crowned king in profile. The word "Pennyroyal" curved above the coin; the word "Press" smiled modestly below it.

Temple sat at her desk skimming the accumulated paper trail on the personalities in the case. Most of the ABA's hubbub had peaked. In twenty-four hours, the five-day mania would end for another year with a whimper. To every thing there is a season.

This was Monday; already some booksellers were leaving. Tuesday afternoon the exhibitors would decamp. On Wednesday the center setup crew would tear down and put up; by Thursday a new crew of conventioneers would throng the vast complex.

And Lieutenant Molina would have an unsolved murder on her books to make this an ABA to remember.

Temple frowned at the photographs of Pennyroyal's reigning authors. Mavis Davis made an unlikely candidate for cold-blooded murderer, and neither Lanyard Hunter nor Owen Tharp had a motive, to hear them tell it. At this point Temple wasn't inclined to credit anyone's declaration of disinterest.

Look at Lorna Fennick, who'd never mentioned her time

as an assistant to Chester Royal. Apparently the experience had been enough to discourage Lorna from becoming an editor and she'd fled to the safer—more ethical?—field of public relations. Then there was the choice of weapon—a knitting needle. The more Temple considered it, the likelier it was a woman's weapon.

Mavis Davis, Lorna Fennick, Chester's editor ex-wife Rowena Novak—all made excellent candidates for the author of the 'stet' scrawled across the dead man's chest.

Stet: Let it stand. In this case, let him end as he began, as nothing. A bitter epitaph even for a murder victim, as if a man's life were only so much editorial dead matter. Or did Royal's death *restore* something in the murderer's mind? Self-esteem? Justice? Who would be bitter in that way but a wronged wordsmith? Possibly a writer, possibly another editor who'd been overruled. Or a would-be editor who'd been abused.

Almost anyone *could* have done it. It didn't require great strength or cunning, just surprise. Anyone could smuggle a knitting needle into the ABA, though a woman would have a better pretext. If Chester Royal had secretly remained behind after the center closed on setup day, someone else could have, claiming an after-hours meeting, say. Getting out later would be much easier than leaving and trying to get in again. Maybe Royal himself had requested the meeting with the killer.

Temple eyed her desk phone, an innocuous beige business model. She ought to look further into Royal's malpractice conviction, but the only one with clout enough to do that was C. R. Molina. She'd rather give a hot tip to Hitler's grandmother. Still . . .

While she was talking to the lieutenant, she could mention the string of cat disappearances—B and T and now Louie. Might as well multiply culpability times humility and beg help across the board. None of this was Temple's business, anyway, except for Louie.

That's what she told herself as she looked up the Las Vegas Metropolitan Police number and dialed. It took ages to get through to Molina. Temple couldn't decide whether she was lucky or unlucky to find the lieutenant in.

"Yes." It was said so abruptly that Temple almost hung up. Instead she gave her name.

"Yes." The lieutenant didn't sound even vaguely interested.

That made Temple mad enough to . . . talk.

"I don't know how the Chester Royal investigation is going—" Pause. Perhaps Molina would tell her. Naw. "But I've discovered something in his background that you may not know about." Pause. Molina was not forthcoming with the encouraging little murmurs that make a phone conversation a two-way street. "Royal was a doctor. Until he was forced to stop practicing medicine because of a malpractice conviction."

"Where? When?"

"Why do you think I'm calling you? You must have access to stuff like this on some computer. Had to have been in the early to mid-fifties, because he couldn't have finished medical school until about 1950, and according to the press release he started dabbling in publishing in 1957. He was an ob/gyn. I bet the case made the papers, wherever it was."

"I'll check it out."

"Great! Could you let me know what you find out?"

A dial tone; Molina had hung up. No chance to mention the missing cats.

"You're welcome!" Temple cradled the phone with an emphasis that could not be termed polite.

"Whew! Who pushed your buttons?"

Lorna Fennick stood in the doorway, with raised eyebrows.

"A public official. I'm sorry you saw me being petty and unprofessional, but the line was dead."

"Don't apologize. I feel like flinging some office equipment today, too." Lorna came over to perch on the desk edge, pushing her lank hair behind one ear.

"Oh?" Temple prepared to be sympathetic.

"The first fallout from Royal's death. Mavis Davis is abandoning Pennyroyal."

"Mavis Davis? She's the last one I'd suspect."

Lorna nodded morosely. "The Reynolds/Chapter/Deuce biggies are hugely upset. When the big fish thrash, we minnows are in for a bumpy swim. Apparently, it's a done deal. Mavis is going with Lodestar/Comet/Orion/Styx."

"Can she do that? Aren't there option clauses?"

"Sure, but option clauses are easy to wriggle out of if you can get big enough money from another house or you do a different kind of book."

"What about her wimpy agent?"

Lorna studied Temple with surprise. "How'd you know about that?"

"Isn't that one of the things that cured you of editing? Watching Chester Royal steer his unknowing authors to an agent who was in his pocket?"

Lorna sat up straighter. "You know that, too? Yeah, he did that, and I left. I never told anyone why. How'd you know?"

Temple shrugged. "I'm around. I hear things. I listen. It's part of my job."

"Please don't breathe a word of the Davis defection. I shouldn't have said anything, but I'm so depressed. This has been a hell of an ABA for RCD. Hell on public relations personnel, too. I had to tell someone."

"I know what you mean. I haven't had the world's best day, either."

"What happened?"

"My cat's missing, for one thing."

"You mean that big black devil from the feature story?"

"Yeah. You haven't seen him, have you?"

"Sorry. But, hey, he was a stray. He probably just ran away. Cats'll do that."

"I know," Temple said with feeling, mentally adding Baker and Taylor to that toll. "But I have a hang-up about critters that skip out on me."

Lorna nodded. "So does RCD. God, it's been frantic. Now Avenour wants me to set up a small memorial service for Chester. I just hope the local police let the staff leave town on schedule."

"There's been no progress on the murder investigation?"

"Nothing visible. Maybe it's the lull before the lasagna hits the plate glass."

"That's what you call it in New York, huh?"

"That's what I call it anywhere—damn messy. Got any ideas where I can stage a respectful service in a hurry?"

Temple ransacked her tote bag and pulled out one of Electra's cards—an embossed blue ribbon tortured into a rococo knot on a pink pearlized background. "Try her; she can switch from white to black in a flash."

"Okaaay. You've got an answer to everything. At least the worst of your work with this circus is done. Hope you find your kitty."

"Thanks."

Temple remained desk-bound after Lorna left, her face propped on her hands, the Pennyroyal Press folder swimming before her vision in a hot metallic haze.

Chester Royal had been the perfect murder candidate: he had hubris and a lifelong history of maltreating people's hearts and minds as well as their bodies. That was the trouble: he was too perfectly odious. Anyone could have done it. Heck, the man had managed to rile Temple in the two minutes their paths had crossed at the ABA. If she had been the sort to get mad *and* get even, she might have grabbed the nearest knitting needle and purled his chest cavity, too. . . .

But only one candidate for killer had made a major lifestyle change for the better since Chester's universally unmourned demise. Temple snagged her glasses and tote bag and headed back out to the acres of exhibition.

A Mavis in Flight

Temple found passing room on the convention floor now. Some attendees had no doubt left town; others had finished their book business and were ranging farther afield in search of bookies and other less-than-literary Las Vegas drawing cards.

Consulting the convention guidebook she pulled from her tote—a tome the size of the Reno phone directory—Temple hunted under the L's. Not long after that she was sailing past the Bantam/Doubleday/Dell consortium under the familiar logo of the red rooster and the entwined anchor and dolphin.

Time-Life Books, long since stripped of the popular navy book bags that were its ABA trademark, reeled by on Temple's right. At Zebra/Pinnacle's booths Temple almost tripped over stacks of giveaway paperback romances featuring equally well stacked cover girls, though the awesomely developed bare-chested heroes gave the heroines a run for their cleavage.

Aisle numbers high above the exhibits were hitting 2400. Temple angled cross-traffic and headed down to 2570–82.

And there the quarry was, chatting happily to all comers: Mavis Davis, already if unofficially ensconced at the Lodestar/Comet/Orion/Styx booths, pumping up the public for her first book under a change of colophon.

"Hello!" She greeted Temple like an old friend, and indeed any familiar face in the press of an ABA soon came to seem like one.

"Hello, yourself. I hear you've been making news."

"But it won't come out until the next issue of *Publishers Weekly*. You can't publicize it." Anxiety was still as much a part of Mavis Davis as her perm-crinkled hair. Her eyes looked even more haunted behind the surface euphoria. Performance pressure, maybe? Or guilt?

"Of course not," Temple said soothingly. "But just in case Lieutenant Molina wants to reach those who worked with Chester Royal, I'll need to put her in quick touch with everybody once you've all left Vegas. You'll be accessible through a new house now."

"Well, yes." Insecurity peeked more boldly through the facade of Mavis's obvious joy and relief. "I wouldn't want . . . the police to think I was making myself unavailable."

"Why don't we get off our feet? You must be exhausted, standing on this hard floor all afternoon. Come to the staff room and I'll get you a soft drink."

"All right." Mavis looked around uneasily, searching for someone to say no for her. "I don't know if I'm supposed to leave, but they really haven't anything planned for me to do here. It's all been so sudden."

"I'd love to hear about it. I couldn't be happier for you," Temple said with sincerity. The poor woman was dying for a sympathetic ear, and Temple had at least two of them.

She steered Mavis back to the same large bland room dominated by a conference table where Temple had met

Lorna Fennick and glimpsed the background for this killing.

"Sit down; I'll get you a drink—diet orange okay? Great. Now." Temple had installed Mavis on a chair near the table corner. She claimed the one across the corner from it. That made the big empty table vanish, made them seem like two friends meeting for lunch at a cafeteria. "Tell me all about your great new publisher."

"It's not only a new publisher, Miss Barr. It's a new agent. The agency is one of the most respected in Manhattan. Imagine. I'm got the same agent who handles Michener!"

"I don't have to imagine it, it's true. How did it happen?"

"Well, my new agent approached me and said that he'd long felt that my career had not been as strongly promoted as it could have been. That I was 'untapped potential.' That he couldn't ethically encourage me to leave my current agent, but that it would serve me far better to have New York City representation, and that—"

"Wait a minute. Your old agent, Chester's friend, wasn't based in New York?"

"No. And he wasn't really a literary agent. He was a lawyer. Mr. Royal said that's all I needed anyway, that the really big authors just have lawyers look over their contracts. He was a friend of Mr. Royal's from way back."

"Where was he based?

"Albert Lea, Minnesota."

Temple gulped diet orange soda that tasted like a chemically addicted tangerine. She could hardly believe her sympathetic ears. Even Temple knew that having a literary agent in a tiny Minnesota town made as much sense as having a film agent in Nome, Alaska.

"Is he here, at the ABA?"

"I guess so." Mavis's seesaw voice wavered into a low range. "I haven't seen him," she admitted. "I don't want to see him! According to what my new representatives are saying, it's clear to me that . . . now you mustn't tell a soul"—Temple shook her head so vigorously her glasses did a bebop on the bridge of her nose—"my ex-agent wasn't exactly doing his best to see that I got what I deserved. Mr. Royal's old friend was . . . behind the times." Mavis's eyes narrowed. "I'm not pleased about it."

And would be even less so later, Temple guessed, when Mavis began to grasp the extent of her editorial enslavement. Or was this just an act? Hell hath no fury—or guile—like a writer ripped off.

"Mavis," she began carefully, "I need to make sure that Lieutenant Molina is aware of all the people connected to Chester Royal who are at the ABA. What's this man's name?"

"I don't want to get anyone in trouble," Mavis said, waffling.

Temple stifled an impulse to point out that she'd just admitted the man had stolen her blind. "You'll get in trouble if you're not forthcoming to Lieutenant Molina, and I'll get in trouble if the lieutenant finds out there were some facts I overlooked mentioning."

"You don't think he . . . iced"—this was intoned with great drama and a surprising amount of relish—"Mr. Royal?"

"I don't think he even flushed him, but I need to know his name."

"Earnest Jaspar—with two *e*'s and three *a*'s. But I don't know where he is. I haven't seen him all ABA."

Temple smiled. "Right now I'd say that's a lucky thing for Mr. Jaspar."

"Yes, it is. I'm not a violent woman, Miss Barr," Mavis said mildly, "but I do think I'd be tempted to, to—trip Mr. Jaspar if I saw him now."

"Heaven forbid."

Mavis looked down at the orange drink can as if she were reading her fortune in its gaudy contours. "You know, I'm beginning to realize that Mr. Royal had some old-fashioned ideas. Styx—that's the house I'll be writing for now—wants me to do a really Big Book. Not two days ago, I'd have said I couldn't have done that without Mr. Royal. Now—"

"Now you think you couldn't do it with him?" Temple prodded gently.

"Yes! He never wanted me to put the doctors in a bad light, but Styx says that people love to know that doctors have Achilles' heels like the rest of us. And, frankly, Miss Barr, I've seen some stuck-up stinkers of doctors." Mavis suddenly recognized her anger and retreated. "Mr. Royal was a bit naïve, I'm afraid."

"It's possible," Temple said with a straight face.

"Still, what if these new people don't know how to edit my books? What if they don't like what I do on my own, all by myself?"

"Didn't you write your first book that way?"

"Yes." Mavis sounded uncertain nevertheless.

"I'll tell you what you do." Temple leaned forward and donned her most emphatic expression. "You think about everything you ever saw or thought in those years as a nurse when nobody—doctors, patients, hospital administrators—thought you were looking and you write it all down to make the most exciting, true story you can. And you don't worry a bit what Mr. Royal might think. He's not here anymore."

"You're sure I can do that? Just write what I know and it'll be all right?"

"Yes, I am, Mavis. Now you just sit here and finish your soft drink. I have to run along. Deadlines, you know."

"Sure. Thank you, Miss Barr."

Temple loved a source who thought you'd done her a favor by grilling her.

She waved goodbye and darted off, only to pause in the hall outside the conference room. Where—or how—would she find a low-profile loner like Earnest Jaspar in the waning hours of the ABA? He wouldn't make a booth his base of operations, and apparently he handled only Royal's authors.

She headed for the exhibit floor again. Had it only been three days ago she'd been tracking a rogue cat through the setting-up clutter? Pennyroyal Press's booth looked as shiny and ferocious as it had Friday morning. The glittering, blown-up book covers resembled graphic teeth about to snap at the idle book browser. Those horrific covers made Temple nervous, brimming as they were with barely hidden hostility and ill will.

And who should be holding up a corner of the display other than Lanyard Hunter and Owen Tharp in rapt consultation? They made such an unlikely pair that Temple stopped to watch them with a smile.

Hunter, tall and angular, slouched into a suit that so replicated his thin frame it seemed to cover hangers rather than flesh and bone. Tharp, shorter and stouter, bristled as he talked, his compact body tense with unleashed energy, his gestures almost abrupt.

Why, Temple wondered, *had* Owen Tharp shaven off the mustache shown on his publicity photo? Was he vain and unwilling to ditch a younger photograph? Did he now think not having a mustache made him look younger? He had to be fifty at least. Or had losing the mustache been a ploy to make himself less recognizable at the ABA? If Molina hadn't spotted him, Temple certainly wouldn't have. He was ordinary-looking to begin with. He could have easily remained behind unnoticed on Thursday night and killed Chester Royal.

And Lanyard Hunter. He acted so resigned to Royal's demeaning little ways, as if constant editorial ego-flaying were no skin off his back. Was he really so cool under that smooth, patrician manner of his?

It was Lanyard Hunter who spotted Temple. He straightened, a movement that alerted Tharp to her presence. Both men stopped talking and regarded her. Some women might have accepted this sudden pall in the conversation as due homage to their beauty and charm, but Temple was just irritated that her chances to eavesdrop had plummeted to zero.

"Still tidying up Chester's messy PR blooper?" Hunter asked. "So crude, getting killed at an ABA."

"It was tidily done, though," Temple said. "The police

still haven't arrested anyone, and you'll all be leaving soon."

"Except Chester," Tharp said roughly. "He was shipped off by Cadaver Express yesterday."

"I can see why you write the books you do, Mr. Tharp. Lorna Fennick said you added a macabre twist to the list."

"Sorry," he said. "I suppose it's in bad taste, but then so's a lot of horror fiction, and I have the bad taste to write it. What I meant was, they flew Royal's body out."

"Where?" Temple wanted to know.

"Who's the ghoul here now?" Hunter put in. There was a touch of pique in his voice. She guessed that her blithe rejection the other night had not sat well with his male ego.

"I just wondered who would claim Chester Royal, since his wives are long gone and glad of it. And there were no children."

"He didn't need children to abuse," Tharp said bitterly. "He could make us writers do what we were told—most of the time—but we're all out of the nest now, and he's dead matter."

"Are you staying with Pennyroyal?"

Both men flashed nervous looks around, but only weary ABA-goers slogged past, book-bloated and indifferent to gossip.

"Sure," Tharp admitted. "Reynolds/Chapter/Deuce is a good house. The imprint might perk up with some new blood running it." He grinned at his gruesome cliché.

Hunter smiled faintly. "Owen, you're a consummate actor, always entering into the spirit of a new part. Now you're the cheeky, press-on employee, eager to support the house in the face of catastrophe. I'll stay if it suits my mood or my wallet." Hunter eyed Temple. "Tharp here was just trying to persuade me to let him ghostwrite a series for me. He thinks my production level could stand beefing up, even if he has to do it personally."

"Will you do it?" she asked.

"If it pays, why not?"

Temple turned to Tharp. "You might be in line for a

promotion under your own name, anyway—or I should say your own pseudonym."

"What do you mean?"

"With Mavis Davis over at Lodestar/Comet/Orion/Styx, doesn't a lead spot open up?"

Both men looked shocked. Hunter's hands came out of his pockets white-knuckled. Tharp's very stillness broadcast his disturbance.

"So Mavis has flown the coop," Hunter finally said.

"With the big bucks," Tharp added. "We may be on a sinking ship, pal."

"Or," Temple interjected cheerily, "dueling for the position of captain—of the *Titanic*."

With that she veered into the dispirited passersby and wove her way to the exhibit entrance and the Rotunda where awaited, like an apple dangling from the Tree of All Knowledge, the registration center.

A lone woman now commanded the long counter that only days before had thronged with eager ABA-goers demanding immediate attention and name badges. Now the attendant watched the occasional passerby through bored eyes adorned with lurid aqua contact lenses that perfectly matched the paint on Temple's Storm. Little did the woman know that she had one shiny red apple to hand over.

Temple approached her briskly.

"Hi. I'm with ABA publicity. I need to contact a member of the convention at his hotel. Can you look that up?"

First the woman looked down at Temple's badge, to make sure it bore a stripe in the proper color. Staff was red this year, red like a Roman Beauty apple.

"What last name?" the woman drawled, letting her eyelids droop over the electric irises.

"Jaspar. Earnest Jaspar. J-A-S-P-A-R."

"Not too many *j*'s," she said grumpily, as if annoyed that she wasn't being put out as much as she could have been by a Smith, say, or even a Jones. "The Riviera," she announced shortly after consulting an encyclopedia-thick computer printout.

"On the Strip?" Temple was startled. There were closer hotels.

"It hasn't moved since Thursday."

Temple went on tiptoe and leaned over the shoulder-high (on her) countertop. "Does it say how long he's staying? Whether he's still there?"

"Sorry." The data sheets were suddenly accordion-pleated into a closed book. "You'll have to ask at the hotel."

Temple checked her watch. Mid-afternoon, the cusp of checkout time. She might just be too late.

Doctor, Lawyer, Indian Thief

She raced back to the office area, people's heads turning at the passing clatter of her high heels, and didn't stop until she reached the employee lot in the building's rear. The Storm sizzled in the sunlight. A trip to the Riviera would barely get its air-conditioning going, but it was too far to walk.

Luckily, all the Strip hotels had humongous parking lots. Las Vegas was a city made for private wheels, even though buses duly plied the Strip at twenty-minute intervals. Unluckily, the lots were so large that one usually hiked the length of a football field to get out of the sun and into the building.

Temple's shoulders sagged with relief as she trotted through the Riviera's always open doors into a wall of icy air-conditioning. Inside, the hotel was luxe and dusky, like all Las Vegas hostelries. The ambiance offered a deliberate contrast to the heat and glare of the sidewalks. This dim, forever-bistro world of glitter and gaming chips was always refuge from the harsh hand of nature.

At the Guest Information desk, Temple waited in line while slot machines chirped and clanked and whirred in the hotel lobby behind her. No foot of the city's floor space was wasted that could support a one-armed bandit with oranges and cherries for eyes and a stainless steel gullet for a mouth.

Slot machines occupied grocery stores and laundromats; they wore the first familiar face you saw in the airport lobby when you came and the ultimate one to kiss your last nickle goodbye when you left. Unless you liked vistas of endless scrub and you drove to Vegas.

"Jasper," the clerk complained, about to say, "it doesn't come up on the computer."

"A-R," Temple said.

Clerkish eyebrows elevated. "Here it is. No, he's not checked out, miss. If you want to ring the room, his extension is 1517. The house phones are—" He had not looked up while delivering his data; Temple had left as soon as she had what she needed.

She clutched the receiver in both hands and braced one high heel against the wall while the extension rang once, twice. Lord knows why she had a hunch that Jaspar was an important person to talk to, but she did.

On five the phone was answered with a simple, "Hello."

"Mr. Jaspar? This is Temple Barr from the ABA. I'd like to talk to you about Mr. Royal. Can you meet me in the lobby?"

He could, and did. Easy as pineapple. She'd described herself rather too thoroughly, but paced in front of the long banks of elevators nevertheless. This was her last chance to dig up an ironclad motive. The ABA was in its death throes. It could very well fade away without revealing the killer of Chester Royal.

That would be a blot on Molina's record—but Temple wasn't worried about Molina's ass. When was that Nazi in pantyhose ever civil to me? she thought heatedly. But she didn't really need to find the murderer first, if only the murderer were found. Why was she so determined to do it herself? She would hardly be righting an injustice in the emotional sense; Chester Royal's death seemed more an act of justice than anything else. So why bother some elderly stranger for what might be nothing? Because someone had messed up her convention, damn it. She was responsible for everything going smoothly, and murder was definitely not smooth. She had to know why—and who.

Jasper was older than she'd expected, certainly over seventy, with a stiff frailty that made her feel like a rotter. No wonder the old boy hadn't visited the ABA floor much; it would have done him in. She had begun looking around for a quiet place to talk when Jaspar squinted in the direction of the lounge.

"I could use a drink. This climate dries out my gullet until I feel like an overbaked turkey on Christmas morning."

"Sure." Temple scurried alongside as Jaspar struck out at a stooped but snappy pace.

The lounge wasn't quiet, but at least they had a table the size of a pizza all to themselves.

"Who'd you say you were?" he wanted to know first.

Lord, she hoped he wasn't half-deaf. "Temple Barr—"

"I know the name. What do you do for the ABA?"

"Public relations."

"What does public relations have to do with Chester's death?"

"I'm helping the local police get a fix on the dramatis personae."

Jasper looked blank.

"The people who knew him that are here."

"I knew him, knew him over forty years." Jasper hoisted his beer at the TV high on the wall that no one could hear.

The President was on-screen, giving a press conference. Temple wondered what hell was breaking loose where, then brought her mind back to Jaspar. "You acted as an agent for several of his writers."

"No, I didn't."

"I beg your pardon?" They were shouting by now. It sounded like an argument, although it was only the usual attempt to communicate in Las Vegas.

"I just dealt with the writers now and again, eyeballed the contracts. Chester was doing me a favor, throwing a little business my way. Wasn't much to the job, but he paid okay."

Another dupe of Chester Royal's? Temple couldn't believe it. "But . . . why?"

"We go back a long time. I helped him with a spot of trouble years ago."

"In Albert Lea, Minnesota?"

Jaspar looked surprised. "Yeah, I was working out of Albert Lea, but Chester's difficulties were in Illinois. Lots of folks wondered why Chester got an out-of-state lawyer. For one thing, we went to college in Milwaukee together—I was older because of World War Two by the time I got to college. For another, I was a good lawyer and he knew it. Everybody thinks there's nothing in Minnesota but snow." Jaspar grinned. "That's not quite true, but it sure's not as hot as this place."

"Why'd you come to the ABA if you did so little?"

"Chester. He wanted me to be around if a writer needed a little reassurance." Jaspar leaned close and enunciated every word. "They're kinda temperamental, writers. Chester explained it to me. Artistic snits. He sure went through a lot of rigmarole to keep 'em happy. I don't know much about this publishing stuff, but if I was you, I'd get out of it."

"I'm not in publishing, I'm in PR."

"PR? Not many Puerto Ricans in Minnesota. Vietnamese, though."

"Tell me about the case you helped Chester with."

"In Illinois?"

"Yes!"

"It was back in the fifties. Sad situation, nasty pickle. You couldn't do things like that in those days, but Chester was always breaking rules. Chester was the ultimate Indian giver."

"What do you mean?"

"If he did anything for you, there was a mousetrap in it somewhere. He had an odd sense of humor. On the surface he looked like a beneficent guy, but deep down everything was not only to his advantage, but it soothed some private sore spot to get the better of someone. An Indian giver—that's what we used to called giving and then taking back, like the government kept grabbing back lands it'd promised the Indians. Chester handed you something with one hand and took something of you away with the other."

"He stole a bit of their souls," Temple said darkly.

"Maybe. But this one time a body was involved. Some woman died. They said it was Chester's fault."

"Was it?"

"Hell, yes! That kind of thing was illegal then. May soon be again."

"Abortion?" Temple held her breath. Could this be the malpractice case she'd set Molina on?

Jaspar nodded and took a swig of beer from the massive mug before him. "Chester was lucky to get off with just his medical license jerked. The DA was thinking of going for manslaughter, but I was pretty sharp in those days; it ended up just a malpractice case. Helped some that the family was claiming the woman hadn't wanted an abortion. Kinda hard to swallow."

"What days? When exactly?"

Jaspar puckered his whole face in indecision. "Early fifties.

"Exactly?"

" 'Exactly' isn't exactly in my mental vocabulary anymore. Maybe . . . fifty-two." Jaspar managed to look both stubborn and grumpy, so Temple tried a different tack.

"But why was the family's claim that the aborted woman was unwilling so hard to swallow?"

"Well—" Jaspar leaned back in the well-padded captain's chair. This question would permit the proper elaboration, the attorney's equivalent of good, old-fashioned gossip. "The woman had almost a dozen kids already. Husband was a switchman for the Great Northern Railway, you know, the one with the mountain goat."

Temple didn't know, but figured the goat wasn't important, so she just nodded.

"Gil—Gil—Gilhooley or some cheesecloth-curtain Irish name. Roman Catholics, of course, but it's one thing to go to church on Sunday and bend your knee and say 'Bless me, Father,' and another to live with ten hungry mouths and another one coming."

"But the family—the husband—insisted she never would have asked for an abortion?"

"Mary . . . Ellen, that's it! Mary Ellen Gilhooley. Women aren't having kids like that anymore. I never did know how they took that kind of wear and tear back then. They don't do it nowadays. Progress."

"Mary Ellen Gilhooley died on Dr. Chester Royal's table during the course of an abortion her husband said she'd never have asked for?"

"That's it. Well, people lose someone close, they don't want to think that person would be driven to do something they're not supposed to. But who knows better than a doctor—or a lawyer—what the client really wants, huh?

"Denial, that's what the psychologists call it nowadays. Those Gilhooleys were into denial up to their face freckles about Mary Ellen and what she needed and wanted, believe me. Husband's name was Michael—that's it! Michael and little Mary Clare, and Eoin and Liam and Brigid and Sean, and—let me see—there was a Cathleen, of course, and maybe a Rory. Irish as they come. Enough kids; Chester was just trying to do a good deed. You can't blame him, 'cept it was out-and-out illegal. So they took his license and he went on to different work. I hadn't thought about that in years, but I remember it clearer than what I had for breakfast this morning. Cost a mint, too."

Earnest Jaspar's pale aging eyes suddenly focused on Temple's. "Don't get old and forget, like me and Chester. Some people, it's like they forget to get old. Others, they just get old to forget."

Temple, lost in the implications of a possibly hot lead, assured Jaspar that she would never forget meeting him. He fussed about planning to attend Chester Royal's memorial service tomorrow once he knew where it would be, but she took his home address and phone number anyway—to justify her snooping to Molina if it should ever come up. She said goodbye and thank you, then paused again in the lobby and phoned home to inquire into the action on other fronts.

"Electra? Have you heard from a woman named Lorna Fennick? Great. What's on in the background? I can hardly hear here and it sounds like you've got a soccer match in your living room." Temple put a finger in her free ear.

"Just the MTV, hon," Electra answered. "I like the sound on high. And I'm on the portable phone in *your* living room. Mr. Marino is home sick so Matt is seeing if he can fix your French door latch."

Temple shifted her weight onto one foot and realized that she was hot, tired and depressed—and that Electra had Matt Devine all to herself in *Temple*'s living room.

"Listen, have you seen anything of Louie? Louie! The black cat. Yeah. Well, look now, please. On the patio, or in the yard."

Temple tapped a toe and stonily eyed the person waiting behind her for the pay phone. Let him go stuff a slot machine, that's what Vegas was for.

"Nothing? No sign? Okay. Yeah, I'm coming home later if the traffic will let me. Keep the MTV warm for me."

Where the devil was Midnight Louie? But she had other felines in the fire. Temple pulled the now-worn Yellow Page from her bag and dialed Eightball O'Rourke. No answer, the same story as when she'd tried the number several earlier times that afternoon. He was probably on his way to the Maldives with Emily Adcock's $5,000.

"You sure know how to pick 'em," Temple admonished herself.

On the other hand, O'Rourke still could be hopping up the money trail in pursuit of the ransom collector. It was possible. Or maybe he'd been hurt—knocked out—by the napper. That was possible, too.

Temple was beginning to feel as flummoxed about the murder of Chester Royal and the snatching of the Scottish folds as she was about the disappearance of the Mystifying Max.

She'd just about had it with being left totally in the dark.

Midnight Louie, Dead Matter

It is hot as hell in this joint, but then I have not seen the Afterlife yet, thank Bast.

(Bast is reputed to be the head deity of cats since Ramses hot-rodded up and down the Nile in a two-tone chariot. Talk about your low-riders.)

I do not ordinarily put my faith in supernatural agencies, especially since those ancient Egyptians used to mummify my forebears—no way to treat a gent of any species. Longevity in a form resembling dried parsley flakes does not appeal to my sense of dignity, not to mention my *joie de vivre.*

However, my sense of dignity has been sorely tried for the past thirty-some hours. Although I am in solitary, there is not enough room in this cell for a fellow to dip his lips in a water bowl without having his posterior doing a bump and grind over the sanitation facility. Sleep—although who could under a death sentence?—is possible only if I knot my limbs into the kind of position I have not assumed since I was a kitten and did not know better, or was a young tom and did—but did it anyway.

My rear extremity, once my pride and joy, is developing a decided kink, not to mention a basketweave pattern from being pressed against these metal-grid walls. Oh, if I had the wings of a bird—I would eat them.

Certainly it would be tastier than the gray-brown swill that is dolloped into my bowl twice daily. There is not enough of this stuff to keep a mid-size hamster going, but I will not touch it anyway. This may be why I am falsely accused of growling by passing attendants who hear the involuntary complaints of my stomach.

I use every opportunity to figure an angle out of here. At least yesterday some would-be animal adopters were trotted through. These folks are mostly in search of kittens, however. We of an enviable maturity attract the occasional window-shopper, but it seems I am considered a hard case and a bad risk for adoption.

For one thing, they carp about my age, which is none of their business. Secondly, they lament the fact that I have not had a certain distasteful procedure performed upon my person. When I hear of this, I shudder, which encourages the onlookers to conclude that I am suffering from some loathsome disease. In fact, the attention I attract is when an attendant points to me and says "This one sure is big. Ever seen one that big?"

"No, indeed, we have not," say the happy browsers. "Sure must eat a lot."

Not for long.

Baker and Taylor get their share of curiosity seekers. Although they have the desired (by some) surgical history, they also suffer from maturity, with funny ears to boot. So I get to keep an eye on them day and night. This is not a pleasant task.

For one thing, they communicate in the most awful mishmash I have ever heard. It makes the caterwaulings of Nostradamus, my Brooklyn-born bookie, sound euphonious. (This euphonious means musical and has something to do with the symphony, I believe.)

"Weel, Baker," I hear Taylor gabble in his Aberdeen burr, "we dinna hae much time left. This wee burrow is less commodious than the fine castle prepared fair us at the ABA."

"Och," flutes Baker, " 'tis true. At least we canna complain that we air not thegither to the last. A shame that our namesake company maun be so wasteful of its funds for naught."

And so on. The dialogue puts me in mind of a road company *Brigadoon*, not my idea of entertainment for my last wee hours on earth. However, I put my paltry time to good use and manage to extract some verra interestin' news from the twit-eared twa from the Hielands, no thanks to them. I begin to plan a breakout for us all.

Then, as the sun pumps out its hottest wattage preparatory to taking its last bow and disappearing behind the mountains, an intruder enters our torpid quarters. It is the attendant I call Jug-ears, accompanied by a well-padded doll of no particular pulchritude but with a kind face. I would have at one time (yesterday) described her as enjoying her middle years, but have become sensitive about such labels.

"I cannot believe it," this indeterminate-age doll trills to Jug-ears. "I have been wanting a pair of cats for my shop—more businesses should have on-site cats; it amuses customers, controls varmits and saves the cats from a life of crime upon the streets. But to think that you have the very kind I want—"

"Right 'cher." Jug-ears stops before Baker and Taylor. "They are growed, though."

"Oh, I could not handle kittens in my place. These darling fellows are perfect! I cannot believe someone just dropped off a pair of purebred Scottish folds."

"Too old for most folks," says Jug-ears, who by my reckoning is fifty if he is a day. "We get lots of adult purebreds. Not cute anymore. Say, we are about to close. Can you hurry it up?"

"How long did you say they have been here?"

Jug-ears grins viciously, but she does not seem to notice. "Almost sixty hours. They was ready for the needle."

"Do you know who brought them?"

Shrug. Jug-ears is not eloquent. "Name is in the book up front. You want me to unlock the cage or what?"

"Of course I will take them. It is incredible; they look just like the Baker and Taylor on the posters. Of course, they are purebreds, so you would expect them to all look alike. The real Baker and Taylor could not be here, of all places."

"Ma'am, we gotta close. Got work to do back here."

Here, I swear, the man turns to gloat in my direction, even though my sixty hours have a good thirty to run. I can count. For the first time I notice that he has a squint and a hunchback. And a mouse-dropping-size wart on his chin. With a long black hair growing out of it.

"Can you carry one?" the woman asks. She has a warm, kindly face, as I say before, and cradles Baker upon her warm, kindly bosom.

Jug-ears takes Taylor and shuffles to the door.

"I am absolutely delighted," the woman croons, patting Baker's runty ears as she leaves. "I run the mystery bookstore in town. You will never know how appropriate to the shop these two are. I am so glad that I took time off from the ABA to come in. That stuffed Baker and Taylor exhibit convinced me I could not live without more cats."

Off they go, my motive for being in this predicament. I find myself in the same state of disbelief as Miss Maeveleen Pearl, for it is obviously she, the *capo* of the Thrill 'n' Quill Bookstore, who has rescued B and T from their imminent demise on the business end of a hypodermic.

Some might think that B and T's salvation is worth my forthcoming personal sacrifice. I do not. My bacon now rides solely on the ability of Miss Temple Barr to think of looking for me in this den of death and dogs. Only the thought of another's misfortune is enough to cheer me up for a fleeting instant.

That snooty Ingram will not be pleased to share a shop with Baker and Taylor.

Chapter 21

Alone at Last

ABA attendees were streaming from the convention center's front entry as if five-thirty P.M. were a Cinderella deadline when Temple cruised the Storm past the Rotunda's flying-saucer-shaped dome. She always expected Gort to issue from the entrance, but only ordinary earthlings ever did. She had to credit the ABA-goers for being a well-ordered, obedient crowd—with the single, startling exception of murder.

Even the rear employee parking lot was a checkerboard of empty spaces. The Storm's air-conditioning fan whooshed full blast as Temple pulled into a slot, blowing the short red curls off her damp forehead.

Bud Dubbs bustled out the back door into the 100-plus, his seersucker sport coat hooked over a finger.

"Where've you been, Temple? That Lieutenant Molina called for you several times."

"I've been trailing the elusive Baker and Taylor. Any message from an Eightball O'Rourke? What about Midnight Louie, anybody see him?"

Bud did a dime stop and a double take. "Not that I know of. *Eightball* O'Rourke? You playing the horses these days? Valerie might have taken a message from O'Rourke. Forget that stray cat. Check your desk. God, it's hot. See you tomorrow."

Bud dived into the front seat of his Celica and punched on his air conditioner.

An uncommon quiet inhabited the center's back halls. Most of the exhibitors must have cut out on the stroke of five-thirty, too. Temple quickened her pace. The security people wanted as few staff as possible around after closing. If she didn't decamp by six, there'd be only one exit door that wasn't on the alarm system, and that would be guarded.

Bud had been right; Temple's desk was pocked with yellow memo forms. "While you were out—" they told her, she had missed calls from everyone but Midnight Louie, it seemed: P. E. O'Rourke, Lieutenant Molina, Emily Adcock, Lorna Fennick.

She tried O'Rourke first, and got only a ringing phone. After she hung up, Temple stared at her cluttered desk. From under the fresh messages Pennyroyal Press's metallic-copper folder winked like an evil eye.

Bud's advice to the contrary, she couldn't forget about stray cats. Louie's continuing absence had become something she simply couldn't let go of.

She hefted the phone book from her lowest desk drawer, grunting, and looked up the City entries. "Animal Pound" led the listings. As she dialed, she eyed her watch with a surge of panic. It was nearly six. Maybe the pound was closed.

The phone rang time after time. Maybe someone was feeding the animals and would take a while to respond. Temple hung on, not really expecting to find Louie there, not really expecting an answer.

"Yeah?"

"Ah, I'm looking for a cat."

"We're closed, lady. I'm just cleaning up."

Cleaning up? From what? The daily executions? "It's important! This cat I'm looking for is . . . famous."

"Yeah?" The voice sounded supremely indifferent. "Look, there's procedures. Call back tomorrow morning."

"It might be too late. He's been missing for over twenty-four hours."

"We hold 'em three days. Lady, I gotta go."

"Wait! Maybe you noticed him. He's a big black cat—I mean, really big, like almost twenty pounds."

"Yeah, could be."

"You *have* him!"

"Maybe. It's not my job—"

"When can I get him?"

"Tomorrow, I told you."

"But what if—"

"We got a lot of cats here; you lost him. You take your chances."

Temple got suddenly desperate. "Listen, he's a material witness. If I get the police—"

"We're not a police agency. We got our own rules. I gotta go."

"You're not . . . killing any animals tonight?"

"Lady, we kill 'em when their time's up, when we get the time to do it. I don't know anything. You're wasting *my* time. Look, I'll be here until seven. I'll let you take a look-see if you get here before I leave. But that's it."

The line buzzed dead.

Temple's mouth was grim. News stories about "pets" being killed by mistake at the pound floated in her mind's eye. She had to know that Louie was safe, but she had too damn many vital things to take care of here to go gallivanting across town in rush hour. She riffled through the memos to find Molina's number. She might be able to tell the homicide detective a thing or two about the Royal murder, but first she wanted a squad car to go to the so-called animal shelter and make sure that Midnight Louie wasn't there and wasn't being executed . . . and if Molina wouldn't do it, Temple would go herself, murder case be damned—! Temple found Molina's number, right on top of another message—typed—that was much more urgent.

"GOT THE DOUGH. IF YOU WANT THOSE CATS, COME TO THE BAKER & TAYLOR SETUP AT 6:30 P.M. TONIGHT. YOU BETTER BE ALONE."

When had this arrived? Temple wondered. Had someone slipped it among her messages after everyone had left? How did the first one arrive, for that matter? Someone here, at the ABA, had left it, that was obvious.

Temple's heart was pounding. She had to leave, to make sure that Louie was not at the shelter, or that he was safe there. Yet her first obligation was to her job: to keep the ABA free of unnecessary bad press. Rescuing Baker and Taylor had become part of that agenda. Why was the kidnapper using her for a conduit again? Keeping her occupied, away from the Royal case, maybe. Keeping her from rescuing Midnight Louie, certainly.

Temple eyed her watch as dubiously as she would an egg timer. She'd never been a fan of deadlines. Six-thirty was forty minutes away. She dialed the center security office. No answer, as expected. Cyrus Dent went home at five like everybody else. Sure, guards patrolled, but not many. Conventions hired local private security forces to police their exhibitions. The building itself was another matter, and nobody much messed with a convention center except passing graffiti artists.

So there were guards around, but where in the vast building? And she could dash out to check on Louie, but what if she didn't get back in time to collect Baker and Taylor? Kidnappers were notoriously impatient. Once the guards had let her out after hours, they wouldn't waltz her back in, not without explanations and interference . . . and that could foul up the return of Baker and Taylor.

But Louie! Temple worried more about him than Baker and Taylor. If the kidnapper was returning them, they were fine. It made sense to bring them back to the scene of the crime; the napper knew the exhibit area, or he'd never have nipped them so successfully in the first place.

Temple's watch showed thirty minutes left to six-thirty.

The phone rang.

She stared at it for a moment. Who'd be calling after hours? The catnapper? Molina?

When she lifted the receiver, she heard an open line. It forced her to say "Hello?"

"Miss Barr?"

She didn't recognize the male voice. "Yes?"

"Eightball O'Rourke. Got some dope on who picked up the ransom."

"I'd been wondering where you were."

"Out trying to nail down the identity of who's got your friend's money. It's taking me longer than I expected."

"You'll be paid for it," Temple reassured him, wondering how much her American Express card would cover. "What happened?"

"The package stayed there for a while. Then a party comes along that acts nervous. Sure enough, one bend and the bait is gone. The trail led to the Last Vegas Hilton."

"You saw the person who picked up the money? That's worth every penny! Who?"

"That's the trouble. The Las Vegas Hilton is the third-largest hotel in the world. It ain't easy getting a make on one person scooting through their doors."

"But you saw the person."

"They was wearing disguising clothing."

"How disguising can it be?"

"Hat, sunglasses. You'd be surprised how hard it is to identify somebody by their clothes."

"Not Electra," Temple mumbled.

"What's wrong with your electricity?"

"Nothing. So you don't know exactly who picked up the money, just that it was picked up."

"Yeah. I been leaning on the Hilton staff, but so far no one can identify her."

"Her?"

"A woman, yeah. Big hat, big gauzy scarf, big dress, not a little woman like you, kinda . . . big. A dumpy, middle-aged woman."

"Do you know how many women in Las Vegas fit that description?" Temple demanded, mentally making her own private list: Lorna Fennick, Mavis Davis, Rowena Novak. Electra Lark, for that matter.

"So I'm working on it. Unless you want me to stop."

"No. I guess the kitty can underwrite a few more hours of detection."

The word "kitty" reminded Temple of her immediate dilemma.

"By the way," she said, deciding to tell Eightball that Baker and Taylor would be back by six-thirty. *Eightball* could check on Louie while Temple was stuck here waiting for the B & T express to arrive!

The line died without so much as a drone.

Temple stared at the receiver incredulously. Did Eightball just hang up once he figured the conversation was over, or had someone . . . cut . . . them off? She held down the disconnect button, then let it up again. Dead silence. How would someone pull the plug on a phone system? Where was the switchboard? Just how well *did* the catnapper know the building?

Better than you, Temple told herself. This was her first convention center job; most of the massive structure remained a mystery to her. She sat back; her stomach felt like a hollow-core door. It was not a pleasant sensation.

At six twenty-five Temple rose from her chair. She dared not show up early for her appointment with Baker and Taylor. Catching the catnapper in the act of restoration would be dangerous.

She hefted her tote bag over her shoulder and moved briskly out of the office. The high-rise heels of her shoes, a snappy pair of Weitzman sandals with multicolored straps, snapped on the hard-surface floor like firecrackers at her steps.

No sense in discretion at this late date, she told herself.

A few fluorescents shone high in the East Exhibition Hall rafters; otherwise, the exhibition floor was darkened. Booths and displays resembled huge, hunkering bears—regularly spaced but rough-silhouetted. Unpredictable.

The zebra-striped carousel figure leaped out of the darkness as she passed and the wan light tangled in its glitter-strewn mane.

Temple didn't scream but her heart was pounding faster than her shoes. What if she got there and Baker and Taylor weren't there? What if the catnapper had defaulted?

Or if she arrived and the catnapper was *still* there? Or if the catnapper was the *murderer*? Well, why not? She could think of no reason why he—she—should be, but Royal had been stabbed with a knitting needle—a woman's weapon. Now a woman had picked up the ransom money.

Baker and Taylor and bears. Baker and Taylor and bears. Baker and Taylor and—uh! Temple breathed again. She backed away from a life-size cutout of Mel Gibson that promoted a series of Mad Max novels. She remembered now. Only an apocalyptic cardboard man.

The Baker & Taylor booth was just ahead. Temple stepped more measuredly, crossing onto the carpeting that defined the B & T area as soon as possible.

The silence was stunning. Her steps had hailed on the hard floor. Now, not even an echo rattled in the steel rafters above. Light reflected from the Plexiglas sides of the Baker & Taylor cat house. Temple saw indistinguishable humps within—real, or Electra's handiwork? She edged closer, hoping, really hoping.

It was too dim to tell; her own reflection jeered back at her, an out-of-focus doppelgänger. Temple leaned her face against the transparent plastic. Come on, Baker, shake a leg! All right, Taylor, *do* something. Twitch a whisker or wash an ear. . . .

No. Nothing but a pair of pillows. A flicker of motion in the murky Plexiglas mirror. Something behind her—

Temple whirled. Something struck her, pushed her into the display case so hard she would have fallen had it not been there. Her stomach hurt, possibly because her bulky tote bag had knocked into her ribs with tremendous force. She couldn't catch her breath, and then it exploded free.

Temple scrambled away, around the booth. She saw no one now, but remembered a presence caroming by, definitely human, not feline.

The carpet continued for the length of a half-dozen booths. Temple edged along on it until she could duck behind another display piece, an island of Formica in an uncertain sea of darkness and silence and danger.

She pulled off one high heel, then another, and jammed them in her tote bag. Her hand brushed the bag's outside and stopped. Something was wrong. There was a hole in the front surface of the bag. Her fingertip circled it in the dark, the jagged place where the tough fabric had given. It was a Goldilocks kind of hole: too small for a bullet and too large for a moth, but just right for a knitting needle!

Temple dug a shoe from the bag and held it by its toe. Its heel made a better weapon than wishful thinking.

She slowly pushed herself upright against the display unit. Playing hide-and-seek as a kid, she recalled, she'd panic as the seeker passed within inches of her hiding place. She'd also believed that if she said "invisible, disappear" often enough, fast enough, she would.

Not here.

Here she'd have to find a way out. Here she'd have to gamble on where would be safe and the best route to get there.

First, no phones on the exhibit floor. Her office? Known to whoever had left the notes. The guards? Somewhere, but where at this exact minute?

All the while thinking, Temple had been creeping in her stocking feet, tote bag over her shoulder and clutched to her side like the shield it had become, her shoe heel a sharp exclamation point in her fist.

She heard nothing but her own unavoidable rustles; the rasp of her breathing. Perhaps the person had gone. But why? She was still helpless, alone, in the dark. Only not quite alone, as Chester Royal had been not quite alone just four days ago.

He had not struggled. Perhaps he hadn't expected a blow. Temple expected one every second. Knowledge is power, but this was a paralyzing knowledge, a knowledge of terror. Temple forced herself to keep moving into uncertainty.

She avoided the rear service areas. She would be expected there. As she plunged deeper into the dark of the convention center she rifled her mind for any memory of a way out. There was always the Rotunda reception area, but it offered no concealment.

A poster flapped not far away. Someone's passage had stirred it. Did he see her? Was it a he? Irrelevant. The person she sensed brushing against her had seemed large, but everyone did to her. The blow had been strong, though. Tightening the grip on her tote bag, Temple's fingertips worried the ragged interruption in the fabric. It was like picking at a scab. She could picture a thin steel needle piercing her flesh and angling up to her heart.

And then she confronted a choice: stay here in the vast outer limits of the hall, or take the corridor that had just opened up beside her. Trap or escape route? Time would tell.

Temple put her left shoulder to the corridor wall and ran along it, feet shuffling along the floor. No slips. No sounds. No panic. Delete that. No *more* panic. No, stet that. Panic!

A soft sound, gentle as a muffled cough, came from behind her. The corridor offered a left turn. She took it. Where was she, damn it!

She looked back, seeing only dim shapes, and her hip collided with an obstacle. A drinking fountain by the cool, smooth stainless steel under her hands. Temple's mouth was parched. Her tongue was sticking to her upper palate; her lips adhered to her teeth.

She moved around the fountain, then clung to the wall again. Looked back and saw a shadow growing, looked ahead to run—and saw it! The escape hatch she'd hoped for: a box on the wall.

She ran, her tote bag slapping noisily against her side. The glass door yanked open more easily than she expected. The big red bar—she had no time to squint at the instructions and get it right—was stiff, harder to move than she thought, and she had only one hand because the other held the shoe uplifted.

An overtaking shadow engulfed her just as the lever hit the backplate with a bang. Something was pressing Temple to the wall by her neck. Blood swelled and thickened to pudding in her ears. A horrible muffled clanging exploded all around. The Weitzman heel hammered down into flesh.

Footsteps were slapping in between the constant clangs. The floor throbbed. The wall behind Temple throbbed. Her head and heart throbbed in ponderous four-four time.

Then Temple was alone with the unholy clamor of the fire-alarm box, and someone wearing a billed cap was running down the hall toward her swearing vigorously.

They were the sweetest four-letter words she'd ever heard.

"I'm sorry, Miss Barr. I thought it was a prank."

Temple sat on a chair in the convention center offices while the same guard who had insulted her ancestry for several generations and in several anatomically inventive ways offered Temple a Styrofoam cup brimming with nice cold water. And ice even.

"I wondered where the guards were hiding," she croaked after a sip of glorious coolness. Her larynx sounded as if it had been operated on by a hacksaw.

Temple swung her bare feet; they never quite touched the floor no matter the chair. She stopped swinging them when C. R. Molina came in with a uniformed officer.

Sweet jumping Charles Jourdans, that *had* been Molina Temple had glimpsed during the chaos when the police had arrived (along with the fire department) only minutes after the guard had found her! She'd taken it for a postthrottling mirage, the Black Dahlia of Death or something come to carry her home, but no, here was Molina in the flesh, poured into an ebony crepe street-length number with a sweetheart neckline and copper sequins festooning opposite hip and shoulder like tarnished orchids. A vintage cocktail dress? C. R. Molina? Lieutenant Molina? On a date? The mind boggled, even if the throat was still sufficiently froggled to keep mum. Temple sighed, punchy and knowing it.

"So you're the fire. I should have known." The lieutenant sounded as crisply disapproving as ever.

"How . . . how'd you get here? So fast, I mean?" Temple knew how George Burns must feel talking after about fifteen stogies. She tried to glimpse Molina's shoes but couldn't crane her neck without wincing.

"You oughta know," Molina said. "You rang. I was off duty."

"I . . . see."

"Apparently you set off the fire alarm."

Temple nodded.

"Apparently someone attacked you."

Temple nodded.

"You'll have to talk."

"But how did you—?"

"It's not important, but when the alarm came in the fire department notified key convention center staff. Bud Dubbs immediately reported seeing you entering the building late. The police dispatcher rounded me up since this smelled of more dirty deeds at the center."

"All that hullabaloo outside was just to rescue me?" Temple was flattered. Not even the guard had been able to restrain her from peeking out front where five squad cars had squalled up under the overhead racket of a police helicopter. That had been only minutes before. Even as they spoke, the convention center and environs were getting a good going-over.

"I'm amazed myself," Molina admitted with a wry glance from under one dusky brow that still could use plucking. "Apparently you really did need rescuing."

"Apparently?" Temple squeaked, indignation forcing her voice into an inaudible soprano.

Molina eyed the adjacent desktops and finally hoisted an empty manila envelope. And something else.

"Hey," Temple protested. "Those are my best summer Stuart Weitzmans!"

"Evidence," Molina pronounced with visible pleasure. She studied the dainty shoes as a German Shepherd fancier might regard a Yorkshire Terrier, with amazed disdain. "We need to do lab work on the blood and hair on the heel. You'll get 'em back. Sometime." She jammed the shoes into the envelope.

"You don't need both of them."

"What are you going to do with one high-heeled shoe?"

"Well, don't scuff 'em."

"Now"—Molina sat on the desk beside Temple—"it's time we had a serious interrogation here."

Temple summoned her best Brenda Vacarro voice. "Not a word. Not a syllable. Not until I get to the pound and see if Midnight Louie's there and all right."

"The cat?"

"I think he's at the pound, but it's closed for the night. The attendant is leaving at seven, and they might accidentally kill him. It's happened! I won't cooperate otherwise."

"We can arrest you and take you downtown."

"Why? You won't get a word that way, either. The pound."

"This is ridiculous."

"It's my cat—kind of. Besides, he's a material witness."

"You're more material. You can talk. And you don't even know the damn cat's there."

"I don't know he isn't—and until I do I don't tell you so much as my Social Security number."

Molina's eyes narrowed to cobalt slits. "You won't *have* any social security if you give the police a hard time."

"What hard time? I'll tell you everything I know on the way there."

"I'd rather get it downtown, where it can be recorded."

Temple smiled. "Then we'd better hurry to the pound before my short-term memory starts fading out from stress."

The guard and the cop, both wearing billed caps with shiny reassuring badges on them, regarded Molina expectantly. Temple, sure of victory, took the opportunity to check out Molina's shoes—black suede pumps that didn't disgrace the vintage dress, with two-and-a-half-inch heels! The nerve of some tall women!

Molina stood, looming even higher above Temple. Despite her civilized appearance, she spoke in her usual professional monotone—flat as a stiff's EKG. "This case has been an operetta since you and that damn cat did a pas de deux with the body on the convention floor. Might as well end it with a wild-goose chase."

Temple rose, barefoot. That made Molina tower like a redwood. She consulted her watch—only 6:53, could you believe it?—and slit her eyes to match Molina's steely blue stare.

"I want to get there by seven, Lieutenant."

"Rawson," Molina instructed the uniformed officer with weary resignation. "We'll use the siren."

Temple on Ice

Temple sat alone in a tiny room equipped only with table and chairs. The sole door had a window in the upper half, smudged as if a lot of noses had been pressed against it. Chicken wire reinforced the glass on a diagonal pattern, looking like fishnet hose.

The dreariness of her surroundings matched her mood. A noisy and speedy arrival at the city pound had found the cupboard bare of Midnight Louie. The surly attendant swore a big black cat had been there, but the indicated cage was empty. Temple believed in her heart of hearts that Louie had been prematurely put to sleep, even though the attendant swore no "terminations" had occurred that night. Whatever the reason, Louie wasn't there.

Temple and Molina had both looked like prize fools, something Temple felt far too depressed to worry about. Maybe Molina wasn't.

As the detective entered the room her impressive brows collided in a frown, reminding Temple that publicly embarrassing a police lieutenant was not a good way to preface an interrogation.

Molina had vanished without a word after their arrival at the police station. Now she again wore her khaki poplin skirt and blazer. The warm interrogation room quickly encouraged her to doff the jacket, revealing a short-sleeved red polyester blouse with a V-neck, in the style called a camp shirt.

"Do I need a lawyer or something?" Temple asked nervously.

"You're not being charged with anything," Molina said. "There's no statute against stupidity."

"Are public servants supposed to resort to name-calling?"

"So sue me."

Molina sat across the scar-topped Formica table from Temple, who felt reduced to an unhappy twelve-year-old called in for a lecture by the big-girl camp counselor. She swung a nervous foot.

She'd been allowed to dump off Lorna's book bag and grab a pair of shoes at the Circle Ritz on the way back to the station. At least this was just an interrogation and she hadn't been fingerprinted and put into jailhouse baggies.

"Why were you coming in so late at the convention center?" Molina asked first.

"I had lots of messages to catch up on."

"Like this one?" Molina produced the catnapper's second note, mounted on a larger piece of paper so no one had to touch it.

"How—?"

"The officers went over your desk while we were busy visiting the local pound. When a citizen is stalked through a public building after hours and apparently attacked, we investigate—seriously."

"What do you mean by 'apparently' attacked?"

"Nothing more than careful police phrasing. The guard

saw someone running away, although our officers found no one. I presume your story will corroborate this fact. So will an analysis of the human tissue samples on the heel of your shoe."

"Do you suppose—?"

"What?"

"Did I actually . . . hurt someone?"

"Not fatally," Molina said with little amusement. "Why would someone attack you?"

"Like Everest—I was there?" Temple tried.

"You were there because of this note. Mind explaining it?"

"Yes, I do. It's a sensitive matter."

"Cats are sensitive?"

"These two are not just cats. They're corporate mascots."

"Right now they're in the middle of a murder investigation, as are you. Tell me about it."

There was nothing even faintly cajoling about Molina's tone, just pure unleavened command. So Temple did.

Molina was not a particularly encouraging listener, but seen across the table and judged as a person rather than an official, and in view of her startling off-duty transformation, C. R. Molina struck Temple as human for the first time.

Her heavy almost blue-black hair, worn in an ear-covering blunt cut more serviceable than stylish, grew wispily around her hairline, an effect that might have been softening had Molina not brushed it brutally back from her face. Her strong brows were unplucked, but after all that was the current practice among fashion models; and yet Temple doubted Molina had noticed. She wore no detectable makeup, except for a wine-colored lipstick that added color yet didn't even flirt with being seductive.

She wore little jewelry: only a class ring on her right second finger, which indicated she had lost weight since getting it. Even seated, Molina was rangy and competent-looking; not awkward, but without fillips of expression or gesture to distract from her grim business. Until tonight,

Temple would have bet that C. R. Molina had neither steady boyfriend nor cat. Her bare left hand said she wasn't presently married even though she must be pushing forty.

"What?" Temple suddenly realized she'd been inventing a life for a person whose job was to probe her own situation.

"I said," Molina repeated evenly, "what made you and this Adcock woman think you could possibly handle this cat kidnapping by yourselves?"

"The Baker & Taylor people weren't sure at first that it *was* a kidnapping. They hoped that the cats had escaped during the hubbub of setting-up and—scared by all the noise—were hiding out somewhere. There's a lot of building to hide out in."

"I know," Molina said, "and so should you after tonight. So you got the first note—and I want that one, too—then hired this O'Rourke to see who picked up the money. How'd he do?"

Temple thought it was mean of Molina to harp on what she'd been through as an interrogation tactic. "You know Eightball?"

Molina nodded and shrugged simultaneously and slightly. "Harmless."

Not exactly what Temple wanted to hear about her chosen private operative. "Eightball called me earlier tonight. Said he'd trailed the pickup person to the Las Vegas Hilton, then lost her."

"Her?"

"I was surprised, too. Maybe she was a shill?"

"She was an aiding and abetting shill, if so. You gave up the money with no guarantee of the cats' return?"

"The nappers didn't leave a calling card. When I got the second note, I figured they were playing fair, so I went down to the exhibit to wait for the return of Baker and Taylor."

"Instead the murderer came back for a second engagement. Is that what you figure?"

"If you say so, Lieutenant. And he did jab at me with a knitting needle."

Molina's luxurious eyebrows rose a millimeter. "Explain 'he' and 'knitting needle.' How could you know in the dark?"

Temple sipped the diet cola she'd been given. Her throat felt bruised. Maybe she'd been wrong to refuse medical attention.

"That's a good question. I thought it was a 'he' on instinct—pure, blind instinct. The person was bigger than I am, but most women are, too. I just had a sense of being up against muscle mass."

Molina actually cracked a smile. "Men move differently, even in the dark."

"And the needle—well, when my bag got skewered, that was the first thing I thought of."

"Bag? Show me."

Temple dragged the tote bag up from the floor. "What else could have caused that hole?"

In the light, the puncture's ragged edge defined a perfect circle the size of a number five knitting needle. Temple shivered.

"I'll need the bag for evidence, too."

"Oh, no! I can't live without this bag. I've practically got my next of kin in here."

Molina shook her head. "Empty it. We'll get you some manila envelopes to take your things home in."

Much as Temple loathed exposing the contents of her tote—her life, virtually—to the lieutenant, the word "home" had a nice, hopeful ring to it.

She dredged out her makeup bag and schedule organizer, both the size of bantam chickens; some crumpled Dairy Queen napkins, her car keys and wallet; three breath mints, about fifteen outdated dry cleaning coupons, a small screwdriver, a wad of tissues; three packets of diet salad dressing, a sewing kit shaped like a strawberry, and assorted miscellanea.

"You planning a trip to the bush?" Molina wondered.

"Listen, this stuff saved my life when the killer took a stab at me."

"Okay. You said it. The killer. What does the killing of Chester Royal have to do with the kidnapping of two cats?"

"Maybe the killer lurks around the convention center every night getting whoever shows up—like the Phantom of the Opera—and I happened to have a rendezvous with the kidnapper and the cats."

"The convention center will love that publicity angle, Barr. The cats never showed. You realize what this means?"

"*They*'ve been gotten by the killer?"

"There never was any intention of returning the cats. It was a ruse to get you onto the convention floor, alone, in the dark."

"That's silly, who would . . . ?" Temple tried again. "That means the killer . . . Me? Why?"

Molina sighed. "I hate to contradict my own instincts, but it's likely that the killer thinks you know too much."

"Me? Just because I stumbled over the body?"

"I think your size fives have been stumbling over a lot more than that these last few days. Bud Dubbs tells me you've been running around on errands of an unusually vague nature, even for you."

"It's my job to keep informed."

"It's the killer's job to see that no one gets too well informed about the murder. After hearing that the murderer used the cats to lure you onto the convention floor tonight, I think that's why the cats were taken in the first place."

"By the murderer? As a . . . diversion?"

"Yes."

"That's dumb. No one knew about them being missing except the B & T people and me. What kind of a diversion is a state secret?"

"No one knew only because you and Emily Adcock were so damn good at covering it up. That's why the ransom was small; nobody wanted the money. What was wanted was a distraction, which you prevented, meanwhile running around and buttonholing everybody and his first cousin about the murder."

"You think I know something?"

"I hate to admit it, but yes. And you probably don't know what yourself, which would be truer to form. You really have a knack for screwing up an investigation."

"Why blame me? It *was* my job to talk to the people involved and I am in a better position to learn the inside story than any police representative."

"It's your funeral," Molina said.

"I see what you mean. Have you evidence pointing to a certain suspect?"

"No." Molina was even more sober than usual. "The key to the crime is motive, and that leaves little evidence—or little obvious evidence."

"Chester Royal was a fiend. Everyone had a motive—his three top writers, his editor ex-wife, his ex-assistant and the current Reynolds/Chapter/Deuce PR director; even, I suppose, his old buddy lawyer," Temple enumerated.

"I know about them," said Molina. "Except for the lawyer."

"Will you tell me what you found out about the Royal malpractice case?"

"You first."

"Earnest Jaspar. Funny old guy from Minnesota. He's staying at the Hilton. Chester had him on hand in case an uncertain author like Mavis Davis needed shoring up. Anyway, Jaspar defended Royal in the malpractice case in Illinois in the fifties: a woman died on his operating table during the course of an illegal abortion her family swore she would have never agreed to. But if you've looked up the case, you know all that."

"Not the details. The press in those days was discreet about abortion scandals. I'm having copies of the court documents sent, but it'll take a while. We *have* been working this case over a weekend, you know, on top of everything else."

Temple figured "everything else" meant her—and missing cats. "Weekend—has it only been a weekend?" She suddenly felt down-to-her-toes beat, as if it would be too much of an effort to say her name.

"I suppose your fevered brain has concluded that a survivor of the long-dead woman is seeking vengeance."

"I don't know if I even thought that far ahead. I just think that a malpractice case in the victim's past is pretty interesting, don't you?"

"Victims usually have a lot of interesting incidents in their pasts. But that malpractice case was decades ago. Pretty farfetched."

"Where is it written that murderers have to strike while their fire is hot? It could be some disgruntled victim of medical foul play. Why not?"

Molina shook her head. "Why *now*, rather?"

"You mean, why wait all this time?"

"Right. We're talking forty years. We're also talking a senior citizen slayer by now."

Temple thought a long, stymied moment, then looked up. "It would explain the knitting needle."

Molina shook her head again. "Sure, a Grandma Moses killer. You're getting punchy. I'll have an officer drive you home." Molina went to the door, opened it, and issued some instructions before coming back to stand over Temple. "I had your car driven back to your apartment, so you'll be ready to go on your dubious errands tomorrow."

"Hey, thanks. That was nice."

A policeman entered with a sheaf of manila envelopes. Temple began shoveling the evicted contents of her tote bag into them. She stood up, her legs feeling rubbery. If only her high heels held up, Temple was sure she'd be fine. Molina saw her to the interrogation room door. "You think of anything, you tell me—immediately."

"Sure." Even if it meant she was cooperating with a . . . Temple looked down and giggled—a flatfoot.

But just outside the door she turned, the manila envelopes clutched to her chest.

"Of course—the sign!" It hit her meandering brain like

a flash of Flamingo Hilton pink neon. "What if Chester Royal was killed for medical, not editorial, reasons? What if the sign on the body didn't mean STET, as in a copy direction, but STET as in . . . short for stethoscope?"

Cool Hand Louie

Only one thing on earth can outperform Midnight Louie when he is doing a solo jazz riff for the ladies in some lonely back street.

That is the siren of a police vehicle. Usually I scram when I hear one coming and that is exactly what I do when I am fleeing my home away from homicide—the pound. I hightail it in the opposite direction.

How I accomplish this unheard-of feat of bustin' out is a tale in its own right. Let us face it, folks, the survival statistics for those of my ilk in such an establishment are nil minus zero.

However common are those greeting cards depicting a quintet of kittens in a basket, gold-fish bowl or some other sentimental environment suitable for framing on kitchen walls, the harsh facts of feline life are that four of those five little sugarpusses will not celebrate their first birthday.

I have not reached my state of ripeness by ignoring odds, even if one is inclined to that sort of idiocy in a city like Las Vegas. And the odds here are that Miss Temple Barr has a lot more on her mind right now than the state of my skin.

One thing my *tête-á-trois* with Baker and Taylor makes self-evident. Miss Temple Barr is right: the napper of the duo with the withered ears is the perpetrator who edited out the old guy I stumbled over on the ABA convention floor so few days and so many lifetimes ago. I decide to take destiny by the flintlock and spring myself to share my information with a larger world. It is the story of my lives: I know more than is good for me and someone is out to get me.

First I size up the villainous attendant whom it has been my ill luck to encounter. This large-eared personage is slovenly as well as slothful; it occurs that I might use this weakness to my advantage. The plan requires risking my second most prized member, but I have not survived this long without a streak of daring-do in my soul.

When Jug-ears arrives with my evening swill, I manage to insert my glorious extremity, which is large, luxuriant and bushy, if I say so myself, into the frame of the cell door.

It takes all of my not insignificant self-control to avoid expressing outrage at the resulting competition between a rock and a hard place. They do not call it the "slammer" for nothing. Suffice it to say that the cell-door latch is not fully caught.

Once Jug-ears continues on his errands, I bat the cell door ajar, bound down to the floor and accept the catcalls of my amazed peers (whom I would spring were not their cell latches too tightly sprung, and their tails too scrawny to cushion any closing blows).

The pavement is still damp from ablutions of a repellent nature as I commence to wend my way far from this unhappy place. An unguarded gate or carelessly unlocked window always awaits the machinations of a fellow with my aptitude for going places, and a stairway of carelessly placed furniture or boxes usually leads me right to it. Once free, I hunker down outside to await the cover of twilight.

The night is warm and dark as I streak through it, invisible and invincible. I expect to make the Circle Ritz before Miss Temple Barr.

As I ramble I contemplate problems yet to come. For one thing, I know the culprit's identity, yet have a long, unshakable tradition behind me (besides my tail) of keeping mum. Yet I am averse to keeping my dainty doll in the dark. A little knowledge is a dangerous thing, some high churchman-type pundit once said, I believe, and Miss Temple Barr knows just little enough to get into big trouble.

So my feet fly over the tepid pavements, my mind churning ways of alerting my little doll without blowing my cover. Even as I ponder the future, I cannot help getting a warm, fuzzy feeling as I dwell on my triumphal escape from the Needles of Death. It is better than a magic act.

Especially my parting gesture. As I bound past, I give the cell door a one-pawed punch. It slams fast in one blow, and I have single-handedly created the LV pound's sole locked-room mystery.

They can scratch their heads over it for days (and they will, given the parasite population tolerated in that fleabag), but my lips are sealed and sent COD.

What we have here is a failure to communicate.

The Name of the Game Is . . . Murder

The pink neon clock in Temple's kitchen announced an incredible hour—ten P.M. Only. Temple's mind and body floated somewhere on the dark side of midnight about sixteen light-years from reality.

She dropped the bulky manila envelopes on her kitchen counter, unmindful when her belongings spewed out like vomit. She'd already picked up her kitchen receiver to dial the penthouse.

"Yeah, home. Just questioning. A *long* story. Oh, Electra, I'm afraid Louie's gone for good! Sure. I'd love company."

Temple had changed into her favorite leopard-print sleepshirt before her doorbell rang—she loved having an apartment with a real doorbell, a melodic caroling that issued from a rank of long bronze pipes. Now it sounded like a dirge.

The lush tropical pattern of Electra's most Hawaiian muumuu vibrated outside her door, but the landlady's chameleon hair was sprayed jet-black, as if she'd known mourning was in order.

When Temple stared, Electra was quick to reassure her. "The hair's for Lorna Fennick's memorial service tomorrow—or rather Chester Royal's. Don't worry; just temporary."

"I'd forgotten about that."

"For you." Electra offered the glass of scotch she clutched.

"Thanks, but I'm not up to it, even after an interrogation at Headquarters. Great hot-shot detective I make, retreating to a tumbler of Crystal Light when the chips are down."

"How down are they, honey?"

"Low-down. I've been stalked through the convention center and grilled by Lieutenant Molina and it looks like Midnight Louie has been—Put Away."

"How horrible!"

"For a while tonight, I never thought I'd see this place again. Poor Louie must have felt the same before they—"

Electra was looking at Temple strangely. In fact, Electra wasn't looking at her at all, which was odd given the emotional fireworks that Temple was providing.

"Dear, what's that on your coffee table?"

Temple glanced over her shoulder into the dimly lit room. Reflected street light shafts slid eerily across the rippled ceiling in shades of aqua and Mercurochrome. The furniture sat hunch-shouldered, downcast somehow. A foothill of silhouettes tumbled across the coffee table's usually sleek glass surface.

"Some novels a woman at the ABA gave me. Want any free books? I'm not in the mood to read medical thrillers."

"Not the books. That thing beside the books."

Temple looked again. "I must have thrown a purse down. I don't remember. I've had an awful day—"

Electra was brushing by, not a hard thing for Electra to do—her capacious muumuus always impinged in passing.

She hit the living room light switch, making everybody blink, including the black cat that reclined Sphinx-like on the coffee table in the sudden spotlight of the ceiling fixture, its hindquarters sheltered by a Time-Life bag and its forepaws splayed upon a tumbled tower of books.

"Louie!" Temple squealed.

He yawned and licked a forepaw.

"Louie!" Temple hurled herself between the coffee table and the love seat, reminded of a similar moment in pursuit of this particular cat.

Midnight Louie was more amenable to supposed capture now; at least he allowed Temple to stroke his head and regard him with the unqualified wonder generally reserved for newborn infants.

"How did you get in?" Temple cooed. "How did you get out? If you ever *were* in the pound—"

Louie had mastered the art of looking wise and keeping mum.

"I wonder how long he's been lounging here while I've been worried sick about him?" Temple mused.

"Long enough to sink a few fangs into those books." Electra deposited the scotch on the coffee table and shuddered for effect. "A creepy bunch of covers. I hate medical trappings like scalpels and surgeon's masks."

"They sell books; some people eat this stuff up. Look, this was written by a nurse." Temple handed over a Mavis Davis tome; Electra examined it dubiously.

"Where? In Transylvania? Now that you've got your kitty cat back I'll toddle along. You should be safe here. Matt fixed your French door lock. M.L. won't get out of it again, and I doubt anybody will get in."

"Where is Matt?" Temple glanced up from admiring Midnight Louie. The hour was late and she looked a mess, but it wouldn't hurt to thank a good neighbor.

"Working." Louie stretched and ambled along the tabletop over the piled paperbacks. "Watch out!" Electra yelled. "He's trying to drink my scotch."

Louie's muzzle was indeed immersed to the whiskers in the low-ball glass.

"Doesn't the ice bother him?" Electra wondered.

"It *is* hot." Temple absently excused Louie's depravity, even as he lifted his damp jowls from the glass. "And he did have a harrowing experience. I think."

Louie deserted the coffee table for the kitchen, where he lofted himself atop the counter to nose among the manila envelopes and their erstwhile contents.

"Watch out, he's in the garbage," Electra warned genially. Obviously her contact lenses were out for the night. "You'd better rest now. The service tomorrow is at ten sharp. Should I give you a wake-up call?"

Temple nodded as she showed Electra out, then returned to the coffee table to survey the damage. Louie had really been taking a bite out of the books, she thought, studying the perforated glossy covers. Apparently people were not the only ones to eat these thrillers up. The major victim had been an Owen Tharp title, *The Origin*, which featured a striking-snake-coiled stethoscope. Perhaps glimpsing this image earlier had subconsciously led Temple to the STETHOscope connection she'd proposed to Molina.

The Origin's subject matter certainly wasn't appetizing: a fiendish physician cloning an army of body-part donors from his unknowing patients. Louie had taken critical exception to it, no doubt, for he had gnawed the all-caps title until it resembled a theatrical marquee spotlight sign that was missing several bulbs; only the —E O——IN were still legible.

The cat thumped down from the countertop.

"You're trouble," she told him in mock disgust. "Not only are your whereabouts usually unknown, when you *are* visible you muck up everything in sight. Think you can manage to spend a quiet night at home for a change?"

Louie accompanied Temple to the front door, where she noticed a brassy new chain lock and spent two minutes trying to make the end piece slide into the groove. Then she gave up and stumbled to the bedroom.

She slept like a kitten, waking briefly now and then to make sure she was warm and limp and somewhere safe. She sensed Midnight Louie as a lump at her feet, then at her side, then gone, then back again.

She started up once—thought she saw a man standing in the filtered night light of her bedroom. Her heart pounded as her mind juxtaposed two unrelated but wrenching events. He might be a still-stalking murderer . . . or the ghost of Max Kinsella. The lighter blurs that were her windows absorbed the illusion. She slept even harder after that.

She awoke again, unsure whether it was late or early. Notions and images floated in her mind, multicolored motes in a golden eye, darting away just as they became detectable. Book covers, words, type, letters, sounds, images. They made a revolving ABA exhibition in her head; through it all threaded a stethoscope and a knitting needle. Butterflies of the brain. And ladybugs. *Ladybug, Ladybug. The lady is bugged and Pennyroyal presses grapes . . . bee's knees and Kankakee and number five knitting needles and Tweedledee and Tweedledum, two of a kind and who's behind*—Temple netted a few, then a few more butterflies from the brainstorm swirling around her, then a few more . . . and then she knew.

Temple switched on the bedside lamp. Louie stared accusingly from the foot of her bed, his emerald-green eyes bisected by black vertical slits. Temple blinked at the sudden brightness as she paged through the phone book, dialed the number, told the man who answered what she wanted.

It took a long time, but C. R. Molina was finally on the line, sounding as if she were speaking from Alpha Centauri.

"It's Temple Barr."

"Do you know what time it is? I sleep, too."

"No, but it doesn't matter. You said you wanted to know—immediately. I know what I *know* now."

"You know what you know . . ."

"Louie told me. He's back and he's okay. Boy, is he

okay. Come to the memorial service for Chester Royal at the Lover's Knot Wedding Chapel at ten A.M. tomorrow, and I'll show you."

"You mean today, damn it."

"Okay; today, damn it. Just come." Then Temple told the homicide lieutenant exactly what she wanted her to bring, besides a few policemen.

Electra had outdone herself.

The chapel's latticework nuptial archway peeked through a cloud of somber crepe. The soft-sculpture people filling the back pews had been attired in tasteful touches of black—arm bands on the gentlemen; veils or hats on the ladies.

Massed sprays of gladioli and other fleshy blooms, courtesy of Sam's Funeral Home, looked fresh from last night's wake and broadcast a torpid, mournful odor.

Temple wore a black linen suit and her Beverly Feldman black leather spikes with furtive touches of jet. An onyx choker circled her neck to hide the beginnings of a bruise. She felt a bit like a heavy metal songstress, albeit tired to her toes.

On the other side of the chapel doors stood Lorna Fennick, wearing a brown dress that underlined her muddy coloring. Lorna's face had thinned and tautened since Temple had first met the PR woman. Only her eyes moved when she nervously studied the assembled soft-sculpture forms, as if expecting them to do something inappropriate. She herself came to sudden life, however, when Reynolds/Chapter/Deuce executive Raymond Avenour entered with an unknown woman on his arm. Lorna escorted them to the front with painful deference. They didn't even acknowledge the forever-silent fellow mourners, as if used to captive audiences.

Temple observed the scene with an odd detachment. Mavis Davis arrived, her permed fleece of hair covered by a skimpy black lace mantilla, her eyes anxious above half-moons of dark maroon. The woman's glance darted around the chapel and finally spotted the posed mute figures, finding nothing to linger upon even in their harmless if slightly loony presence.

Rowena Novak came in accompanied by Earnest Jaspar—that combination startled Temple. But then Rowena had been Chester Royal's wife. Likely she'd met the friend that had outlasted all of Chester's wives. Perhaps the reason for that longevity could be found in the shameful secrets of the Gilhooley trial. Guilt cements strange fellowships.

At ten minutes to ten, Matt Devine materialized from the breezeway to the Circle Ritz. He had procured a black suit somewhere and took his place at the organ with a properly subdued air. He looked gorgeous in black.

Temple was still contemplating Matt's unexpected participation when Lanyard Hunter arrived, his patrician voice preceding him as Lorna went to meet him.

"A wedding chapel! Ironic—like holding Chester's memorial service in a neighborhood bar he'd been kicked out of repeatedly."

Hunter's silver pompadour brushed the crepe swagging the top of the arch as he stepped under it and drew Lorna's arm through his. She led him to the front.

The next arrival surprised Temple. Claudia Esterbrook, licking her lips nervously, wearing a blatant red suit and her usual mask of impatience. She nodded to those already assembled and sat sullenly, as though obligated to be here. Temple wondered why.

Owen Tharp came last. He briskly waved away the solicitous Lorna, nodded to Temple—the only one who did—then strode halfway down the short aisle. He deliberately sat next to one of Electra's mute congregation, a well-stuffed matron whose wide-brimmed hat today trailed black satin roses and midnight veiling with bridal panache.

Temple consulted her watch. The little hand was on ten and the big hand was edging toward twelve. Where was Lieutenant Molina? Temple caught Electra's eye at the front of the house . . . er, chapel. This was not a theater, after all, and Temple was no longer doing PR for the Guthrie. That didn't mean she couldn't stage-manage a bit. So she eyed Electra and tapped her wristwatch with a forefinger.

Stall, the gesture said, you know.

Electra knew—not what was going to happen, but that something more than a memorial service and a morose scent was in the air. Still, she had all the relevant press releases stacked on her lectern and was prepared to ruminate long and loudly on Chester Royal's life and death as well as the nature of things physical and spiritual.

Totally unexpected, the last guest ambled through the ever-open breezeway door: Midnight Louie, his coat freshly groomed to its fullest, most funereal glory, his white whiskers spanking clean after a morning repast of shrimp.

But where was Molina?

The long hand ticked the twelve and there was no postponing the moment of truth *and* consequences.

Electra nodded solemnly to Matt, who coaxed a series of doleful sounds from the Lowrey's liquid throat. Louie deserted the vicinity of the organ for Temple's ankles. Temple didn't recognize the melody, probably some Michael Jackson ditty played at thirty-three-and-a-third speed, but it was ripe with ponderous chords.

She swallowed a smile. From the back of the house—the chapel, that is—the dummies' showy black was reminiscent of a mob funeral.

The chapel had never held so many living spectators. Las Vegas weddings were famed for their lack of encumbrances—waiting periods, blood tests, expensive attendants and witnesses who might not forever hold their peace. The ceiling fans spun with syrupy laissez-faire. The room was warming up with the crowd and the day, or maybe Temple was just nervous about what she was about to do.

Or about Molina's continuing absence . . . didn't the woman know the meaning of the word "important"?

"We are gathered today," Electra began, "in this city of

extravagance, to honor a life that has not so much ended as evolved onto another plane."

Heads swiveled toward each other at this overoptimistic invocation. No one present was eager to imagine Chester Royal as evolved in any respect, especially if it meant his survival, his transportation via some unearthly airline that might return any residue of his noxious personality back to earth.

"He is not gone," Electra declaimed, "he is . . . removed."

Temple glanced at Matt. He had spun away from the organ and was watching Electra with polite wonder. Well, Electra was on the money. Someone had "removed" Chester Royal, all right.

"We must not mourn," she continued vehemently. "Even now Chester Royal may be floating in the ether of our vaguest thoughts, a constant presence seeking a welcoming place. As you think of him, so he shall be with you all. He was a man to remember."

With loathing, Temple thought, imagining the unspoken sentiments of the gathered "mourners."

"An . . . endlessly affectionate human being."

Five ex-wives.

"A brilliant entrepreneur of art and business."

Who blended the crassest concerns of both into a mediocre hash.

"He always had time to consider a friend."

And how to whittle a friend's ego to matchsticks.

"A man responsible for the success of many beyond their wildest dreams."

Their wildest dreams included killing him.

"Who asked nothing for himself."

But others' total surrender.

"And whom we shall all miss and mourn deeply."

Even as we celebrate our freedom.

"And whom we will never forget."

Until we can get out of this hot-plate town and home to business-as-usual. . . .

Electra paused to gauge her audience's numbness level. She eyed Temple, who looked at her watch, the door and shook her head. Electra forged on. "And now, ladies and gentlemen, I would like to discuss the healing power of crystals for those troubled by grief."

A stifled groan came from someone among the congregation. It acted as a secret signal. Both of the chapel's outer doors whisked open. Light flooded in like a blare of trumpets as Molina and three uniformed officers entered the back of the chapel.

Temple rushed over. "Have you got it?"

Molina flourished a handful of limp fax paper. Temple reached for it. Molina wasn't about to let go.

"Why don't you just tell me what's going on?" the detective suggested sweetly, with rock salt under the sugar.

"Because if I'm wrong, you won't end up looking like a fool again."

The slick papers strained between their hands. Then Molina let go and Temple had sole custody. Hurriedly she glanced through them. Aha! The one she was sure would be there!

Heads had turned to note the new arrivals, so Temple beckoned the emissaries of the law aside.

"Everybody who's involved in the case is here," she told Molina in a stage whisper. Temple nodded to Midnight Louie, who had leaped onto a pew to sit beside a well-stuffed gentleman in a top hat. "Even my missing, er, associate, who discovered the body in the first place."

"Everyone except the catnapper," Molina said.

"Even the catnapper."

"Good. I wouldn't want to miss booking anybody on a major charge like that," the detective said sourly. "Can we get on with it? I'm tired and I want to go back to headquarters and do paperwork."

Temple nodded at Electra, who finished up with a rhetorical flourish about surviving personalities, channeling, loving thy neighbor and the benefits of brown rice.

Temple's footsteps sounded ominous on the aisle's

white tile flooring as she approached the front. Whispers rose among the living members of the congregation. One of these nice people had tried to kabob and throttle her just last night. Molina and one officer followed her. The other two policemen stationed themselves at the chapel's two exits.

Electra faded to the sidelines as discreetly as a woman of her size and personality could manage, as Temple reached the front and turned. "I have some final words to say about Chester Royal," she said. "I'm sure that none of you want to leave Las Vegas with his murder unsolved."

This statement, expectedly, brought no response.

"A sign bearing four letters was found upon the body. Only the murderer, the police and myself, who was the first person upon the scene, would know that."

Temple produced Exhibit A from Electra's lectern, a placard she had prepared that morning, and held it up.

"You all know the meaning of this term 'stet,' with the possible exception of Mr. Jaspar." He nodded gratefully. "Let it stand." She paused. "Someone did not want to let Chester Royal stand. Someone struck him down. That's what editors say when they delete type, they 'strike it out' when they turn it into dead matter. And another thing some of you may not know. The murder weapon was an old-fashioned steel knitting needle."

Temple lifted an example off the podium. This time gasps greeted her display.

"It was used by someone who knew where and how to thrust it, someone with medical knowledge. Almost all of you had the access to that knowledge, through your association with Chester Royal, if nothing else."

"Wait a minute," said Raymond Avenour. "If this is a round-'em-up and declare-'em-guilty session, I respectfully withdraw. I know nothing of medicine, and little of Chester Royal personally. I'm here representing my publishing house, period, not to attend an amateur detective melodrama."

"I am an amateur," Temple agreed, "but a very real

police detective is present to take matters in hand if necessary. And I have genuine evidence to present."

"A mock-up of a sign and a knitting needle you bought in the five-and-dime?" Claudia Esterbrook said scathingly. "Get real."

"I borrowed this needle," Temple said, "from our esteemed . . . officiator. And whether this is the needle that killed Chester Royal doesn't matter. It was always a symbolic weapon anyway."

"Symbolic?" That was Molina, sounding disgusted.

Temple nodded. "I assumed, rather sexistly, that the use of a knitting needle indicated a woman perpetrator. No matter that anyone could easily smuggle it past the guards onto the convention floor. Never mind that, properly directed under the ribs and up into the vital organs, it could be swiftly fatal. Discount the fact that the bleeding would be internal and therefore discreet, or that the eccentric choice of weapon would baffle the police."

Molina started to say something, but Temple pushed on.

"Some of you may not have known that Chester Royal was a practicing physician long before he was a nonfiction writer, a packager, an editor and the publisher of an imprint."

The right faces showed apparent surprise: Lorna Fennick's, Claudia Esterbrook's, Mavis Davis's—all the women in the case except Rowena Novak, who sat as if carved from headstone granite. She knew, she had always known.

"How did you know, Mr. Hunter? And you did, didn't you?"

"Lanyard," he corrected with oily grace and a condescending smile. "From my many medical masquerades. Chester showed a knowledge far beyond the enthusiast's. I can smell doctors; I make quite a game at cocktail parties out of correctly identifying their specialties."

"And Chester Royal, how did he react to your amazing ability?"

"He was not amused." Hunter glanced rather fondly at

Lorna Fennick, who had come to sit beside him. "Lorna was his assistant then, and quite innocently ran across his medical degree stuffed in a drawer. Chester was furious."

Temple turned to Lorna with new insight. "So he fired you because you knew too much."

Lorna nodded reluctantly. "I was ready to leave anyway. I'd had enough of his manipulations. He hated me because I managed not only to stay on at the parent company, but achieve a responsible position there."

Temple saw another light. "And *you* tipped Lanyard Hunter off to Royal's Achilles' heel!"

"I didn't 'tip him off,' Temple. I complained bitterly to him about Chester's unfair treatment. We were seeing each other, though Chester didn't know it. Lanyard had just submitted an autobio on his medical charade. Chester said he wanted to buy it, in the meantime trying to convince Lanyard to suppress it and try fiction instead."

Hunter nodded. "When Lorna told me how angry Chester had been at her discovery of the medical degree, I knew he had something to hide."

"So that's how you became a favored author—you blackmailed him."

"Nothing so obvious. He knew that I knew and walked more softly, that's all. I didn't know anything, other than that he feared something in his past. That was enough to give me an edge; like anyone in an author-eat-author world, I used it."

On the other side of the aisle, Owen Tharp snorted derisively. "You ever consider simply writing well as a method of career advancement?"

"Why?" Hunter shot back. "That never mattered that much to Royal, or he wouldn't have put out so many of your books."

Temple watched the infant ghostwritten Hunter/Tharp collaboration combust before her very eyes in a puff of surly smoke.

"I can't believe what was going on at Pennyroyal Press," Mavis Davis said. "It was every man for himself and exploit the women. I'm glad no more of my books will appear under that awful imprint."

"Nor will any others." Avenour suddenly spoke up. "I'll deny it if anyone leaks the news, but R/C/D is deep-sixing the imprint. I'd advise Mr. Hunter and Mr. Tharp to find new publishers."

"What about my sales figures!" Hunter blurted out. He got no reply.

"I've been very patient," Lieutenant Molina put in, shifting her weight.

Temple held up her palms to quell the objections. "Just a few more points." She turned back to the audience. "Certainly Chester Royal was unique in the ill will he managed to foster through Pennyroyal Press—but his murder had little to do with authorial or editorial ego, or business exploitation, or publishing, period. Which, of course, is why it happened at the ABA, where everyone—even the police—would presume that it did."

"What about the 'STET' you said was written on the body?" Owen Tharp asked.

"That 'stet' cuts both ways. It was a decoy to underline the publishing connection, but the killer was cocky enough to make a play on words at the same time. It's also an abbreviation of the doctor's most notable prop, the stethoscope."

Lorna Fennick was frowning. "Temple, you've got a megacreative imagination. Even if it implied a stethoscope, so what? Everybody knew Chester Royal put out medical thrillers, so that leads right back to publishing."

"Not . . . necessarily. This killer was sending a message, one that had festered for a long, long time. The knitting needle was more than a crude attempt to focus suspicion on one of the many women in the case, such as Mavis Davis, or Rowena Novak, or even you, Lorna, because the killer knew of Chester's misogyny. The knitting needle was as symbolic as the 'stet.' A knitting needle especially fit the crime for which he was paying with his life."

Exit a Murderer

"This is ridiculous!"

Lieutenant Molina stood with her fists on her hips, her dark head lowered like an angry bull's. She looked ready to close down Temple's act.

"A minute! I promise. Just a minute." Temple snatched up the knitting needle. "This is not just a knitting needle. It did something else in times past, something awful."

"My God . . ." The voice was low and shaken. Rowena Novak was burying her face in her hands. Finally she looked up at Lieutenant Molina.

"She's right. I never thought of it, and it was so obvious! Chester hid his medical past because of a malpractice suit. He'd performed an illegal abortion on a woman years ago, in the early fifties. In those days there was no safe alternative to unwanted pregnancy except the filthy back-alley abortionist, or homemade methods like coat hangers and knitting needles."

Molina grew stern. "You didn't mention your ex-husband's former profession—or legal difficulties—when I interviewed you."

"It happened nearly forty years ago. Chester was decades removed from it when I married him. I forgot about it, that's all. Not even the knitting needle reminded me."

"The knitting needle was a message from one killer to another," Temple said. "Chester's death was an execution."

"Why do we have to be here?" Avenour asked. "If this has nothing to do with publishing?"

Temple held her temper. "The murder has nothing to do with publishing, but the *murderer* does."

"Then you're still saying it's one of us," Claudia Esterbrook said angrily.

Temple eyed them all. "Yes. I'm saying it's one of you."

"And you know *who* it is." Lanyard Hunter's silver head had lifted like a hound's scenting the air.

"I know who it is."

Silence held. Someone cleared a throat.

Temple had them, her whole audience, including Electra on the sidelines and Matt, who completely abandoned the organ keyboard to turn around and watch. Even Midnight Louie had paused in his grooming, his black hind leg slung over his shoulder like a shotgun.

"Get it over with! Tell us!" Mavis Davis burst out nervously.

"I have to show you—and the police. Mr. Jasper, except for the Pennyroyal authors, you don't know these people?"

The elderly lawyer shook his head.

"But you knew Chester from college days. You knew him better than anyone?"

"Longer, anyway," Jaspar said with lawyerly qualification.

"Then tell them about the Gilhooley case."

Jaspar leaned forward to adjust his body on the hard pew. His eyes grew watery and reflective.

"I lost the case. You always remember the ones you lose.

Of course, defending an obstetrician/gynecologist against malpractice charges involving an illegal abortion in the fifties was fool's work. I was practicing law in Albert Lea, and I knew Chester, so I did it. For some damn-fool reason, maybe money, Chester aborted one Mary Ellen Gilhooley, who was pregnant with her eighth or ninth child. I can't remember. They had big families then. Anyway, she hemorrhaged. It couldn't be stopped and she died. I didn't get Chester off. He lost his license to practice medicine for doing an illegal abortion. He never blamed me. It was the breaks."

"Did he do it just for the money, Mr. Jaspar? Several women here have told me that Chester was pathologically hostile to women. Why would he have risked his license to help a woman—or is that when he became bitter?"

"Chester was always railing against somebody or something. It was his nature. He never told me why he did it. But you must remember that he was a doctor in the old days when folks—especially doctors themselves—really thought they did know best. If you ask me, he suffered from a high-handed streak."

"Didn't you tell me that the Gilhooley family claimed that the mother—Mary Ellen—never would have sought an abortion, that it was against her religion, against her wishes and her will?"

"Yeah, but families get hysterical when something like this happens. The fact is that she was on that operating table and she died. Nobody's ever questioned that Chester Royal was responsible and was violating the law at the time."

"Wait a minute!" Lorna Fennick sat forward. "I see what Temple's getting at. Knowing Chester much later as well as I did, seeing—and enduring—the full flower of his misogyny . . . did anybody then ever ask whether the doctor might have deceived the woman?" Lorna pushed her bangs back as if to clear her thoughts. "Anybody ever consider that he got her on the table on some pretext and then did what *he* felt *ought* to be done? Didn't matter that she wanted this baby, whatever number it was: *Dr.* Chester Royal had decided she'd had too many. He planned to abort her and say it was spontaneous. Maybe he was even going to sterilize her if she hadn't hemorrhaged. Doctors used to do things like that. It would be just like him! That man was so . . . twisted about women!"

Avenour was frowning, too. "What about the husband, the dead woman's husband?"

"He'd be dead himself by now," the unidentified woman with Avenour objected.

"Or surviving children?" Lanyard Hunter asked, his face screwed into speculation. "How old would they be?"

They all looked to Temple. She glanced to the impatient Molina and picked up the faxes.

"According to clippings on the case that Lieutenant Molina received this morning, the father was Michael Xavier Gilhooley. The children ranged in age from toddlerhood, Mary Clare, to the mid-teens. Mr. Jaspar remembered some of their names. Want to see how you do against the clipping?"

"Mary Clare," he confirmed. "Tragic—little girl like that without her mother. They were all Irish names, old-fashioned Irish names, don't ask me to spell 'em or say 'em right. There was Liam and Sean and Eoin—"

"Ee-oh-eye-in? That sounds like a strange name."

"That's how it was spelled. I wouldn't forget a monicker like that. They were named in the suit, though, of course, we never saw the kids in court. Eoin, like I said, Brigid and Cathleen. How many's that?"

"Six."

"There were more. Funny, it's like the names of the seven dwarfs; can never remember them all. Mary Clare, Brigid and Cathleen, Eoin, Sean and Liam, and—Maeve! That's it, and another funny name. Maybe Rory. That's eight."

"And Kevin," Temple finished. "Nine Gilhooley kids. Even little Mary Clare would be forty-one today. The oldest would be past fifty."

Everyone eyed each other nervously and computed their likely ages.

For the first time, Lieutenant Molina smiled. "So which Gilhooley was undercover at the ABA? Was little Mary Clare working in the registration Rotunda? Sean in the maintenance brigade? This isn't a game of Clue," she warned a bit sternly. "If you make accusations you have to back them up."

Temple turned to her. "You said the key to this case was motive, and I've provided a plausible one. You also said that it made no sense to wait nearly forty years to commit a murder of vengeance. Last night I asked you to check on any news stories about the Gilhooley clan since the trial, and you came up with one."

Temple picked up a fax in the tense silence. She pushed her glasses from the top of her head to her nose.

"Here it is. A *Chicago Daily News* item dated May fifteenth of this year. An obituary for Michael Xavier Gilhooley, seventy-three. Mary Ellen's husband is dead now, too. No matter what happens, he won't have to see one of his children accused of murder, though the killer didn't expect that. Chester Royal's death had been planned for a long time, and it should have been foolproof. That Michael Gilhooley died on the eve of the ABA was just frosting on the killer's cake. Where better to disguise a motive than among twenty-four thousand conventioneers?"

"What a story!" Lanyard Hunter's eyes blazed. "I'm going to write the nonfiction book I wanted to do in the first place, and it'll be about this case. Eat your heart out, Avenour; any big publisher will snap up a true-crime piece like this. I don't need Pennyroyal Press or R/C/D."

"This has been most instructive," Owen Tharp said. "And, Lanyard, I'll beat you to press on that book. The only way you'd get a good idea is by being hit over the head by it."

"Don't back off, Lanyard; that's a great idea!" Claudia Esterbrook virtually jeered. "Unless *you*'re the Gilhooley in disguise. You never did say whether you wrote under a pseudonym or not."

"None of your business!" he snapped.

"That's the question, isn't it?" Temple felt wrung out. The faxes were crumpled in her hand, she had held on to them so tightly. "Who is the child who has never forgotten a mother's wrongful death, who never believed that she would act against her conscience, despite the evidence? Mary Ellen's death robbed a young family of its mother—and worse, of its self-respect, for that mother died under circumstances society regarded as shameful."

"You sound like the defense attorney for the killer," Molina noted.

"In the killer's mind, over many years of agony and planning, the crime came to seem justified." Temple took a deep breath. "The identity of the killer was staring us in the face, like the placard with 'stet' on it. We just didn't know how to interpret it."

" 'We'?" Lieutenant Molina said. "Keep it in the first person singular."

"Okay. Think back to the Gilhooley children. Don't some of their names ring a bell?" A long pause, during which Temple whipped out another visual aid, a list of names. "Something bothered me when Mr. Jaspar first mentioned them, but I couldn't figure out what. Then I did.

"These Irish names," she asked Jaspar, "they're old-fashioned, as you said, but aren't yuppie couples going back to names like Sean? And everybody knows that, though it's pronounced 'Shawn,' it's really spelled 'S-E-A-N' as if we would pronounce it 'See-an.'?"

Jaspar nodded. "Hell, even I know that. Knew it then, too. But most of the time, that Irish spelling throws people off."

"I know. I worked at the Guthrie Theater when the Irish actress Siobhan McKenna appeared. Her first name struck me as one of the ugliest I'd even seen printed on a theater program—until I heard it pronounced, 'She-vaughn.' It's a lovely name."

Jaspar wasn't the only puzzled onlooker, but Temple plunged on. "And now there's Sinead O'Connor, the hot pop singer. Most people murder that one—'Sin-ee-ad." But it's really 'She-nayde.' Isn't that prettier?"

"If you say so," Jaspar grumbled. "This newfangled naming is pretty silly to my mind. Girls named Meredith and Tyler and—"

"Temple?" she prompted. Jasper shut up. "Even Maeve has come back. Once I would have said 'May-eeve,' but I know better now. It's 'Mayve.' "

"What are you getting at?" Lorna asked. "Are you implying that one of us is a Gilhooley daughter who changed her name?"

"Sometimes a name changes itself. Did you know that many Celtic names are variations of each other? Take something as basic as the English 'John.' The Scots use 'Ian,' and the Irish, 'Eoin.' You say every letter—but fast, not so every letter stands out, as Mr. Jaspar said it a few moments ago. Not 'Ee-oh-eye-en,' as if you were reciting vowels, but fast: 'Eoin.' The Welsh, on the other hand, spell it in a way we all know how to pronounce: Owen."

The congregation sat like stones, suddenly staring at one man.

The silence prevailed until Owen Tharp spread his hands in resignation. "I didn't expect to be found out," he burst out, "much less tripped up by a name, but I'm glad Da was dead before I did it."

Even as he spoke the police were converging on him. He offered no resistance, and stood to be handcuffed. In a moment an officer was mumbling the ritual Miranda warning, a grimmer sort of rite for the Lover's Knot Wedding Chapel.

"Chester ended up with quite a lively wake. I wouldn't have missed it for the world." Claudia Esterbrook rose to smooth the wrinkles in her scarlet skirt. "I assume the rest of us can go now?"

Molina nodded. Temple watched people stand, looking lost and a bit ashamed. Not Claudia. She swaggered up the aisle ahead of Avenour and his still-anonymous ladyfriend, and Earnest Jaspar. No one else left, and no one met Owen Tharp's eyes except Temple.

"Even though you tried to kill me, I . . . regretted giving you away."

Tharp shook his head bitterly. "After Royal, I really didn't have it in me to kill again. It was reflex; a murderer is supposed to care about his own skin, his freedom. I found out I don't." He turned on Lanyard Hunter. "But I *do* care about my writing. And if you lay one incompetent finger on my story, I'll sue the pseudonym right off you!"

"You should have time to write now," Rowena Novak noted thoughtfully. "I'd be happy to be interviewed for your book."

"That did it?" Lorna Fennick asked Temple in some awe. "You figured out that his pseudonym was the key?"

"Every creative person wants to make his or her work known in some unique way," Temple said. " 'Gilhooley' had never been a good candidate for a book cover—too long, too vaudevillian, too bitter to Owen Gilhooley. So he used Michaels. He was Michael's son, wasn't he? And he used the more recognizable Welsh version of his baptismal name as a last name; and then as a first name. Tharp contains the word 'harp'—a metaphor for the Irish storytelling bard. Through the years he made word-games of his pseudonyms, and they eventually led back to his past."

Temple turned to Lanyard Hunter. "You said it yourself, when we had dinner: the best kind of lie is the truth that nobody takes seriously. It will never catch the teller and will seriously mislead everybody else. Owen Tharp's choice of pseudonyms both veiled and memorialized his past. Chester Royal never tumbled.

"He'd donned many personages during his journey through genre fiction. But the true personality, the one that had never changed over the years, was the young man who'd seen his mother needlessly taken away. That was the person who killed Chester Royal."

"Close enough," said Tharp to Temple's diagnosis, his

head turned away. He wasn't about to share the mystery of his own actions, the history of his mania. Maybe he was saving it for the book—and probably the motion picture, too.

"What about the catnapper?" Lieutenant Molina was still waiting, arms folded, looking unimpressed.

"As you suggested, Lieutenant, the kidnapping of Baker and Taylor was a diversion Tharp engineered to distract the ABA and the media from Royal's death. Except Emily Adcock and I failed to cooperate. We didn't publicize it. So he left a ransom note on my desk hoping to force me to go public, but Emily whipped out her American Express Gold Card and paid the ransom, further frustrating his purposes. Then he promised the return of the cats to trick me onto the convention floor for his halfhearted attempt at mayhem. I'd like to think he was out to confuse matters rather than kill me. I may be wrong."

Tharp said nothing.

"What about the woman who picked up the ransom money?" Molina persisted. "That's a lesser crime, but she's still out there. Who is she and where's the money?"

Temple shrugged uneasily. "I don't know everything, Lieutenant. Got to leave something for the proper authorities. She's probably a mere hiree, like my Mr. O'Rourke. I wish you luck in finding her, Lieutenant, if Tharp won't tell you."

Molina was about to say more, but Temple turned quickly to Owen Tharp. "But there's one thing I *do* deserve to know, Mr. Tharp. Those cats are the innocent victims of all this. Where are they?"

Owen Tharp looked truly shamefaced for the first time. "I had to lose them as soon as I could. They're . . . at the pound."

"How long have they been there?"

"Since Friday," Tharp muttered.

"Good Lord! They're goners by now," Temple said with a lump in her throat and a glance at Midnight Louie reclining on the organ bench next to Matt.

"Oh, poor Emily!" Lorna Fennick came over to commiserate.

"Thanks for Tharp," Molina said curtly as she and her troops led the man out.

Lorna hugged Temple's shoulders. "Don't listen to that sourpuss. This was a tour de force, Temple. Better than "Murder, She Wrote." I hope you get the credit you have coming for this."

"Well, it's been exciting, and risky, and I'm glad the ABA doesn't have an unsolved murder hanging over it. But addictive as puzzle-solving is, I'm just realizing that this one ends with a man facing years in jail. I kind of liked Owen Tharp, even if he did try to knit and purl my tote bag, and he certainly had his reasons—in triplicate. And—poor Emily!—I'm just sick about Baker and Taylor being killed at the pound. I really blew that. Look—Louie's come to rub on my legs and comfort me, haven't you, Louie? I can't bear to tell Emily."

"You'll have to," Lorna said warily. "Here she comes now."

Emily was barging through the double doors, her purse over one shoulder, a huge shopping bag over the other and a cat carrier dangling from either hand, and jammed herself helplessly in the doors. "Temple—thank God I caught you. I'm on my way to the airport, but look—"

Temple and Lorna ran to free her.

"Your darling stuffed Baker and Taylor are in the shopping bag," Emily said breathlessly. "We don't need them anymore." She lifted the carriers. "Look! The right one's Baker, and the left, Taylor. Thought you deserved to see them in person."

"You got them back! Oh, Emily, how?"

"The woman who owns the local mystery bookshop bought them from the pound, can you imagine? This weekend. She was tickled to get such good 'look-alikes' for her shop. When she compared them to the posters she realized she'd somehow bought the real McCoys. Well, she came to B & T at the convention center when we were clearing out.

I'm afraid I borrowed your cat carrier for Baker. Maeveleen, the bookstore owner, gave me one of hers, so we three are outa here in a limo to McCarren and a plane to—don't ask me where; it's hush-hush. Gotta go. See you at the next ABA in Vegas!"

Emily backed up and barged out the doors as Lorna and Temple braced them open.

"Forget the carrier," Temple shouted at Emily's back, as she raced for the white limo hugging the curb. Corporate kitties traveled in style. She glanced at Midnight Louie, who had trotted over to nose Baker and Taylor through their carrier grilles. "I don't need it anymore." She dropped her voice. "But what about your five thousand dollars!"

Baker's and Taylor's carriers were disappearing into the limo's back seat on disembodied hands. Emily Adcock dived in after them, pausing only to flash Temple an ecstatic smile. "Don't worry! The company will reimburse me—or the librarians will raise the money. I don't even care. I'm just so happy to have them back. 'Bye."

The remaining ex-suspects trickled out the chapel doors into the glaring midday heat.

Lanyard Hunter donned dark glasses and drew Lorna Fennick's arm through his. "This has been an eventful ABA, thanks partly to you, Temple. I'll have to dedicate a book to you."

"I've enjoyed working with you," Lorna said with a farewell handshake. "Sort of. I've got to get out of town, too."

They ambled away, renewing old acquaintanceship and maybe more. Mavis Davis came out last, her unshielded eyes puckering against the sunlight. She looked ten years older.

"I—" She fell silent, gazing miserably down the Strip where the others were vanishing into a haze of heat and shimmering signage.

"When did you change your name to Mavis?" Temple asked quietly.

The nervous eyes fixed on her face at last. "Why . . . you know that, too?

Temple smiled. "Maeve Gilhooley was an impossible name for a book jacket. Even a newcomer to publishing like you knew that. Besides, you wanted to escape the past. I imagine you went by your foster family surname for so long that 'your' name didn't seem yours, so why not use another? That's why you wouldn't take a pseudonym when Reynolds/Chapter/Deuce asked you to. Mavis Davis already was one. And Mavis is Celtic, too, as in the old Scottish song, 'I have heard the mavis singing.' Like your brother, you kept your original identity in some way. Guess writing ability ran in the family."

"I didn't know the truth about my mother's death, or even that I had a father—or all those brothers and sisters. Imagine!" Mavis smiled, but sudden tears filled her eyes. "The scandal shattered the family, which was poor to begin with. Eoin, like the other older boys, left home to earn money. Us younger ones were parceled out quietly to other families. You could do that without official interference in those days. Eoin has told me that Da was never himself after Ma died. He drifted, drank. Eoin sent what money he could. He never forgot, never forgave. Of course, I was too young to remember the trial and the troubles."

"Eoin told you all this? When?"

She reached up to remove the sad mantilla. "Eoin came to me only two days ago. It was like one of the thrillers we wrote that I never really believed—a long-overdue reunion, sins of the past, revenge. He'd deliberately begun working for Pennyroyal Press to wait for his chance. He had kept track of me through the years, of all of us, though he never contacted us—"

"That's one way he betrayed himself," Temple put in.

Mavis frowned. "By keeping track of us kids?"

"I overheard him tell Lieutenant Molina that you were from Kankakee. But how did he know? Later, it hit me. That information wasn't in your author bio. That's when I figured out there must be a hidden connection between you and Owen Tharp."

"Poor Eoin. He may be a murderer, but he didn't tell me sooner about our relationship because he didn't want the rest of us to suffer for his crime if he were caught, though he thought he'd go free. He was newly furious about how . . . Mr. Royal was treating his sister. When he told me everything, when I saw how I'd been lied to all my life—denied my own mother's memory, kept from knowing my father and family, and from believing in myself—when I realized that Chester Royal had managed to ruin my life twice . . . well, it made me angry, too, so I did what Eoin wanted. He was my brother."

"All you had to do was play dumb and pick up the ransom money, though?"

She nodded. "I'll send the money to Emily Adcock."

Temple grinned. "Pseudonymously, I hope."

"You mean—?"

"No one needs to know. Why do you think I kept my mouth shut? You didn't do anything wrong except abet a relative in a catnapping; that's hardly Murder One. You're finally free of Chester Royal. Certainly you've paid in advance for any wrong you might have done, simply by working with the old ogre all those years. Just go home and write that Big Book."

"I won't abandon Eoin now that I've found him. Our mother's death marked the older ones, and I can't blame them. Sometimes, Miss Barr, ignorance is bliss. I'm glad I didn't know what Chester Royal was earlier. I might have done what Eoin did."

"I doubt it." Temple bent to pick up Midnight Louie. "Oof, what an armful."

Mavis daubed at her eyes with a lacy corner of mantilla. "Thank you. Goodbye, and thank you."

Temple watched Mavis Davis join the migration up the Strip, her back straighter than Temple had ever seen it. Most of them would be racing back to hotels and into airport limos. They'd soon forget the Las Vegas ABA.

Meanwhile, guess who was stuck here? She turned and lugged the cat inside.

Electra was flitting among her fiber people, removing their mourning garb.

"That was more exciting than a wedding any day," she said. "I thought that lieutenant would never get here. Not very grateful, if you ask me. And those publishing people! I had no idea they were such a kinky bunch. 'Course, when you consider what goes on in some books nowadays. . . . I bet you're glad this ABA job is over and you can concentrate on normal clients, like the mud-wrestling federation."

"I'm going back to the apartment, Electra. I'm ready to collapse, and Louie wants his lunch."

"Fine, fine." A matronly dummy lost her swath of veiling and her wig in one sweeping gesture.

Tired, Temple ambled through the breezeway, the cat at her heels. The tepid halls were deserted. She felt she moved in warm Jell-O, like a dreamer wading farther and farther away from the shoreline of reality.

When the elevator stopped on her floor, Louie paused midway in the door to consider his next move.

"In or out, you lug? Make up your mind."

He finally deigned to amble along the arc of the building's central hallway. When Temple reached the long shadowy passage that led to her door, she stopped.

Matt Devine, now in civvies, was leaning against the wall, with what looked like frosty margaritas in both hands.

"Thought you could use a refresher after the show. That was quite an ordeal."

Temple perked right up. "Great idea, thanks. Say, what was that slow-tempo funeral march you played at the beginning of the memorial?"

He grinned. "Curiosity will be your downfall. How do you know it wasn't Mozart?"

"It wasn't."

Matt sighed, and studied the contents of his glass. " 'A Whiter Shade of Pale.' Procol Harum."

"One of my favorite songs! Really?"

Matt nodded, then pointed to the business card Temple had put into her nameplate slot. "I saw this when I was installing your chain lock. I think it's wrong."

She stared at her card as he handed her a hand-chilling glass. "I don't see anything wrong with it."

Matt's glass clicked against hers. "It should read 'Temple Barr, P.I.' "

She liked the sentiment, and the compliment, and especially the source, but she said modestly, "No, not really. Never again. I solemnly swear." She was actually contemplating matters more intimate than detection.

Midnight Louie, ignored at their feet, didn't believe a word of it. He indolently stretched his forelegs all the way up to the doorknob and gave it a royal whack.

Louie's Last Meow

No one is happier than yours truly that this ABA thing is over. For one thing, I no longer have to worry about being nabbed on a homicide charge. Although I sport a couple fistfuls of switchblades, few even in this town would confuse any one of them for a knitting needle.

I have also reached a satisfactory arrangement with Miss Temple Barr on my domestic accommodations. She now leaves the guest bathroom window open just enough so that I can shimmy in and out of an evening.

At first I am afraid that Baker and Taylor's close call in the city pound will encourage her to curtail my, ah, movements. But she lightens up once the wrong-doer is caught—and even more once Mr. Matt Devine makes a friendly overture—and I have no trouble swaying her to my way of thinking.

So I am out and about these days and even stroll up the

Strip to the Crystal Phoenix, where I am made much of, seeing as how even a little of Midnight Louie goes a long way.

I am doing fine, but I am not too sure about my pal Ingram. His muzzle turns a shade lighter in one day, I swear. The close call with Baker and Taylor preys upon his mind. He is not one to share his territory. His person, Miss Maeveleen Pearl, has severely undermined Ingram's confidence in her good taste and sense. He is often to be found curled upon those noxious tomes known as self-help books, such titles as *People Who Love Pets Who Love Their Creature Comforts* and *When Good Things Happen to Bad Dogs.*

"Uncivil accents, Louie," Ingram rails when I come around for a stoopside chat. "No decent ears to speak of. Called me 'laddie.' In my own place!"

I can see the whites of his eyes.

It does not help that Miss Temple Barr, in one of the diplomatic gestures she is known for, has bestowed Baker and Taylor—the shills—on Miss Maeveleen Pearl, whose whimsy it is to arrange their floppy bodies in various spots throughout the Thrill 'n' Quill. Ingram is never sure where they will turn up next, perhaps in his very own bed.

Desist, I tell him, after hearing these complaints for the nth time. It is no use telling him that discussions in stir with the live Baker and Taylor on their abductor's apparent gender—as well as the Scottish name Ian, and its kinship to the Gaelic Eoin and the Welsh Owen—enabled me to nail the ABA murderer.

Some might marvel that I, in my usual toothsome way, should emphasize as a clue the very word that is the culprit's long-forgotten baptismal name.

The likes of Electra Lark would attribute my mystical moxie to previous lives (a viable theory, if you ask me), the deep spiritual powers of my kind going back to the time of the Pharaohs, or plain old feline intuition.

The fact is, I cannot masticate an entire title, leaving just Owen Tharp's byline, in the time I have available.

Also, too often the attempts of my species to communicate are dismissed as outright destructiveness. Call it a game of subconscious charades. By removing the other letters to leave an odd-looking remnant, "—E O——IN," I created a memorable impression on Miss Temple Barr and produced what the literati might call a homophone of the murderer's current moniker, or a halfway homophone, anyway. (This homophone is not a communications device for dudes of a specific sexual persuasion but is a fancy word to say that Owen and Eoin sound the same but are spelled differently.) Let the method fit the madness, in this case, the chaos of the ABA and all things literary.

To sum up, as Miss Temple Barr is most fond of doing, what the hell—it worked, did it not? Thanks to my usual blend of physical heroics and intellectual discernment.

Speaking of discernment, Lieutenant Molina, useful at last, has since checked the pound casualty list and found the name signed by the person who deposited B and T on the sadly substandard premises: Gil Hooley. Owen Tharp was playing word games to the last. And so the last nail is pounded into that coffin. I only regret that it is not one of my own.

Having settled my most pressing affairs and seen that all is right with the world, mostly, I can proceed to entertain myself in my customary fashion: I troll for carp in the pond behind the Crystal Phoenix, an enterprise all the more enjoyable for the necessity of avoiding the hotel chef's roving meat cleaver. (Chef Song is a great fancier of carp, like myself, but after that there is a splitting of the ways, you might say.) My various lady friends require attentions of a censored nature. I have hopes of impressing them with my exploits, but true to past history, I do not get proper credit in the matter of solving the Royal murder. (That is always the case with us sleuths, from Sherlock Holmes on.)

It is lonely, dangerous and unsung work (not to mention unpaid), which is why I take the precaution of writing my own memoirs. Though I am a bit long in the fang I have no intention of going quietly, even if it is true that I wax more contemplative of late as I lounge about my retirement condo in Miss Temple Barr's absence. She is out on the town with Matt Devine, hopefully gliding on the Goliath Hotel's infamous Love Moat. Above me comes a gentle thump now and then from Miss Electra Lark's penthouse, which I notice often during Miss Temple Barr's absences—either our esteemed landlady has poltergeists or she is entertaining gentleman callers of an athletic persuasion.

Speaking of which, I spend many happy hours recalling ladyloves I have courted, rivals I have scratched off the map (so to speak) and my widespread, numerous and thankfully-ignorant-of-my-existence offspring.

Which brings to mind the rumor I heard when I finally caught up with Sassafras, who is strictly an old acquaintance these days. Street talk is that starlet Savannah Ashleigh has come so far down in the world since she made "Surfer Samurai" that she has slunk into Vegas to make a cheapie flick about a stripper and will show her stuff in the buff at the Lace 'n' Lust downtown. I could not care less about the state of either Miss Savannah Ashleigh's film career or her unveiled epidermis, neither of which has ever struck me as having promise. Skin has never been my style. But when Miss Savannah Ashleigh previously visited Vegas, she stayed at the Crystal Phoenix and was accompanied by the sweetest platinum doll I have ever laid hopes on—the Divine Yvette, a petite aristocratic number up to her mascara in silver chinchilla fur. I definitely would strain my stride to see more of this little doll and her big blue-green peepers, not to mention her little pink nose and other more discreet parts of her anatomy. I will have to look in at the Lace 'n' Lust at the first opportunity.

It is on such a trip down memory lane that I inadvertently stir and depress the On button on the television's remote control mechanism. Thus my ears are blessed with an extremely racy exchange from the daytime drama *Lays of Our Lives.* Or perhaps I mishear the title.

My ears are not what they used to be, and then again, I am often told I was born with a back-alley mentality.

Midnight Louie Bites the Hand that Feeds Him

I am not often invited to address a captive audience, unless it is lunch. So how can I resist finishing off the foregoing literary exercise by unmasking its so-called author? At least the subtitle got it right: "A Midnight Louie Mystery."

There is no mystery about this novel. I say straight off that this Douglas dame owes it all to me. I teach her everything she knows, and then some. Her father was a Pacific Northwest salmon fisherman, so she had one thing going for her from the first. And I am pleased to add some genuine class to her act through this sort of telepathy that we have had since Moses was knee-high to a Munchkin.

We first met during her sixteen-year stint as a pencil-pusher for the local rag in St. Paul, Minnesota. That was the seventies, when she was a mod young thing and I was . . . ah, in my usual prime. I caught her eye right off—it took three inches of tiny type to list my many attractions in the classified "Pets" column. From the start she saw that I was meant for bigger things than ending up as a birdcage liner, so she called to check out my vital statistics: eighteen taut-muscled pounds, catnip-green eyes, raven-black hair and lots of it; a well-manicured four-on-the-floor and fully equipped from the factory.

Naturally, she does this big story on me, and I end up on a Minnesota farm, doing time with the moo concession. Meanwhile, my partner in crime-to-come is finding journalism confining, since little dolls are not considered promotional material in that racket, where little has changed since *The Front Page* days.

So this Douglas doll writes these twenty-three novels all by herself. I sneak a peek during a pretend-snooze on her bookshelves and find she writes about history, mystery, fantasy and science fiction, and even romance. That is okay by me. Louie's *l'amours* are legendary. (I often get myself into risqué positions. I love danger.)

Happily, those of the feline persuasion make frequent guest appearances in her fiction, like that snaggletoothed Felabba in *Six of Swords* and her SWORD AND CIRCLET trilogy. (A Samoyed dog named Rambeau gets the leading furred role in her new TALISWOMAN fantasy trilogy: I am all for equal rights and animal rights et cetera, but am glad she is back on track with my solo gig in these here mystery books. It is my exploits on mean streets that will really bring in the Bacos around here, if you ask me.)

As for this author doll, what is to say? She leads a dull life compared to mine. She now hangs out in Fort Worth with the same husband, Sam the "D" (as in Douglas), she's had since they met acting in some play in St. Paul. He's an artist who makes unique acrylic kaleidoscopes. Ho-hum. If I want to see something colorful running around in a circle, I would prefer a spray-painted punk gerbil. This writing doll also collects dainty vintage clothes, which are not good for anything but running my nails through, at which point she gets hysterical for some reason.

Unhappily, I am not the sole feline in her life; also count two alley bozos, Longfellow and Panache (sixteen and fifteen pounds respectively—no threat to *my* heavyweight title), and a pair of platinum Persian purebred dolls, Summer and Smoke, who are more than somewhat luscious, but have undergone this awful involuntary operation and pay me no mind at all. Their loss.

But there is only one top cat in Las Vegas and in this Douglas dame's books. Remember that, and I will refrain from reminding you by initialing your epidermis.

(signed) Midnight Louie, his mark

Carole Nelson Douglas Strikes Back

First of all, Louie's description of our relationship should be called a "Tall Tailpiece." He owes his current fame and good fortune solely to my literary efforts. In fact, Midnight Louie was on the auction block for a dollar bill when I found him in 1973 in the fine print of the classified ads.

This "big, black Tomcat" was obviously a handsome fellow, and just as obviously had been a discipline problem. His current custodians described "a con artist and eighteen pounds of cuddly pussycat, very versatile and equally at home on your new couch or in your neighbor's old garbage can." They admitted that he'd been reared on "purloined goldfish" and claimed that he "understood," but didn't speak, English.

All they asked was that Louie's new keepers allow him roaming room and that he remain the ladies' man he (also obviously) always was. Unsure where a *roué* like Louie would fit in the Family Life section where I wrote feature stories, I called his foster parents for an interview.

They were frank to a fault. At 2 A.M. one morning, Louie had attached himself to the wife near the Coke machine at a respectable Palo Alto motel where Louie was copping carp when he wasn't playing gigolo with the female guests. The motel manager was about to change his place of residence from goldfish pond to city pound. So the infatuated wife air-freighted Louie (in a borrowed puppy transport he much despised) to St. Paul.

Once there, Louie accosted her lawyer husband; tried to molest their altered Siamese female, Pooh; engaged in a rumble with the resident Hoover vacuum; and decided that the litter box was the nearest route to China but no place to commit an act of personal hygiene.

Soon the couple noticed that domestic security had reduced Louie to a mere fifteen pounds, as well as their apartment to rubble. They advertised, at length. Readers were shortly clamoring to adopt the disreputable feline. Louie graduated to an obscure, bucolic existence after I wrote my feature story. My first mistake was letting Louie loose in his own words for most of the piece.

I began writing novels in my off hours within three years, but Midnight Louie didn't sneak into my mind again until 1984, when I began writing fiction full time. I then persuaded him to relocate to the bright lights of Las Vegas to narrate a quartet of romances with an ongoing mystery that was solved in the last book, published as *Crystal Days* and *Crystal Nights* in 1990. Louie took to Vegas like a duck to bottom-dredging. He also took umbrage when the romance editor unilaterally lopped forty percent of his . . . er, pride and joy—print time—out of the books. Readers clamored for more, not less, just as Louie predicted.

Louie done wrong is not a civil or pretty sight. I had no peace until I agreed to let Louie get his claws into the real thing: Mystery with a capital "M" for murder. (Given his editorial truncation, it's no coincidence that Louie's first foray into crime fiction involves the icing of an editor at a booksellers' convention.) Louie is fond of saying that there are eight million stories under the naked neon of Las Vegas. This has been one of them. He intends to tell them all, at length and in his own words, as long as his "mouthpiece" lasts.

Collaborating with Louie has been exhausting but fascinating, and, what the heck, some soft-hearted dame somewhere is destined to play patsy for the big lug. Oh, lordy, it's catching. . . .